Kitty McKenzie's Land

AnneMarie Brear

Chapter One

Sydney, Australia. 1866

An hour after dawn, on Saturday, the tenth of June, the *Ira Jayne* sailed between two cliffs forming the mouth of a beautiful, wide harbour. The journey had taken ninety-one days; the longest voyage undertaken by the ship and her captain. To everyone's pleasure, they experienced an uneventful trip along the east coast of Australia. Now, as they sailed through the harbour's heads, pink and gold streaked the horizon, but for once the sky held no interest for Kitty or the ship's inhabitants.

She rose early and joined a few passengers to lean against the deck rails, eager for the first glimpse of the small city. They all delighted in spying little bays with golden beaches, rocky cliffs, inlets and thick forest. Every now and then in the distance, a small cottage materialised at the water's edge. Kitty soon learnt from a sailor that the township was further up the immense harbour.

Kitty watched a small boat approach bearing the harbour pilot. It was a wonderful sign of life beyond the ship. As the pilot climbed aboard and took control of the vessel, a cheer went up in his honour.

Swallowing her emotion, she smiled. She had done it. She had brought her family safely to the other side of the world. Impulsively, she kissed them all, laughing and crying happy tears. Her hands shook as she cupped Rosie's face. This was for all of them not just her. Their future lay here, she was certain of it.

Connie hitched Charles higher in her arms as he struggled to get down. 'It looks wonderful, lass, don't it?'

She nodded. No words could describe the joy she felt.

The passing shoreline changed. The countryside became more populated and cottages appeared in vast numbers and even signs of crude, dirt roads showed through the trees. Closer to the city, the more the country showed promise of civilization. The forest thinned until eventually buildings and dusty streets replaced it and, at last, the sight they all had waited for, crowds of people.

The ship groaned to a standstill in the mouth of the quay at the edge of the city. Watercrafts of all sizes and shapes crammed the large harbour. Kitty dared not move from the rail. She craned her neck to observe absolutely everything, determined to never forget the scene.

Eventually, the quarantine officer boarded and spoke with the captain. He toured the ship, inspecting the steerage passengers for any health problems. After another hour in which the ship berthed alongside the wharf, he declared the vessel safe and allowed the first-class passengers to disembark.

Kitty stared out over the city's rooftops. Gentle undulating hills covered by townhouses, cottages and buildings dotted the landscape. In the distance, the grey-green forests, or bush, as the locals called it, fringed the city. However, the bustling scene on the quay below soon captured her attention once more.

Somewhere down there was Ben... Hopefully.

The docks teemed with people of all descriptions. Workmen loaded and unloaded ships, small boats, wagons and carts. They cursed, swore, laughed and whistled. Smart, gleaming carriages drove by with fashionable occupants, and hired cabs went to and fro along the dock picking up or dropping off customers. Kitty's senses swam as she tried to absorb the plethora of bewildering sights and sounds, delightful aromas and not so pleasant smells.

She wanted to look at everything at once, as well as search the crowds for a glimpse of Ben. Had her telegram from Melbourne reached him? Doubt burnt her throat like acid.

What if he no longer loves me?

'Kitty, lass, please!' Connie cried, from the saloon doorway, at the same time pushing an eager Joe back inside so he wouldn't get lost in all the confusion. 'We've t'get everythin' out of the cabins an' the bairns are drivin' me mad.'

'I'm coming.' She lingered for a moment more, her heart frozen with fear that Ben had changed his mind. However, come what may, she must start her new life with courage.

Kitty welcomed the hectic hour of last-minute packing and organising. It kept her thoughts free of anything except the business of disembarking. A porter was sent for, and with the help of a few sailors, her crates and chests were brought up from the hold and placed on the dockside. The children were so excited they got in everyone's way and pestered the adults with questions no one knew the answers for just yet.

Finally, after saying goodbye to the other passengers with vague promises to keep in touch, Kitty and her party took leave of the captain, officers, seamen and lastly the ship.

At the head of the gangplank, she balked. She was stepping from her old world into a new one, and for one suffocating moment, her courage left her. She nibbled her bottom lip. Then, holding her head high and her back straight, she strode down and stepped onto Australian soil.

On the dock, the noise hurt their ears after the relative quiet of the ship and the ocean. Kitty frowned at the multitude of faces passing by. They left their luggage piled on the wharf and a seaman from the Ira Jayne said he would keep an eye on it while they sorted themselves out.

'Stay together,' Kitty said, taking Rosie's hand and hustling her family over to the immigration depot to join the queue of first class travellers.

When, at last, Kitty and her family left the building, it was with great relief and tiredness. They made their way out into the midday sunshine and back to their luggage. The children complained of hunger and the babies needed changing.

'What are we to do now, Kitty?' her sister Mary asked, who, at seventeen, was fully aware of the sailor's whistles coming her way as she lifted her violet skirts away from the open drain running down to the water's edge.

Connie jiggled Adelaide in her arms. 'I know I need a cup of tea.'

Kitty put her hand to her forehead. 'I thought Ben would be here by now. What if he hasn't received my telegram?'

Mary searched the crowds. 'There's so many people, I bet he can't find us.'

Kitty walked a few paces, looking for the man she'd crossed oceans for. Suddenly, she stopped and frowned. Her stomach twisted, for behind her somewhere amongst the mass, someone called her. She spun around and only just made out her name being called again. Some sixth sense raised goose bumps upon her skin.

Standing on tiptoe, she scanned the crowds. There, just a flash of a cheek, a hat set a certain way, but it was enough. Kitty gathered her skirts and pushed through the throng. She saw a gap and made for it, her walk turning into a run. Tears blurred her vision and she dashed them away impatiently.

'Kitty!' Ben dodged people and luggage.

The crowd thinned. He paused and then slowly walked to her, as she now walked to him.

'I tried not to believe the telegram. I dared not consider that you would be soon with me,' he told her, crossing the open space until there was no more than twelve inches between them.

A moan bubbled from her lips. Her darling Ben stood before her with his love, his heart plain for her to see. 'Are you glad I came?' She risked his rejection, but was certain he still felt something for her, because it glowed in his beautiful blue eyes. He was all she wanted.

'All I wished was for you to be by my side.' Emotion made his voice heavy. He reached up to touch a loose tendril near her cheek. 'God, you are so magnificent. The sun has lightened the copper in your hair...'

'I thought you might never return to England, so I came to you.'

'I didn't intend to stay away much longer, but you have made me the happiest man alive coming here.'

'I'm not alone.'

'If you were one amongst a hundred, I wouldn't care.'

Kitty's tears flowed freely down her cheeks. 'I have wondered whether you might still want me or have found another.'

'It is you I love. No one can take your place.'

She sighed, relieved, aching with love for him. 'Ben...'

He crushed her to him and held her tight. She cared nothing for propriety, cared nothing for the looks and stares that came their way, for at last Ben held her.

Seagulls soared overhead, dipping and raising as they caught the warm air currents. Their cries mingled with the yells and cusses from sailors and dockmen as they went about offloading the newly arrived ships. Cranes swung heavy netted cargo across the quay to the shrill whistles of the guiding labourers, but none of it mattered as they stared at each other.

Kitty grinned as Ben held her close. The noise of the dock drowned the words they whispered; words that had waited many months to be expressed.

Ben's eyes glistened with emotion. 'I never thought this day would come.'

'Nor I, my love. I still find it hard to believe we actually made it here.'

He glanced behind her at the entourage that watched them. 'They've lost the paleness of York. Your brother and sisters have grown.'

Kitty smiled back at her family, sisters Mary, Clara, growing fast at age ten, four-year-old Rosie and her twelve-year-old brother Joe. Behind them stood her dearest friend, Connie, holding her twins, Adelaide and Charles. To the side of them, their mouths agape at the strangeness of this new land, were Alice and Hetta, befriended servants. 'Yes, the sunshine on the voyage benefited us all.'

He looked back at the Ira Jayne, moving gently at the restraints of the mooring. 'I owe that ship so much. It and the captain brought you safely to me.'

For a moment, Kitty thought of the past weeks, being cooped up in the ship and of the voyage from England to this very different life. She pushed away the memories of those left behind, her missing brother Rory and the friends and loved ones buried in churchyards...

'Come, let me take you to your new home.' Benjamin squeezed her hand. 'I long to show you everything.'

Within minutes, he'd hired hackney cabs for the party, and a cart for the chests and crates. They travelled through the jostling city streets, gazing at the buildings and people.

'Everything is so exciting, even the air smells differently, crisp and fragrant.' Kitty sniffed deeply and laughed.

Benjamin told her, Mary, Joe and Clara as much as he knew about the eucalyptus trees, tea trees and others permeating the air with their scents. He informed them of the difficulties of living in this country and also the advantages. He pointed out the great parkland called the Domain, where ladies strolled, nannies pushed perambulators and brass bands played on Sundays.

The road passed Government House with its tended ornamental gardens and strutting peacocks. The city, in all its diversities, flashed in glimpses before Kitty's eyes. She was enchanted until they spied the edges of the slum areas, where thin children with dirty bodies ran around in rags and she remembered the cellar back in York and how close they came to ruin.

Soon, the cabs pulled to a halt outside a large terraced house in lower Forbes Street, close to Woolloomooloo Bay. The three-storied terrace, built of pale sandstone blocks, was one of ten houses built along the street towards the water. Tall eucalyptus trees dotted the edge of the street until they multiplied into a small woodland closer to the water.

Kitty paused on the cab's step and looked around.

Benjamin smiled, his gaze lingering on her as he helped her down. 'No regrets?'

She returned his smile with one full of love. 'None at all.'

'It's all so different,' gushed Alice, turning to help Connie with the babies.

Joe stumbled and giggled. 'I keep swaying. The ground won't keep still.'

They all laughed and tumbled into the small front parlour where a shifty-eyed maid hovered.

'Susie, tea, please.' Ben guided Kitty to a chair.

The maid bobbed a curtsy and left the room.

Kitty knew, from Ben's letters, that the house consisted of three bedrooms and two attic rooms. Downstairs contained the parlour, dining room and small study. At the back of the house, a scullery led off from the kitchen. Suddenly she thought of Martin, her seafaring brother. 'Have you seen Martin? Has he contacted you?'

'Yes, he came to see me the day after he docked. He was well and happy.'

'Is he still in Sydney?'

'No, my dear. His ship left almost immediately for India.'

Joe sidled up to her. 'I'm hungry.'

'Well, we cannot have that, young man.' Ben held out his arm. 'Kitty, my love, I hope you are all hungry for my dining table is groaning under the weight of all the food I have brought in.'

He led them into the dining room, and she gasped at the plates of fresh food awaiting them; bread, boiled chicken, eggs, fruit, sandwiches and cheese. Joe and Clara's eyes grew large with want.

Ben selected a large, crimson wildflower from the centre arrangement and gave it to Mary. 'A native waratah, Miss Mary.'

'Oh, thank you.' She showed it to Connie.

He turned to pull out a chair for Kitty. 'I shall arrange for the maid to make up beds in the attic. I did not expect to house so many, but we shall manage I am certain.' He grinned.

'It will not matter where we sleep, Ben, just as long as we are on dry land.'

Later, after unpacking, Kitty found Ben sitting at his desk in the small study. She hesitated in the doorway, wondering if he'd received the news from his grandmother about his father's death. 'My darling...'

He looked up and held out his hand for her to join him. 'How I have missed you.'

She crossed to him and took his hand in hers. 'And I you.'

8

'Nothing will separate us now.' He kissed her hand and winked.

She lowered her lips to his, savouring the feel of them. Suddenly, Hetta's voice could be heard in the kitchen and they sprang apart like naughty children. Kitty felt the heat in her cheeks as the servant Susie walked by carrying a broom.

Ben gazed at Kitty, his smile soft and devoted, and her heart soared. How she loved this man.

'Shall we go out for a meal tonight?' Ben smiled. 'Or are you too tired?'

'I am rather tired. I think Connie is already napping with the babies.' She gazed at the papers littering his desk and remembered the news she had to break. 'Did...did you receive Dorothea's letter?'

'About Father?' He nodded, the light dying from his eyes. 'Yes. It arrived two weeks ago. My father was dead for three months before I even knew about it.' Ben released her hand, opened a drawer and took the letter out. 'The shock of it staggered me for days. I should have been there.'

Kitty held him close. 'He was a fine man, my love. I spoke to him only a short time before he died. He was so proud of you. He loved you so.'

Ben sighed heavily. 'I shall always miss him, Kitty.'

'Of course.'

'I never got to say goodbye...'

She kissed the top of his head. 'I'm so sorry.'

'Tell me, is...is my mother well?'

Kitty pulled out of his arms to look at him. 'She took your father's death badly, but Dorothea is taking good care of her. I am...afraid I cannot say much more, for your mother has no kindness in her heart towards me. Sadly, we did not become friends.'

'I had hoped you might but did not really expect it.' He stood and kissed her forehead. 'Never mind, darling, we are together now and always will be. Mother...will cope. She has Grandmamma.'

'Will we be married soon?'

'Tomorrow, I visit a friend of mine, who is a vicar, and I will organize a date.' Ben kissed her fingers. 'It cannot be soon enough.'

Chapter Two

Kitty left the bedroom she shared with Mary, Clara and Rosie, as Alice descended the steep narrow stairs from the attic. 'Good morning, Alice, did you sleep well?'

'Aye, not bad, Miss.' Alice smiled, despite her troubled expression.

'Is there anything wrong?'

'Aye, well... It's just Hetta and me don't feel right about going on the picnic Mr Kingsley has arranged for the family.'

Kitty placed her hand on her arm. 'Why?'

'Mr Kingsley is a gentleman and well... We, me and Hetta that is, don't feel right about sitting down with him and pretending we're the same as you. We're working class and he knows that, and—'

'Please, Alice...' Both the women turned as Ben spoke coming out of his bedroom.

'Mr Kingsley, we mean no disrespect, but Hetta and me don't feel it right to...well, to...'

'Hobnob with the gentry?' Ben laughed.

Alice smiled. 'Aye, sir, something like that. Besides, we want to go and look for work.'

'Work?' Kitty stared at her. 'We only arrived yesterday.'

'I already have a solution to that.' Grinning, he took Kitty's hand. 'Susie, the maid here, is not an adequate cook. I eat out most of the time as testament to that. So, with me soon to be a married man,' Ben winked, 'I shall need a good cook. I happen to know you are quite accomplished in that area. Therefore, I would like to offer you the job. I will also need a housekeeper. I believe Hetta would be available for such a task, would she not?'

'Oh, Mr Kingsley!' Alice clapped her hands in delight. 'We'd be honoured to work for you and the new Mrs Kingsley. I'll run up and tell Hetta now.'

Kitty linked her hand through Ben's arm. 'What a fine man you are, Benjamin Kingsley.'

'I want you to be happy, and you wouldn't be if your little fledglings left the nest. Am I right?'

She laughed. 'Yes, you are right. They left England to start a new life with me, I owe it to them to see that they are content.'

He kissed the top of her head. 'As much as I like your extended family, I do ask for you to curb your gathering of stray chicks before it's standing room only in the house.'

'Oh, tosh!' She chuckled. 'Come, stop your nonsense and let us go on our picnic.'

Benjamin took them to a secluded little bay with its own sandy beach. A flat rock shaded by a tea tree served as a grand table for the wicker baskets full of food. Later, the children removed their shoes and stockings to play at the water's edge. Screaming and laughing, they became much wetter than they should have.

'Imagine having a picnic by the water in the middle of winter back home?' Joe declared to their amusement.

'The winters are milder here.' Ben crunched into an apple. 'No snowfalls in Sydney.'

After the simple diet onboard the ship, the family thoroughly appreciated the wonderful display of food before them. They ate a variety of breads, cheeses, fruit and salads.

Connie laughed watching the twins touch the sand and grass for the first time. 'How Max would 'ave loved this.' She sighed and took a small stick out of Charles's mouth.

Kitty smiled, thinking of the wonderful, hulking man who'd left this life too early. She grasped her friend's hand. 'Yes, he would have, but he'd be happy knowing you and the twins are well and cared for.'

The following day, Ben insisted that Kitty and Mary go on a shopping spree to buy new clothes for the family, at his expense. The cab driver dropped Kitty and Mary off in George Street, one of the largest thoroughfares in the city. Ben was to meet some business associates he had forgotten about in the excitement of Kitty's arrival, and he left them to shop alone.

Kitty hesitated to use Ben's money, but common sense won out. He was wealthy. She was not, and as she saw so much that the family needed, she threw caution to the wind for once. After all, she would soon be his wife.

Towards noon, they were hungry and thirsty. Hot, dry dust coated everyone and everything. Standing in the middle of busy, unfamiliar streets, Kitty had a moment of unease at becoming lost, but after a short meal, she decided to catch one of the horse trams plying the streets and tour the city. It surprised them to see such beautiful and grand buildings in a relatively new city. They viewed quaint churches of all denominations and pub-lic buildings of classic architecture. These were interspersed by grand, solidly built houses of the merchants, shopkeepers and tradesmen. Indeed, some of the stunning houses owned by the wealthier families of Sydney would not be out of place back in York.

The opposite of this unexpected grandeur was the slum areas. The Rocks, an area of crime and poverty, were the worst areas and Kitty possessed no wish to explore it further. Ben had mentioned this place to her in letters. The rough and disorderly inhabitants of this vicinity showed no respect for the law or other people. Old, rickety huts leaned drunkenly against their neighbours, remnants of the early settlement of years ago. Here, the filth of open sewer drains and rubbish mixed together to flow from one hovel to another. Ben had told her rampant diseases took the young and the old, and cheap gin houses and illegal opium dens lined the lanes and alleys. The people of this quarter held little in the way of comforts, children played in the dirt with scraps of clothing clinging to them for covering, while the adults lingered in doorways either drunk or with the blank-eyed stare of the hopeless.

'We must never stray to this locality by ourselves,' Kitty murmured, grabbing Mary's hand tight.

'Let us go to the quay. Perhaps the *Ira Jayne's* sailors are at work.'

They alighted from the tram near Albert Street and strolled down to the circular quay. They gazed in wonder at the graceful ships docked and at the ones anchored further out in the harbour. It brought a smile to their faces when they found the Ira Jayne, riding at anchor some distance away. They walked until blisters grew on their feet, and at last they admitted defeat. They could not look at everything in the city in one day. Exhausted, they caught a hansom cab home as the sun slipped behind the hills west of the city.

'Really, lass. The first dress you tried on was as good as t'third. Benjamin's gettin' impatient.' Connie tossed her head and hung up another discarded dress.

'I want to look extra well tonight, Connie. I must make the right impression on Ben's friends.'

'An' you will.'

'That damned seamstress said the dresses would be ready by this afternoon. I cannot wear the dresses I brought with me. None of those are suitable for dining with the town's finest.'

'I know, lass, but there's nowt we can do.'

Kitty examined her image in the mirror. Powder and soft rouge covered the tan she acquired on the voyage. She fingered her hair. Newly washed and brushed, its copper tones twinkled in the lamplight. Mary had arranged it superbly on top of her head, leaving a few tendrils to drift around her face. This party, her first amongst Sydney's society, filled her with nervousness. Being sociable with strangers was a pastime she had not missed while being poor. She lacked no social graces, except the fact of wanting to be social.

Her greatest fear was to become the scandalous social butterfly her mother had been. Eliza's flirtations, extravagant lifestyle and risqué acquaintances all drew rumours of her wildness. Kitty wished her father had curtailed her mother more, but he had loved Eliza unconditionally, thus letting her reign in unencumbered freedom.

Her mother's legacy stayed with her, and she was determined her sisters would never become their mother's image. This new life with Ben would change many things, but Kitty refused to be changed by it.

Susie came in carrying a large box. 'It's here, Miss McKenzie. It's just arrived.'

'Praise the Lord.' Kitty took it from her and placed it on the bed. Every passing minute tortured her plunging confidence. 'Has Miss Mary received hers?'

'Yes, Miss. Hetta's taken it in,' Susie replied, sullen.

'Thank you, Susie, that will be all.' She dismissed her, not liking the housemaid very much. Susie had a sly way about her that irked Kitty.

A short time later, Kitty whirled in front of Connie. 'Well? Will I do?'

Connie grinned. 'I'm lost fer words, lass.'

Kitty glanced down at the off-the-shoulder, pale lilac dress with short sleeves edged with lilac lace. The whale-boned bodice showed her slender figure to great advantage, and a tasseled fringe of at least six inches, in a deeper shade of lilac, skirted the hem. Dainty silver slippers peeped from beneath the dress.

'Here, lass, put this on. He's waitin' for you.' Connie placed a fine silk traveling cape of moonlight silver with white fur trim around Kitty's shoulders.

As Kitty descended the stairs, Benjamin stood talking to Mary near the front door.

He turned and smiled. Love and admiration radiated from him. 'Words fail me.'

Pleasure filtered through her like hot water through snow. 'I fear you are biased, sir.'

'Absolutely.' He winked.

Kitty grinned at Mary who looked beautiful in a watery lemon-coloured dress of satin and lace. Her jet-black hair, so like her mother's, was curled and arranged on top of her head with white rosebuds placed in amongst the ringlets. Kitty, keenly aware they had not dressed so graciously since before their parents' death, took a deep breath. She wanted her family to have the best in life. By marrying Ben, she would finally be able to give it to them. All her risky decisions, all they had endured, had been worth it. They were to meet the best of Sydney's society; they were on their way.

Their hosts, the Freeman's, lived in a large house in Macquarie Street in the heart of the city.

As they travelled in the hired carriage, Ben reached over and took Kitty's gloved hand in his. 'My sweet, you are shaking.'

'I am nervous, Ben.'

'Do not be. Dan Freeman has become my closest friend.'

'Have you told him about me?'

'Of course. His wife, Ingrid, is a wonderful woman. My hope is that you will find a friend in her.'

Kitty nodded as the carriage rumbled to a halt. 'So do I.'

A crowd waited to be shown in through the front door, which led off the street. Ben helped Mary and Kitty down from the carriage. He waved to an acquaintance and then tucked Kitty's hand under one arm and Mary's under the other. Laughter danced in his eyes. 'Dan and I, being perceptive businessmen, recognized the same intelligence and ambition in one another. Together, we started the import and export company my father sent me to establish. Dan has introduced me to influential people of the town.'

Mary hesitated; her eyes wide. 'Oh, Kitty. I thought you said it was to be a small dinner party? I'm not officially out yet.'

Kitty bit her lip. 'That's true. Ben what will we do?'

Frowning, Ben stared at the arriving guests. 'I'm sorry. Dan did promise something small.'

He smiled at Mary. 'Can we pretend this is her coming-out party then? It appears Dan has invited half of Sydney.'

'Would you be happy to consider this night your coming out, Mary?' Kitty squeezed her hand.

Mary smiled, delighted. 'I'd like nothing more.' She kissed Kitty's cheek.

Light illuminated each window on all three floors, sending a comforting golden haze over the street. A humming of noise filtered out to them.

'Did Dan go exploring with you?' Kitty asked, gathering her skirts out of the street dust.

'Yes, he did. We travelled to Melbourne and Hobart and most of the country in between. We have achieved a great deal in the last year. The business proved immensely profitable and it gave us the freedom to invest our time and money into other things.' He grinned down at her. 'Together and individually, we have bought and sold property, mills and factories. At present, we are putting in tenders to build new roads and bridges throughout certain areas of New South Wales.'

In the hallway, a footman took their outer clothes. It was evident from the numerous carriages lining the street and the noise that the house was full of people.

They made their way down a short hall and into a spacious room crowded with happily conversing guests. It seemed so long ago, another lifetime, since Kitty had attended such a gathering. So much had changed in that time. She suddenly felt alien to these people. It was unlikely any of these beautifully dressed citizens had ever buried both parents and then, due to bankruptcy, been forced to leave home and live in a cellar. Still, she had been taught from birth how to be a lady and was here for Ben and her family's sake. She wouldn't let them down.

'Ben. Ben.' A man of average height, with sandy-brown hair and serious hazel eyes came towards them, a frown lining his face. 'I do apologize, my friend. I did tell my wife to invite only a few people, but alas she is wont to talk to all and sundry. As a consequence, the house is full.'

'Never mind, Dan. We'll enjoy an intimate meal at my home soon. Now, let me introduce you to my fiancée, Miss Katherine McKenzie, Kitty to her friends, and her sister Mary.' Ben brought them before him. 'Kitty, Mary, this my good friend, and our host, Dan Freeman.'

Dan's solemn eyes crinkled a little in a shy smile as he took Kitty's hand. 'I'm pleased to finally meet you, Miss McKenzie. We have heard nothing else but your name being praised.' He turned and bowed over Mary's hand. 'Miss Mary.'

Kitty smiled. 'I am honoured to meet you, Mr Freeman.'

'I hope you enjoy Australia and all her beauties, Miss McKenzie.'

'Oh, I do already, Mr Freeman. I think I fell in love with it by the books I read and the paintings I saw long before I set foot on this soil.' She sensed this colonial man was proud of the land to which he had been born.

Dan Freeman held out his arm, and Kitty accepted it. He led them through the throng until he found his wife standing by a serving table laden with silver, offering an array of food. 'My dear, may I introduce you to Miss McKenzie, Ben's fiancée, and her sister Mary. Miss McKenzie, this is my wife, Ingrid Freeman.'

'At last we meet you, Miss McKenzie. You are very welcome here, as is your family.' Ingrid Freeman smiled at Kitty and Mary. She was a tall woman, finely boned, thin and angular with it. Her face had a serene look, though a closer glance revealed laughing eyes.

'Thank you for inviting us to you home, Mrs Freeman.'

'Benjamin has talked about nothing but you, Miss McKenzie. We were all quite excited when the Ira Jayne docked, knowing we would soon meet you.'

'Since my arrival, I have heard a great deal about you and your husband. It comforts me that Ben had the great fortune of acquiring genuine friends in his time away from home.'

'Shall I get you something to drink, Kitty?' Ben asked, and at her nod, he turned to Mary as the quartet struck up some music.

'Come, Mary, I believe we shall dance our way over to the refreshments table where I know the excellent wine is served.'

Laughing, Mary let Ben lead her out to the small area set aside for waltzing.

Ingrid swept her hands over the table behind them. 'Miss McKenzie, can I offer you something to eat?'

'No, not at the moment, thank you.' The thought of food choked Kitty. Though her anxiety had diminished, she doubted she could eat.

Ingrid's gaze softened. 'Please, do not think we judge you. I know how people can smile at you one minute and in the next whisper your downfall. Nevertheless, this society is made up of people from so many different and, shall we say, diverse backgrounds that to make hasty judgments could quite easily ruin you.'

'To be honest, Mrs Freeman, I have a great fear of failing Ben.'

'Nonsense. From what he has told us about you, I doubt anything you could do would change his opinion of you.'

Kitty stiffened. What had Ben told them?

Ben and Mary returned to her with flutes of wine. Other couples joined them, and introductions were made. Ingrid smiled and lightly squeezed Kitty's hand in reassurance. It did nothing to help her from fretting. What had Ben said and to whom? Her head pounded. She wanted to put the past behind her. How could Mary, Clara and Rosie eventually find good husbands if word got out about them living in a cellar?

The sound of breaking glasses took Ingrid from them as she hurried towards the disturbance. Dan asked Mary to dance while Ben conversed with another man in their group. A small cluster of elderly women moved close to Kitty and moaned about being away from England. They then regaled her with tales of how to best cope with the lack of society in Sydney. Kitty hated to appear rude, but she desperately needed some fresh air. The closeness of the full room and lack of food made her head swim.

She stepped into the hall, in search of a back door out into the garden, when a woman wearing a beautiful pink and black satin dress, sashayed towards her. The woman possessed dark sultry features with a glint in her catlike eyes that spoke volumes. In her small, dainty hand, she held a closed fan; this she tapped gently against her cheek. She was a sensual woman of the world and all who saw her knew it.

'We have not been introduced.' Her voice was deep, exotic.

Intrigued, Kitty paused. 'No, we have not.'

The golden catlike eyes narrowed. Her gaze sauntered over Kitty. 'Ahh, you are darling Benjamin's bride–to-be?'

Her intimacy was not lost on Kitty. 'Yes, I am, and you are?'

'The woman who has been keeping his bed warm.'

Kitty blinked, but other than that, she remained motionless on the outside while inside her stomach churned. 'Is that so? I am much obliged, however, your services will no longer be required.'

'You think you can keep him satisfied? You, a cold, little Englishwoman?' Her throaty laugh straightened Kitty's backbone.

'You forget, an English wildflower survives under all conditions unlike the exotic blossom that dazzles for a short time and then fades.' Kitty turned on her heel and walked blindly into the nearest room, which thankfully, was empty.

Breathing in deep gulps of air, she held onto the back of a nearby chair to steady herself. How could he? Did the gypsy-like woman speak the truth? Were the doubts she experienced in York coming true? She trembled as shock warred with her budding anger.

She spun around as the door opened.

Ingrid entered and rushed to her side. 'Are you all right?' Ingrid took her hands. 'I witnessed what happened. I am sorry, but she has gone. I told her to leave immediately.'

Kitty sucked in a breath. 'Is it true? Is that woman Ben's mistress?'

'Please, Miss McKenzie, I know nothing of that, though I do not believe it to be true. She charms the men, but rarely does she give herself to one man completely. Rather, she likes to keep them dangling. She is married to an elderly, wealthy gentleman, who keeps a strict eye on her. He is no fool and knows exactly why she married him. Anyway, she is not important, believe me.'

'It is important to me!'

'Come sit down.' Ingrid led her over to an olive-green sofa under the window. 'I really do not think it is true. She is an unusual woman, but I doubt Ben even looked in her direction. He is besotted with you.'

'I was not here, she was.' Kitty jerked to her feet. Pain lanced her. 'I knew something like this would happen.'

'Miss McKenzie, Kitty, please, do not torture yourself over her. She is nothing.'

Kitty blinked away her tears. 'You think I should just dismiss it?'

Ingrid sighed. 'If there was something between her and Ben, it would be known. Nothing is kept secret for long in this town.'

She tilted her chin. 'Like my background?'

'Ben told us how he met you when you and your family lived in a cellar. We know, through hard work, you managed to buy yourself a business.' She chuckled. 'My Dan thought you a paragon to do that as well as raise a family.'

'I did not want people knowing of my struggle. I want my family to rise again to our former status.'

'And married to Ben you will.' Ingrid flicked an invisible speck off her apricot silk dress and glanced up grinning. 'You can relax now.'

Kitty paced, wondering if she would ever unwind. 'For Ben's sake and my family's, I need to be accepted.'

'Well, they do accept you already. Your background is between us. No one else will know. I promise.'

Kitty looked keenly at her. 'Ben desperately wanted you and I to be friends.'

Ingrid sat straighter, her face pale. 'You think it impossible?'

She sighed. This night had not been as she hoped. However, the woman seated before her seemed genuine. 'I think...it will not be a chore.'

Ingrid burst out laughing. 'Oh, you are so refreshing! I am so happy you have come.'

Chapter Three

Kitty wondered where the weeks of that first month in their new country went, as the family settled into their new lives. Benjamin acquired a place for Joe in King's College, a private boy's school near Parramatta in the southwest. Thus, Joe boarded at the school during the week and came home on the weekends. Kitty enrolled Clara at the young ladies' college, situated in William Street, not far from the house. It was the type of school Kitty had always hoped she would attend.

The house became a hive of activity when Ben and Kitty announced their intention to wed on the first Friday of August.

After the Freeman's party, Ben introduced Kitty and Mary to more of his friends and acquaintances. They dined with the beautiful Ashford-Smith couple, Gil and Pippa, whenever they were in Sydney and were invited to visit their country home at Berrima. Kitty did her best to push the image of the dark, sensual woman to the back of her mind. She was not in doubt of Ben's love, for he showed it plainly, and she had no wish to quarrel over someone who no longer mattered. Despite such reasoning, at times Kitty pondered the betrayal and whether it actually happened, but she did her best to conceal her thoughts.

With each new day, Kitty and Mary found themselves receiving ladies for morning and afternoon tea. These new acquaintances insisted Kitty should join them in all social gatherings and she found her time being monopolized more than she cared for.

Her relationship with Ingrid Freeman grew strong. She liked the woman and enjoyed her company, but she found her time increasingly hard to manage and desperately tried to set a routine. Lengthy periods spent with Connie or the babies were rare, as visitors never stopped ringing the front doorbell. Her days were now so busy, that an hour or two was all she could spare for Connie, Clara or Rosie.

Even her nights were no longer hers to call her own. They attended balls and dinner parties, musical soirées, theatre plays, poetry readings and a hundred more gatherings Kitty couldn't put a name to. Many a night, she did not reach her bed before two or three o'clock in the morning. Her head swam with the names and faces of people she was introduced to at picnics, days sailing on the harbour, carriage driving into the country and so much more.

Sadly, she was becoming tired of it. Though she could not say she was unhappy, for how could she when with Ben? Nevertheless, she also knew she couldn't keep going like this. Her character fought this busy, impersonal way of life. She ached for direction and quiet, peaceful days.

In contrast, Mary blossomed like a flower after the rain, much to the family's surprise. Through introductions at different parties, she developed friendships of her own age. She gained a small set of acquaintances and now spent her life as it would have been had their parents lived. The quiet, shy Mary had gone, replaced with a young woman intent on living life to the fullest and for some reason it frightened Kitty.

The one unadulterated delight for Kitty came at the end of July when, after his ship docked, Martin visited Forbes Street. Everyone laughed at the surprise on his face when he entered Ben's house and found his family in residence. Kitty cried with happiness as he swung her around the room. Very mature at eighteen, he looked so much like their father that sometimes it hurt to look at him. The sea life suited him. His tanned skin and overlong black hair matched his muscled arms and wide chest. Martin was a brother to be proud of, and if the ghost of another brother lingered sometimes, she accepted it and moved on. The pain of Rory's abandonment when they were at their weakest had diminished somewhat.

The Sunday before her wedding, Kitty sat on a hard-wooden pew in the local church. Religious instruction hadn't played a large role in her life since her parents' death, but Mary insisted they should all go every Sunday for morning and afternoon service. To please her, Kitty suffered it.

The uninteresting sermon allowed Kitty's mind to wander. She glanced around at the congregation. Leaning forward a little, she looked past Mary's bonnet and winked at Joe. He also fidgeted in his boredom. She gazed at the stone block walls and marvelled at the convict-built structure. Stifling a yawn, she noticed, a little further down, a grizzling baby being held up over its mother's shoulder.

Wide-eyed, the baby stared at Kitty. The child's face reminded her of someone, and it puzzled her. The baby put its thumb into its mouth.

Rosie.

The baby uncannily resembled Rosie. Goose bumps spread across her skin. *No, I must be going mad.* Obviously, her tiredness from all her social activities was catching up. Even so, she could not stop staring at the child. The woman turned to soothe the baby, and Kitty glimpsed the side of her face more clearly. The woman was not young, and obviously not the mother, with wisps of grey hair poking out from her shabby felt hat.

'Kitty, darling, are you all right?' Ben whispered.

She turned and nodded at him. 'A little tired, I think.'

'You need to be well rested for Friday, my love,' he murmured, squeezing her hand, his eyes full of love.

The service came to an end and the worshippers filed out into the weak sunshine. Scattered dark clouds forecasted rain. Kitty searched the throng to catch a better glimpse of the baby resembling Rosie, but there was no sign of the woman and baby. With a frustrated sigh, she turned back to her family.

Waking early the next morning, Kitty left the house to amble down to the harbour. Rain, fallen during the night, had dampened and refreshed the street. The bushland edging the water sharply scented the air with eucalyptus. In the east, the sun rose in a cherry-streaked sky.

She stepped along the path, which followed the water's high tide mark, feeling at peace. Behind her, all was quiet, as though the city had not yet woken. The only sound came from the native birds as they rang out their morning chorus. On the water, in the middle of the harbour, one or two boats sailed by. It was a scene worth painting. She strolled along a twisting dirt pathway that snaked through the trees and around outcrops of rock. She wore stout boots and held up her dark blue woollen skirts so as not to trip.

After a couple of miles, Kitty stopped and rested on a large rock. She glimpsed a few cottages hidden in the thick bush. A dog barked somewhere in the distance.

A smile lifted the corners of her mouth as thoughts of her wedding day surfaced. After all this time, she was going to be Ben's wife. Hopefully, one day she'd be mother to his children. She felt ready for marriage, in fact she longed for it. She was aware of a physical ache inside that yearned to be satisfied whenever Ben's gaze lingered on her. Also, it would be a relief to share the responsibilities of the family with a man. All the decision making had been hers with only Connie to discuss issues with. The family had lacked a man's presence since Max's death and Martin's departure. For too long all the worry had been hers alone.

Close by, a beady-eyed bird with a large beak flew down to sit on a log. Kitty studied it. She marvelled at the wildlife in this country and picked this bird to be a Blue Kingfisher as shown in her books. In a sudden flash of blue-green, the bird flew close to the gentle, lapping water and pulled a worm out of the muddy ground and in the next moment it was gone.

Breathing a contented sigh, she raised her head to view the harbour and the land on its other side. The colours of this land seemed old, immoveable. greys, slate-greens and earth tones spoke of a place older than man, and it gripped Kitty by the heart. In moments like these, when she had time to sit and be still, she soaked up the ambience of her adopted country.

With reluctance, she rose. A busy day awaited her, engagements with two ladies and the final fitting for her wedding dress. Stepping over a rock, she glanced up as a figure rounded the bend along the path. Kitty paused, recognizing the woman from the church with the baby that looked like Rosie.

The woman stopped and peered. 'Are you the McKenzie woman, from York?'

Kitty couldn't have been more shocked if the woman had grown two heads. How does she know who I am?

'Well? Are you?'

Kitty stared. The woman was much older than she first thought, at least sixty, with thin, grey hair and hard, but wise eyes, revealing she was not easily fooled. She wore a drab, faded black skirt, a not-so-clean yellow blouse with a black knitted shawl thrown over her shoulders.

'Yes, I am Miss McKenzie.'

'Aye, I thought so. I checked around see, once I 'eard the name mentioned. I couldn't believe me luck though, that you were his sister.' The old woman cursed and spat on the ground at Kitty's feet.

'I...I beg your pardon?' Goose bumps sprinkled upon her skin. 'I am afraid I do not understand your meaning, Mrs?'

'Me name is White, Bess White. I 'eard your name being spoken at the market, just by accident like, by the maid at the house you live in. Anyway, I pressed a coin in her hand to see if she would tell me about you, because I've an interest in the name McKenzie.' Bess White's face warped into an ugly sneer. 'Well, this lass was a find now, wasn't she? She told me all about you, about how you've just got off the boat from good ole England.'

Kitty bristled at the woman's tone. 'I am sorry, but what is it you wish to know and why? We have not met before.'

'Over a year ago, your brother came to this country and ruined my lass. He promised her the world, he did! But delivered nothing but a bairn, an' me lass is ruined because of it.' Again, she cursed and spat at Kitty's feet.

Kitty narrowed her eyes in disgust. 'I am sorry for your troubles, but how am I to know you are telling the truth?' Swiftly, it dawned on her and she raised her chin challengingly. 'And I am afraid I do not believe you, because my brother Martin only arrived in this country at the beginning of this year. There is no way that he could be the father of your daughter's child. I saw you in church yesterday and that baby was maybe six months old or more.' Kitty triumphed that she had plucked herself out of a sticky situation.

Bess White stepped closer. 'I ain't talking about your sailor brother, and yes, I know about him too. Oh, no, I'm talking about the other one.' Hatred burned in her eyes. 'The one with all the airs and graces, but don't have a coin in his pocket.'

Kitty staggered backwards, her hand going to her throat. The blood drained from her face. 'No. I do...not believe you.' A trickle of fear like ice-cold water ran down her spine. 'What was his name?'

'Rory,' the woman spat. 'Rory bloody McKenzie!'

Kitty had no memory of walking back to the house, but she must have done so, because she stumbled through the front door and fell into Ben's arms where he stood in the hall putting on his coat.

'Sweetheart, my love, tell me what happened to you?' He begged as he half-walked, half-carried her into the sitting room.

Hetta, polishing the mantelpiece, raced from the room crying for Mary, Connie and Alice.

Kitty became dimly aware of them hurrying around the sofa.

Ben knelt before her, rubbing warmth back into her hands. 'Darling, please tell me what happened? Were you attacked?'

Slowly, she recovered from the shock of the old woman's words. Anxious faces hovered close and she wanted to ease their worry. 'I...I am all right. I...I met...someone on the path down by the water...'

'Who? Who did you meet? Did they hurt you?' Ben leapt to his feet, ready to do battle, only to sit down again and hold Kitty's hands on seeing her tears. 'Oh, my darling.'

'I am fine, Ben, really. It is just this woman—'

'A woman attacked you?' He was incredulous.

'No, no. The woman was the one from the church, the one with the baby.'

Mary's eyes mirrored the bewilderment of the others. 'Kitty, you are not making any sense. Did you hit your head?'

'Mary, she saw him!' Tears filled her eyes and tripped over her lashes. 'She says he made her daughter with child.'

'Good God, lass.' Connie folded her arms. 'Who you talkin' about? It's too early ter play guessin' games.'

'Rory, of course! She said our brother Rory was here, in Sydney.'

Mary gasped. 'Rory? Here?'

Kitty took her handkerchief out of her pocket and wiped her eyes. Taking a deep breath, she told them about her encounter with the old woman.

'So, where is he now?' Ben asked as she finished.

'The woman doesn't know. She thought I might know where he is. She is awful mad at him for abandoning her daughter and wants him to do the right thing, but he obviously took his leave when he found out about the baby and has not been seen since.'

'Your brother sounds like a charmer, Kitty,' Ben commented sadly, standing.

'He was not always like that.' Kitty felt honour bound to defend him.

'Yes, yes, he was, Kitty. Mama spoilt him as he was her golden-haired boy,' spoke Mary quietly. 'Only you never saw it because you and Rory were always close.'

Kitty sat straighter, annoyed at them for slandering Rory. 'I know he ran out on us when I decided we would live in the tenement's cellar, but he was frightened and couldn't accept the situation. It was a shock to us all, remember?' She stood and tidied her hair. It was amazing to believe he had come to Australia. Now more than ever she was determined to find him. He had been gone too long and she wanted her brother home. She was ready to forgive anything, just as long as they were all together.

Connie cocked her head to one side. 'Lass, you all were shocked, but you didn't walk away. You stayed and toughened it out, like he should've done.' Connie shook her head then left the room. Hetta and Alice followed suit.

Kitty ignored the comments and took Ben's hands. 'I want to find him, Ben. The old woman has hunted for him for a long while now, and there has been no trace, but we have the money to do a comprehensive search.'

He nodded. 'I will put out the word that we are looking for him. However, this is a big country and he might be anywhere. If he has no money and he wants out of the city, then he may have gone to the bush to find work or gone to Melbourne or Hobart, the possibilities are endless.'

She raised an eyebrow. 'I shan't be deterred.'

'How did this woman know you?' Mary asked.

'She heard about us from the maid, Susie.' Kitty walked to the mantelpiece and tapped her fingers on the polished wood. 'Susie needs to be dealt with, Ben. For a few pennies she told the old woman all about us. She has no loyalty.'

Ben sighed. 'I will speak to her, dismiss her if I must, but now, I must go. I am late for an appointment. I will be back later this afternoon.' Kitty walked with him into the hall. 'Will you be all right?'

'Yes, of course.' Kitty gave him a dutiful smile, but her mind was reeling. Rory...

For the remainder of the morning, Kitty wandered restlessly from room to room. She cancelled her fitting appointment at the seamstress's shop and told Mary to go and visit the ladies by herself. She was in no mood to listen to prattling women.

After their midday meal, Kitty offered to take the twins and Rosie for a walk to give Connie a break. As they prepared the babies upstairs, a knock sounded at the front door. Kitty groaned, hoping Susie would remember her instructions to tell whomsoever it was, she was not home today.

Hearing a squabble of voices and shouting, Kitty exchanged a puzzled glance with Connie.

'I'll go down an' see what's it all about.' Connie sniffed. 'That Susie ain't worth feedin' in my opinion.'

Hetta hurled into the room. Being a large woman, she wasn't used to rushing about and she gasped, holding her side.

'What is it, Hetta?' Kitty scowled.

'Oh, Miss Kitty. There's a woman downstairs, an' she's got a babby. She says she's leavin' it here an' you can take care of it!'

'Oh, my Lord,' whispered Kitty. 'It is Rory's child.'

'Hetta, stay an' look after the twins for a minnit.' Connie grabbed Kitty's hand and they rushed downstairs.

Kitty stopped short as Bess White stood in the hall with the baby.

'Now, listen 'ere.' Connie strode up to the old woman. 'You can't go droppin' babbies off on doorsteps. We don't know you from Adam, an' we're not tekken your word Rory McKenzie 'tis father of that babby, so you can 'op it. Go on. Out!'

Bess puffed out her chest, an arthritic finger pointing at Connie. 'I'm telling you the truth. This child is Rory McKenzie's!'

Connie put her hands on her hips defensively. 'Surely your daughter wants 'er own child?'

'Me daughter died an hour ago. She's had consumption for two years and having the boy only weakened her more. I've done me bit, now it's your turn.'

To Kitty, it seemed as though Bess White had aged even more since early that morning. In the room's stunned silence, the shabbily dressed old woman lowered the baby to the mat and with a last look at Kitty, walked out the door.

'I'll be back, she can't do this.' Connie huffed, ready to march through the door. 'We'll get t'police on 'er.'

'No, Connie.' Kitty murmured, gazing at the baby. There was no doubt in her mind Rory fathered this child, for he was a McKenzie. The child possessed her brother's sandy-blond hair and the same blue eyes.

'What you talkin' about? She's ter be made t'come an' get him!'

Kitty slowly bent down, picked up the baby and looked into its innocent wide eyes. 'Can't you see the resemblance?'

Alice had come in from the kitchen wiping her hands on her apron. 'He looks like our Rosie, Miss.'

Connie stepped closer. The child, content in Kitty's arms, sucked its thumb. 'Aye, I suppose you right.'

'What are you to do, then, miss?' asked Alice.

Smiling down into the soft, but not-so-clean face, Kitty planted a tiny kiss on his forehead. 'Why keep him, of course.'

'Nay, you're mad,' cried Connie, horrified. 'You're ter be married at end'er week. Yer can't start you married life lookin' after a stranger's kid. You'll 'ave your own before too long.'

'Stuff and nonsense, Connie. This is my brother's child, therefore a part of my family. I could not turn away from this child, any more than I could from your twins. There is enough love inside me for any number of children, whether they be my own or someone else's.' She turned to Alice. 'Heat some water. This little man needs a wash.'

'An' what about Ben?' Connie wouldn't give up.

'Ben will understand.'

***

Ben did not understand. As dusk coated the town, he arrived home and found the baby in Kitty's arms.

The family left the parlour quickly, taking the child with them and leaving Kitty to explain.

'I cannot turn my back on this child, Ben. He is Rory's son.'

Ben stepped into the room, his face set. 'You have no proof.'

'He is the image of Rosie, and the others, as babies. Mary and Connie can see that, just as well as I can. There is no doubt in my mind he is a McKenzie.'

'He is not our responsibility, Kitty. He should be with his mother's family.'

Anger simmered in her at Ben's selfish attitude. 'His mother died today. The grandmother doesn't want to take care of him anymore, so what is there left to do? Send him to an orphanage?'

'Well yes. We could find a decent and loving family for him.'

Fury flushed her face. 'He is my nephew! I cannot believe you want me to send him away when he is all I have of my brother. How can you suggest such a thing?'

'Kitty, try and understand my point of view. I don't wish to be saddled with a baby that is not my own. Good God, I have already accepted nine members of your family and five of those are not even related to you.' Ben ran his fingers through his hair in frustration. 'Christ, I think I have done well so far.'

'Oh, I see. I am sorry, Benjamin, I never meant to burden you with the people I love. In the morning, we shall be gone to lodgings of our own. I would so hate to inconvenience you for another moment.'

Ben's face paled as he fought his anger. 'Do not be so bloody high and mighty, Kitty. Did you think of me in this matter? I'll be bringing up another man's son. I feel like I shall always come second, or third or way down the list in comparison to your family.'

'How can you say that? How can you stand there and say such vile things to me?' she cried. 'I came from the other side of the world to be with you. Were you in any hurry to return to me? Or were you content to leave me behind? Did the gypsy whore fill my shoes, did she?'

'What are you talking about?' Ben's face screwed up in puzzlement. 'What gypsy whore?'

'We met at the Freeman's party. She was quick to inform me of your liaison. Do you prefer her to me? Do you still see her?' Kitty's temper cooled with the surfacing hurt.

'There has never been anyone but you. You know that.'

'No, I do not.' Kitty turned on her heel and strode to the door.

Ben marched over and reached it before her. He leaned against the door barring her way. 'Listen to me, please. There has never been another woman, and you know I did not mean those harsh words I said, but have you thought everything through. I—'

'Let me out, please.' Kitty spoke through clenched teeth.

'Try to understand—'

'Oh, I understand you quite plainly, Ben. I am only pleased I have found this out before Friday. After all, once we married you could quite easily have sent my family away and I would not have been able to do a thing about it.'

'You know I am not like that. You are making me out to be a hard-hearted blackguard,' Ben snapped. 'I will not let you do this to us, Kitty.'

'I would like to go to my room.' She looked at some point over Ben's shoulder, knowing if she looked into his eyes she would break down and cry.

Slowly, Ben moved away from the door, but before she opened it, he took her hand and placed it to his lips. 'You may keep the child,' he whispered. 'I will not lose you over this. So, I give in to your wishes.'

'And I should be grateful?' Kitty held her head high. 'Sorry, Ben, but I know your true feelings on the subject, and therefore it would always come between us.'

Ben smiled, and then chuckled. 'Oh, how glorious you are, Kitty McKenzie!' He crushed her to him and kissed her fiercely. 'I love you and because of that I will grant you anything you desire.'

Kitty sagged with relief against him and welcomed his kiss. It awoke a deep hunger inside her, and she ached with yearning, for the intimacy they would soon share. She wanted to be loved properly. Need pulsated through her body. She ran her fingers through his thick ebony hair as his tongue plunged into her mouth. A moan escaped her.

When he released her, she leaned back. 'Will he and the others come between us? I need to know.'

'No, my love, they will not. Because there will come a time every night, when I will close our bedroom door and you will be all mine until morning comes again.'

'Oh, Ben.' Kitty sighed against him. 'I cannot wait.'

Chapter Four

The sun shone like a golden jewel. The stormy weather of the day before had cleared. The city glowed pristine in the sunlight of a lovely, crisp winter's morning. Birds flew against the clear blue sky, calling out to each other in what seemed to be great joy.

Organized chaos reigned in the Kingsley house on Forbes Street. Holed up in her bedroom with Hetta, Mary, Clara and Connie fussing around her, Kitty dressed in her wedding finery.

'Is Martin here yet?' Kitty went to the window and peered up the street. He had agreed to give her away, but his boat was late by two days coming into port.

'No, he isn't, but I'm sure he will soon be, lass,' Connie soothed, packing the last of Kitty's belongings for her honeymoon in Tasmania.

'Well, if he doesn't make it, Dan Freeman said he would do the honour, if need be.' Kitty turned to Mary. 'Is my hair finished?'

Mary put the last tiny white rosebud into Kitty's hair, which was arranged up on top of her head and held with mother-of-pearl tortoise shell combs. Kitty admired the gold high-lights shining in her copper-coloured hair, they were a legacy from spending days on a sun-soaked deck. Her dress was off the shoulder, consisting of white tulle skirts overlaid with a long, brocade satin skirt trailing into a short train. A row of seed pearls was sewn down the back of the whale-boned bodice. Around her neck, she wore a white silk choker, which held a topaz cameo, a wedding gift from Ben.

'I put your posy with mine downstairs, I will go and get it.' Mary grinned. She looked lovely with her long, straight black hair arrayed into a coronet of ringlets inserted with pink rosebuds. Her and Clara's dresses were violet, and Rosie's was light pink.

Kitty nodded and turned to Hetta. 'Could you go down and check on Alice? She has all the babies in the kitchen.'

'Aye, Miss Kitty.' Hetta moved to the door. 'No doubt young Charles will be lording over proceedings.'

Connie snorted. 'Little devil, that he is.' She bent to straighten Kitty's silver slippers and helped to guide her feet into them.

A sudden commotion on the landing heralded Martin entering the room. He halted by the door. 'My, my, where's the witch that changed all of you into beautiful women? She deserves a gold coin.' He laughed as Kitty rushed to embrace him.

'I was so worried you would be too late.'

'For such an occasion? Never.' He winked and then marched over to twirl Connie around the room.

'Give over, you daft sod.' But she kissed his cheek, nonetheless.

Martin's expression sobered. 'Downstairs, Mary told me the recent happenings. Do you truly believe the child is Rory's?'

Kitty nodded. 'Absolutely.'

'So, our wayward brother made it to this country then, when he should have returned to us.'

Connie tutted. 'Don't spoil the day, Martin. What Rory has done can't be changed.'

39

'And again, we are left with the consequences.' Martin took Kitty's hand. 'The child is well?'

'Very well. The doctor says he is in excellent health. He has grown in only a few days.'

Connie straightened Kitty's skirts. 'Aye, of course he would, now he's gettin' properly fed.'

'We have named him Rory.' Kitty waited for Martin's reaction.

'Seems sensible, but let's call him Little Rory. Happen the poor chap might not want to emulate his father completely.' Martin brightened and held out his arm. 'Come, we have a wedding to attend.'

During the short journey to the church, Kitty experienced last minute nerves and smiled wryly at Martin, who squeezed her white-gloved hand.

The carriage turned into the last street and rumbled to a stop some distance from the church.

Mary craned her neck to stare out of the window. She gasped at the carriages lining the way. 'So many people, Kitty. We shall have to wait for them to be seated.'

'I hardly know most of them.' Kitty grinned at Clara opposite.

They waited for five minutes before Martin opened the door and balanced on the carriage's small step. 'What's the hold up, driver? I have a sister wanting to be married.' He laughed.

'Nay, sir, I'm not sure,' the driver called back. 'But it looks like some kind of accident. A fruit cart has gone over I think.'

'Can we not go past it, man?'

'No, sir, at least not by carriage.'

Martin bent back inside to Kitty. 'I will go and have a look. There might be away around it.'

'No, Martin.' Kitty chuckled. 'Wait a few more minutes. I am sure it will soon clear. I was early anyway.'

He patted her hand. 'Yes, but at this rate we shall be decidedly late. I will be back shortly.'

An anxious feeling in the pit of her stomach made her feel slightly sick. Kitty took a deep breath. Soon, she would be Mrs Kingsley. For a fleeting moment, she thought of her parents and then of Dorothea. They and she would have treasured being here this day. Kitty missed the three of them, especially her father. She remembered the witty conversations and discussions they shared. Emotion caught in her throat. He should be the one walking her down the aisle, but thankfully she had Martin.

'What is the matter?' Mary asked, taking her hand.

'I was thinking of Mother and Father.'

'Yes, I was too, earlier. Mother would have enjoyed the occasion and the chance to sparkle. She was always very good at doing that.' Mary's eyes softened.

Clara frowned at them. 'Sometimes, I am frightened that I will forget what they looked like. I think I already have.'

Mary hugged her. 'You won't, I promise.'

A hubbub of noise reached them, and Kitty noticed the amount of people coming and going all around them. 'Where is Martin?'

They continued to wait and with each passing minute, the knot of apprehension grew tighter in Kitty's stomach. Abruptly, a shout sounded close by. A scream rent the air, making them jump in their seats.

'What could be happening?' whispered Clara, her eyes wide in her small face.

'I do not know, pet.'

'Where has Martin got to?' Mary muttered in annoyance. 'We are going to be really late.'

Minutes passed until Kitty could not stand it a moment longer. She gathered her skirts. 'Enough of this. I shall not be late for my own wedding. We will walk to the church.' She quickly descended from the carriage and gathered up her skirts. Mary and Clara followed close behind.

People mingled around. A strange wailing drifted to them from somewhere further up, but there was so much confusion it was hard to determine where from. Carts, carriages, wagons and gigs were left abandoned in a haphazard fashion. Men and women stood shaking their heads, children talked excitedly to each other and dogs ran wild barking at everyone and everything.

Kitty lifted her beautiful skirts high so as not to foul them. Her heart thumped against her ribs. A feathery touch of fear tingled her spine. Something unknown made her slow her pace until she stopped altogether. Mary bumped into her from behind.

Ahead stood people she knew, people whose homes she visited and parties she attended. They gathered in groups and she recognized the Clearys, the Weatherbys, the Ashford-Smiths and the Havershams. Kitty frowned. She wished they would stop dithering and enter the church. They were now dreadfully late.

All at once, her guests turned to stare at her. Horror etched their faces and Kitty took a step back. She blinked as her vision wavered. A few guests broke from the crowd and walked towards her with blurred faces. The throng moved. She looked past them. Close to the church front, carnage littered the street.

A large cart lay on its side. Fruit, spilt out of broken crates, blanketed the road. Near to the broken horses, still tangled in their harness, a man sat on the roadside crying so hard it made Kitty wince. A woman also sat on the road. In her arms, she rocked a small child, bloodied, mangled and obviously dead.

Martin squatted by the upturned cart. He nodded to Dan Freeman, who knelt beside him. In his lap, Dan cradled Benjamin's head and shoulders. A mist clouded her vision, she saw rather than felt Connie put her arms around her and croon in a soothing voice.

A scream pierced the air, a scream so shattering Kitty wanted to put her hands over her ears to shut it out. Hazily, she realized it was she who screamed.

Strangely, all noise stopped. In the silence, Kitty walked forward. Slowly at first, then faster and faster until she was running, running to Ben.

He was trapped from the waist down. The cart broke on impact with the road as it overturned. A piece of broken wood had pierced straight through Ben's chest, pinning him to the ground. Crates laden with fruit and vegetables showered him, but it was the piece of wood sticking out of his chest that did the damage. He was bleeding to death.

Kitty, helped by Martin, knelt beside Ben's head. From her silk wedding purse, she took an embroidered satin-edged handkerchief, given to her as a wedding present from Mary. Gently, she wiped the crimson blood from the cut on Ben's handsome face. Her tears dripped onto his bloodied cheeks, the salty water of them mingled with his blood and ran down into his hair.

'My love, it's Kitty,' she whispered. 'Sweetheart, open your eyes and look at me.'

The women standing around her wept inconsolably.

'The doctor is on his way,' Martin murmured, his face a ghastly colour.

Kitty ignored him, concentrating on Ben. 'Open your eyes, Ben,' she demanded harshly of the broken man she loved. 'You can do it. Do it for me. Open your eyes.' She knew if he'd just open his eyes he would live, simply because she would not let him close them again. She would breathe her life force into him. 'My darling, I need you to look at me, please. Please look at me, my love.' She returned to pleading softly to him, but a terrible anger took hold of her. 'Ben. Benjamin. Look at me!'

The doctor arrived opposite her and she stared at him, silently imploring for him to work a miracle.

Martin took hold of her. 'Come away. Let the doctor—'

'Leave me, Martin, leave me,' she begged him, pushing away his hands.

'Let the doctor see him,' His voice broke at her pain.

'No. Ben needs me.'

'He needs the doctor's help more.' He and Dan Freeman forcibly pulled her away, but she fought, screaming and tearing at them. Didn't they understand that she had to be with him?

Crazed, she flung herself about within their restrains. 'Let me go, please!'

Two gunshots exploded, making everyone jump. The thrashing horses now laid still. Martin and Dan caught Kitty as her world went black.

Connie sent Hetta home with the children, leaving Mary, Alice and herself to wait until it was their turn to see to Kitty. At the moment, she was in the two men's arms in case she bolted for Ben.

Ingrid Freeman organized for the guests to leave and, with some other members of the wedding party, began clearing away the onlookers and the poor children, who scrambled about gathering the fallen fruit.

The mother of the dead child, whom Ben had tried, in vain, to save from the cart's wheels, was taken home. No one neither knew nor cared where the driver of the cart was taken. Everyone's attention was on the man who lay dying on the road, on his wedding day.

With the cart lifted off his chest, the wound with the piece of wood still sticking out bled freely. It bled much faster than the doctor could staunch it. The doctor worked frantically.

A small, bright crimson river crept its way to where Kitty stood engulfed by her family. Calmer, she disentangled herself from Dan and Martin and stepped towards the man who should have been her husband by now. Her beautiful white gown was stained ruby around the hem. Her hair hung loose down her back. She knelt by Ben's head and gently cradled him on her lap.

The doctor leant back on his heels and wiped the perspiration from his brow. 'I'm sorry, my dear, terribly sorry, but his wound is too great. I can't stop the bleeding. He needs immediate attention, hospitalization, but to move him would be fatal. Then again, he cannot remain here, that piece of wood needs to come out.'

'It is all right, doctor. I am here now, and I will take care of him.'

'My dear, your young man is close to death. In fact...he will not last more than a few minutes.'

'Go away.'

The doctor blinked. 'Pardon?'

'Go away.' She bent her head once more to Ben's face. She kissed his closed eyes. Her beautiful man...

Kitty sat on the road, rocking slightly while stroking Ben's hair. She felt frozen in mind and body, too shocked to cry. 'Ben, I need you to look at me, just once more, my love. I'm wearing my dress, it's so lovely...' Her chin quivered, but she straightened her back and tossed her head. She had to be strong, but slowly the realization was filtering through the ice encircling her brain and heart. 'I imagined our children would have your cornflower blue eyes...'

Ben shuddered and she tightened her arms about him as he went limp and died. He never opened his eyes for her. He never said goodbye.

Chapter Five

Kitty sat on the sofa staring into the fire. Mesmerized, she concentrated on the dancing flames to block out the humming of voices in the room. Thankfully, the other guests had gone and only the Freemans remained. Clasped in her hand was a small posy of white and blue lilies. She had thrown one similar onto Ben's coffin as it was lowered into the ground.

Tiredness pulled at her bones due to sleepless nights. Sleeping frightened her now, for dreams haunted her, dreams of red rivers. Ben's life force flowed to her, encircling her, drowning her. But whether she was asleep or awake, she continually relived the memory of holding his head on her lap on that dreadful day. So much noise. The screaming, shouting, a dog barking, the awful grunting of the horses as they suffered and then finally the merciful two shots from the rifle.

She rocked back and forth, hugging herself. Will I ever wake up from this nightmare?

Almost afraid to, she glanced at the black drapes hanging at the window to let passersby know this was a house of mourning. Outside on the footpath, straw had been put down to quieten foot traffic. She hated it all. Overwhelming grief surged through her body. She wanted to rip out her hair, beat her chest, smash something, anything to make the hurt go away.

Without drawing attention, Dan Freeman made his way to her and sat opposite. 'Miss McKenzie, I—'

'I am Kitty, Dan.' She glanced at him then back to the fire. 'I think we have been through too much to stay on polite terms, you must agree?'

'Yes. Yes, of course.' He cleared his throat as a flush stained his neck. 'You are not alone in mourning Ben. We were like brothers and I too feel the pain of losing him.'

She shifted in her chair, refusing to acknowledge or share his hurt. She had not cried so far on this appalling day and had no wish to start now.

Dan pulled at his starched collar as though it choked him. 'Ben adored you, and I admire you for your courage.'

Kitty leant over to grip his hand. 'Thank you.'

'Ben gave me this...' He fished inside his mourning coat pocket and took out a rolled document tied with a red ribbon. 'He gave it to me on the morning of your...wedding. I was to wait outside the church and give it to you before you went in. It's his main wedding gift to you.' His hand shook as he held out the document.

Kitty looked at it as it wavered slightly in the air between them. 'What is it, do you know?'

'Yes. Title deeds.'

'Title deeds? To this house?' Kitty blinked back the swelling of tears.

Dan's gaze locked with hers. 'No, not for this house, for land, five hundred acres of bushland, up north. It's an investment.

Something for you so that you'd be secure should anything ever happen to...to Ben.'

She covered her face with her hands, and she rocked in the chair. It was laughable. A gift of security...

'I'm sorry, really.' Dan voice deepened in his grief. 'I should have waited a time before giving it to you.'

Ingrid, Martin and Connie hurried to her side. Kitty took a deep breath to gain control of herself again.

'I think we should go, Ingrid,' Dan said on a rush of breath. The colour of his face changed to putty.

At this, Kitty sat straighter, away from Martin's arms that held her gently. 'No please, Dan, Ingrid, I apologise for my...my behaviour. Please stay a little longer, I beg you.'

'Dan didn't mean to upset you, dear.' Ingrid took her hands in her own.

'Of course, I know that. It is just... I did not expect...' Kitty glanced at the papers Dan held. He gave them to her, and she crushed them against her chest. 'This is the last present I will ever receive from Ben, and the knowledge of that is...is quite overwhelming.' A solitary tear escaped, and she bit her lip so hard she tasted blood.

'The deed is in your name, Kitty,' Dan said. 'You are an owner of a property you can sell whenever you wish.'

'Security,' she whispered. She would rather have Ben.

Three days after the funeral, Martin sailed away on a voyage that would take over three months. With the house in mourning, the women did not go visiting nor did any visitors come and see them, except the Freemans. Dan insisted on taking care of them and Kitty allowed him to. For the moment, she had no strength to face the world alone.

Ingrid came every two days to check they were coping. It was she and Dan who took Joe back to school near Parramatta. Clara returned to her young ladies' school, and with the return of their normal routine, the family started to pick up the pieces of their lives again.

Kitty received a visit from Ben's solicitor. He was in charge of tying up Ben's interests and needed Ben's personal belongings so they could be shipped back to his mother. Kitty remained unmoved by his request. She knew Georgina would suffer greatly over the tragedy, coming only eight months after John's death. However, Georgina also got her wish. Kitty never became Ben's wife.

As the months dragged by, one by one, the family lived a dull existence in the terraced house on Forbes Street. When the weather was fine, Kitty sometimes walked along the foreshore of the harbour either late in the evening or early in the mornings, but mainly she stayed in the house.

She paid the rent from the money left from the sale of the teashop, but other than that, she held no interest in any material or financial matters. What the family ate, wore or did for entertainment no longer concerned her just so long they left her alone. She refused to be involved in anything that caused her to become part of the real world, a world without Ben. She loved playing with the babies, and she enjoyed her reading, which kept her mind occupied, but she wasn't ready to take on the load of being responsible for everyone and everything again.

One sunny Saturday morning in early November, Alice stormed into the sitting room. 'Miss Kitty, I really need to talk to you.' Her flushed face and irate stance alarmed Kitty as she glanced up from her book.

'Speak to Connie, please, Alice.'

'No, I can't, miss!' Alice's harsh tone cut through the quiet room. 'I'm sorry to disturb you, but you need to know a few things.'

'I really do not wish to be—'

'Do you know Hetta and me haven't been paid since Mr Kingsley died? Not that it matters as much as bills not being paid.' Alice threw a pile of bills onto the small ornamental table near the sofa.

Kitty winced and shrank back. 'Alice, I—'

'Do you know, miss, that all the grocery bills are paid by either meself or Connie? And now we have no money left of our own and the bills still keep on coming.'

'Surely there is...is...um...' The book fell onto her lap as she rubbed her temples. She tried hard to concentrate on the matter and say something to reassure Alice, but nothing formulated in her brain. The numbness of it frightened her. She blinked and then swallowed. Her breathing became rapid and the blood drained from her face. Wide-eyed with panic, she stared at Alice.

'Miss Kitty?' Alice grabbed her shoulders. 'Miss Kitty!'

Kitty gasped. 'I-I...I cannot...breathe...'

Alice ran screaming into the hallway calling for help.

Within moments, Connie, Mary and Hetta surrounded Kitty.

'She can't breathe,' Alice yelled at them.

Hetta pushed them all out of the way and cupped her hands over Kitty's mouth. 'Listen to me. Breathe in. Breathe out.' She stared into Kitty's eyes. 'Breathe in. Breathe out.'

Panting, Kitty managed to calm down enough to let the air enter her lungs. Her fear receded and she gripped Connie's hand. 'Thank you, Hetta. I...I'm all right now.'

Alice burst into tears and threw herself onto her knees before Kitty. 'I'm so sorry.'

Kitty hugged Alice to her, hating herself for her cowardice. 'No, it is my fault.' She frowned, worried at what she had done to her family. 'I am sorry for abandoning you all.'

'Alice will get you some tea.' Connie indicated for the others to leave.

As the room emptied, Kitty reddened in embarrassment. 'I am so ashamed I let you all suffer.'

'We didn't suffer too badly, Mr Freeman helped us.' Connie sniffed, business-like once more. 'But 'tis been four months, lass. 'Tis time ter move on.'

'I-I cannot do it. I cannot...'

Connie wrapped her arms around her shoulders, hugging tightly. 'Nay, lass, you're strong an' you know that life 'as t'go on. You've done it before. We all have at some point, haven't we?'

'Not without him.' She shook her head. 'He meant everything to me.'

'I know, lass, I know.'

'He was mine...' Kitty croaked into Connie's chest.

'Aye, lass.' Connie kissed the top of her head. 'We all thought the world of 'im.'

'I want to die.'

'Nay, lass. I'll not 'ave you sayin' owt like that.'

Kitty shoved Connie away. Anger choked her. 'What have I got to live for now he is gone, answer me that?'

'Why, you've got your whole life ahead of you. Then there's this family, it's falling apart without you. 'Ave you forgotten Little Rory? He's your responsibility now.' Connie's voice had risen, and she quickly lowered it. 'Do you think Ben'd want you t'throw it all away? You've got t'mekk him proud, lass.'

Kitty slumped back against the sofa and closed her eyes. 'I cannot do it. I simply cannot live without him and I don't want to.'

'Aye, lass, don't you think I don't know 'ow you feelin'? But if I can manage without my Max, then so can thee.' Connie's distress brought out her accent even more thickly.

She opened tear-filled eyes. 'Does the hurting ever go away? Because I think I will go mad at the thought of my life without Ben in it.'

Connie sighed heavily. 'It tekks a long time, lass. I still wake up an' think Max is sleeping beside me, but then we were together for a long time.'

'Unlike Ben and I.' Kitty swallowed back more tears.

'Everyone grieves in different ways, lass. Only time can heal you, an' it does eventually, I suppose.'

Kitty studied her clasped hands lying in her lap. Something happened to her this day, she knew. It was impossible go on the way she had. For months now, she denied there was life outside the house. She must join the world and live her life again. The thought depressed her. Without Ben, she was robbed of a lifetime of happiness being his wife and mother of his children. She'd been so close to having everything and then having it suddenly snatched away from her was the cruellest thing to experience. Why did the fates decree this? Why do I have to live my life without the man I love?

Clara entered carrying a tray. 'I brought the tea. Alice thought you might like some scones too.'

'Lovely, thank you, dearest.' Kitty smiled, wiping her face dry with the back of her hands.

Connie stood and smiled at Clara. 'Did you enjoy school to-day?'

'Yes, I did.' Clara set the tray down on the table before pouring the tea from the small silver teapot.

'Good, lass. Right, I'm off up to see the babbies.'

Clara watched Connie leave and then turned to Kitty. 'Alice is awfully upset. Are you better now?' She passed the cup and saucer to Kitty.

'Yes, pet. I am.' It appalled Kitty that she had no idea if Clara was coping at the young ladies' college. Where had the time gone? She patted the sofa. 'Come, sit beside me and talk to me. How is school?'

'I like it very much. My piano playing is greatly improved, though my spelling and Latin could do with some work, apparently.' Clara giggled, deepening her dimples.

'It's a shame we don't have a piano.'

'I wish you could attend our concert next week.' Clara glowed with excitement and enthusiasm. 'It's a penny donation at the door and all proceeds go to fixing the roof, which leaks. What fun it shall be. I am reciting a poem by Tennyson. Mary has been helping me. She and Martin are coming to see me perform.'

Kitty frowned. She knew nothing of this. 'Why can I not go?'

Clara frowned, puzzled by the question. 'Because you aren't well,' she said, as though Kitty was a little slow-minded.

Kitty placed her cup and saucer on the tray and walked to the window. She was annoyed with herself and also frightened. Her family was quite happily going about their lives while letting her wallow in self-pity. Well, not for much longer. 'I am going to your concert, Clara. I am now quite recovered from...from... Well, let us just say that I am better.'

Kitty took the tea tray back to the kitchen and placed it on the centre worktable.

Alice turned from the oven and tentatively smiled at Kitty. 'Are you all right, Miss?'

'I am fine, thank you, Alice, but we must talk. Can you come into the study in a minute when you are finished here?'

At the study door, Kitty hesitated. She had not been in the study since before her wedding day. This room was Ben's. Swallowing the lump in her throat, she reached out and gripped the doorknob.

'Lass? What you doin'?' Connie marched down the hall.

'I-I need to...um, there are the accounts to be sorted and...' Ben loomed large in her mind. 'Alice said that...'

'Aye, I know. Do you want me t'deal with it?' Connie placed her hand on Kitty's shoulder. 'Why don't you go up an' rest? I'll see ter it.'

Kitty was tempted but shook her head. 'No. I have to face it and begin my life again.' She smiled, trying to be brave. 'I cannot let you shield me anymore. I am responsible for this family. I have spent months doing nothing but indulging in self-pity. It's time I stood on my own two feet and stopped leaning on you and the others.'

'Nay, lass, that's what we're 'ere for.' Connie snorted.

'I need to do this. You do understand?'

Connie nodded. 'Right you are, then, lass.' She boldly opened the study door.

The room held a slight aroma of the cigars Ben sometimes smoked when discussing business with his friends. His favourite books still lined the bookcases, and on the walls hung the much-admired English paintings of country scenes. Kitty ran her fingers along the desk's dark polished wood. She touched his silver ink well. 'Oh, Ben,' she whispered.

A timid knock sounded at the door.

'Come in, Alice.' Kitty nodded.

For two hours, they worked at the ledgers and the pile of bills Alice placed on the desk. First, Kitty paid the butcher and the grocer. Next, they began with the bills for the cobbler in Bridge St., the seamstress in George St., the wood deliverer, the milliner in Elizabeth St. and the newspaper store that still delivered Ben's newspaper every day. Last of all, Ben's library books had to be returned.

Kitty sighed, replacing the pen back on its stand. 'I might visit the Freemans. I need Dan's advice on the money I have left. I also need to see Ben's banker. Ben opened an account for me, but once all these bills are paid, I think it will be empty.'

'The Freemans have been true friends, Kitty.' Connie dressed in black crepe stood by the desk. 'Dan and Ingrid haven't known us very long an' could've easily washed their hands of us, but they didn't. I think you should invite them over, ter thank them.' Connie cocked her ear on hearing one of the babies' cry.

'You are right. I will send a note today inviting them to dinner on Monday. It will be short notice, but I mustn't let another day go by without telling them how much I appreciate their kindness.' Kitty looked from one to the other. 'I also need to know what is the amount owed to you both.'

'It wasn't much, Miss Kitty, really. Let's leave it,' Alice mumbled, making for the door and back to her safe domain of the kitchen.

'No, Alice.' Kitty forestalled her. 'If you paid my bills, you will be reimbursed, and then there is also your wage, Susie's and Hetta's. You'll be back paid and settled up to next week.' She held up her hand to stop Alice arguing. 'You both must be due for days off no doubt. So, you take tomorrow and Hetta can have Monday.' Kitty turned to Connie. 'How much do I owe you?'

Connie stood with her hands on her hips and glared. 'Don't you dare ask what you owe me, Kitty McKenzie. I'm family, what's mine's yours an' so on!' Indignant, she stormed from the room to return to the babies.

'She will never change.' Kitty huffed but then smiled at Alice, for they wouldn't want Connie any other way.

Martin's ship docked the following day. He had been gone since the funeral and was sadly missed. The women savoured the sound and sight of a male in their midst after so long. Mary insisted they go for a picnic by the water to celebrate. Kitty persuaded Connie to join them and leave the babies in the care of Hetta and Alice.

For the first time in many months, Kitty spent a few hours in quiet laughter, free from the cloud of grief. With her hand linked through Martin's arm, they led the way home as the sun descended behind the distant blue hills to the west and threw a pinkish haze around the land. The streets teemed with folk strolling in the pleasant evening weather and Kitty uttered a deep sigh. It was a sigh of acceptance. Her life and happiness was her family. Their comforting chatter, coming from behind, was satisfying to hear. She gazed at the gardens and houses they passed and breathed in the scent from the roses and other flowers permeating the air.

'How are you really?' Martin whispered, leaning close.

Kitty peeped up at him from behind the short veil of her small black hat. 'Good, I think. At least, I am becoming better all the time. You coming home has helped.'

'I've been so worried throughout the whole voyage.' He patted her hand where it rested on his arm.

'Do not be, dear brother. Life has a way of moving forward, whether you want to go along with it or not. I have my family's love and support, what more can I ask for?' She shrugged. 'If I must live my life without Ben, then I must. I will miss him and never forget him, but more importantly I must live for him. My life has to be worth that of two.'

'Kitty—'

'Let us talk about something else.' She gave a wry smile. 'Tell me about your trip.'

'It was fine. I bought you all gifts from India.'

'Splendid. It must be so exciting visiting such places of interest.'

'Yes, it was... Kitty...I think there is someone who wishes to speak to you.' Martin indicated to an older woman standing on the path waiting.

Alarmed, she stared at Bess White. 'What do you want?'

'I heard about your troubles, and I wanted you to know that I'll have the boy back if you want.'

'Have him back?' The thought of handing Little Rory back to this woman horrified her. 'Never will I give him up. You were only too ready to be rid of him.'

The old woman's gaze did not waver. 'Well, I might have been a bit hasty like, but if you're willing to pay me a few shillings for his keep, then I'll have him.'

'So, it is money now, is it? Little Rory has a price on his head, has he? Well, too late. He is mine now and you will never see or have anything to do with him again!' She gathered up her black skirts and marched past the woman. Her frustrated anger, never far from the surface, gushed to the fore demanding release.

'Kitty, wait,' Martin called and rushed to catch up. 'You were a bit harsh, don't you think?'

Kitty spun, furious. 'No, I do not. She was eager to give Little Rory away and speak ill of our brother.'

'She had cause to and she was grieving for her daughter.'

'Little Rory is ours, he will be brought up to be a gentleman and be loved by his family. This family! Imagine the life he would have with her, if money is all she wants him for.'

'All right, calm down.' Martin took her arm, but she shrugged him off and strode away to the house.

Again, he caught up with her. 'Little Rory is all that woman has of her daughter. I thought you might be a little more understanding.'

At the front door, she glared at him. 'And he is all we have of Rory.'

'Rory isn't dead, Kitty.'

'How would you know? Nothing has been heard or seen of him since he left this town over a year ago. Anything could have happened to him by now. None of our advertisements have received a response.'

'He deserves nothing from us as far as I am concerned,' Martin snapped.

Kitty gave him a scathing look before going inside and straight upstairs.

Connie paused as she passed Martin and put her hand on his arm. 'Leave her be, lad. She'll never give that babby up, so there's no use tryin' ter talk ter her about it. That White woman medd her choice. Only now, she realizes she could've medd money with him.'

'Surely not, Connie?'

'Aye, lad, it's hard t'believe some people are like that, but that's life.'

'I hate to see such anger in Kitty. She has never behaved in such a way before, yelling in the middle of the street like a common fishwife. She might have been brought down low before, but she was always a lady and considerate of other people.'

In the hall, Connie took off her black lace shawl. 'She's still a lady, Martin, but she also knows how hard you have ter be ter survive in this world. She's been dealt some knocks, startin' with your parents' deaths. She's tekken the brunt of it ter shield you all from it. So, think on, lad.'

Kitty pushed her bacon around her plate, her hunger gone. Her gaze strayed to the mail sitting beside her. No doubt, they were mostly bills. Sighing, she picked up the first one and discarded it.

The next one was from Ingrid Freeman accepting the invitation for dinner that night. She opened the next letter. It was from Kell & Gateby Associates, Solicitors. Kitty read the letter with growing dread. The owners of the house had instructed the solicitors to sell. The family must vacate the premises by the New Year.

'What's up, lass?' Connie and Mary entered the dining room for breakfast.

'There is a letter from these solicitors.' She indicated the letter in her hand. 'The owners of this house want to sell it, and we have to leave by the end of December, in just six weeks.'

'Oh, no, Kitty!' Mary rocked back in her chair. 'What will we do? I thought Ben owned it?'

'No, he just rented it.'

'Can you buy it, do you think, lass?'

She shook her head. 'I don't think so. Even if I could, how am I to keep us going?' She rubbed her forehead in despair. 'We are in the same situation as in York.'

'Are you saying that we have to buy a shop again and work for the rest of our lives?' Mary groaned. 'I cannot believe you are asking us to do this again.'

'Nothing is decided yet, Mary.'

'I like the way we live now, the way we should have always lived.' Mary crumpled her napkin. 'I will not work again, Kitty. Do you realize I will lose all my new friends? They will not want to socialize with me once I am working class.'

Connie waved her teaspoon at her across the table. 'There's nowt wrong with the working class, me girl.'

Mary scraped back her chair. 'I shan't let you do this to me again, Kitty. I won't.' She ran from the room.

'That lass needs a good hidin'.' Connie folded her arms.

'Leave it.' Kitty rose and gathered her letters. Susie came in carrying a pot of tea, and Kitty asked her to go on the street and find her a hansom cab. 'I might go see Dan at his office in Castlereagh Street instead of speaking about this to him tonight.'

Before long, Kitty was heading into town. Castlereagh Street ran parallel to the major streets of Pitt, George and Elizabeth. Early morning shoppers and the cabs, carriages, horse drawn trams, bullock wagons and carts passing through the city stirred up the dust. As the sun rose higher, the heat shimmered off the stone buildings. Kitty found it hard to believe it was only nine o'clock in the morning.

She paid the driver, and lifting her navy linen skirts from the dust, went inside the cool, dim building. She waited a moment for her eyes to adjust after the brightness of outside.

A tall youth, in a starched suit, rose from behind a desk and asked whom she wished to see. Within minutes, she was sitting in Dan's office.

'Kitty. Is everything all right?' Dan hurried into the room and took her hand.

'Yes, except there are some business matters I wish to discuss with you, if that is all right, and you have the time?'

'Of course, I have the time.' He relaxed and sat in his brown leather chair. 'So, what can I help you with?'

She passed him the letter from the solicitors and let him read it. 'I wanted to know whether you might help me decide what to do next.'

'I understand Ben left no will, so it makes it difficult. All his money, property and any other assets, go to his nearest living relative, his mother.'

Kitty nodded. Georgina. The woman haunted her from across thousands of miles. Georgina would be happy to see her ruined, penniless once more. Kitty shuddered, imagining the woman crowing to her friends that the McKenzie chit didn't get her hands on her son or his wealth.

Dan sighed, and leant back in his chair. 'Do you have any money?'

'Some, from the sale of my shop in York. Only, it will not last forever and I am worried. I could rent a small house and make us all live very frugally. It is not as though we haven't done it before. Even so, I am loath to do it. Maybe you might know of some other solution to my problem?'

'Not off hand, no. Let me think about it today, and we can talk some more this evening when Ingrid and I come to dinner.'

'Thank you, Dan. It helps to talk to you about it.' Kitty rose from her chair, while Dan came around to lightly kiss her cheek. 'Until tonight then,' she said, and walked out of his office.

Leaving the building, Kitty strolled down the street. As usual, most of the streets running south to north led to the harbour. The offices and shops held no interest for her as she passed them, and the heat became more intense. By the time she reached the water's edge, she was hot and perspiring. In a small park area, she sat under the shade of a large pine tree. Kitty took out her handkerchief and wiped her damp forehead.

She closed her eyes and leant against the tree trunk. Her life was once again in turmoil and the family would be disrupted. She was tired of worrying and hurting. Sometimes, she thought she'd manage, and then the next moment, she was so down in spirits she could barely eat.

Kitty stared out over the glistening water and idly watched the boats and ships go by. She adored the harbour, the sight of it and the activity, the noise and the smell, but sitting here wouldn't fix her dilemma.

'What am I to do, Ben? Help me,' she whispered, looking out over the rippling water. She ached to have him hold her and murmur that everything would be all right. Suddenly, an idea began to form in her mind, hesitant at first and unclear, but with each passing minute the conception grew, becoming more defined.

———*ee*———

After finishing a tasteful meal cooked by Alice, Kitty lingered by the door until all were seated comfortably in the parlour. As Ingrid and Connie discussed knitting patterns for young children, Kitty smiled at how easily Connie mixed with the Freemans. Gone was the shy, but hard, undemonstrative woman whom Kitty first bumped into so long ago. Her hair, newly washed and arranged neatly in a bun at her nape, made her look like she had always lived well and been a part of society. That was until she spoke, and one heard her broad Yorkshire accent.

Mary, Martin and Dan passed around the Sydney Morning Herald newspaper, each commenting on public's response to the recent Drunkard's Punishment Bill being passed. Hetta looked after the babies and Clara had gone to bed. Only Joe was missing, being at school.

Kitty stepped over the small table, placed in the middle of the room between the sofas and, picking up the large silver teapot, began to pour out cups of tea for everyone. She waited until there was a slight pause in the conversation and plunged in. 'I have been giving a great deal of thought to the present predicament this family happens to be in, and I have come up with a solution.'

'Really? What is it?' Martin sipped his tea.

She looked around at their expectant faces. 'We are going to live on the land Ben gave to me.'

'What?' Martin gasped, nearly choking on his hot tea. 'Are you mad?'

'Why is that madness?' She raised her chin in defiance, ready to battle.

Dan lost all colour. 'That land is in the middle of nowhere. You simply cannot go north and live in the hut there.'

'Dan is right.' Ingrid nodded. 'Surely there must be another solution?'

Kitty shrugged. 'There could be. However, this is the course I wish to take.'

Martin's manner dismissed her foolishness. 'It is ridiculous to think of you living out in the wild bush totally unprotected. It is complete folly! And what exactly are you going to do once you are out there, become a farmer?'

'Yes, if I must. Though, I am sure I can hire someone who can do that for me. All we need is to grow enough food to feed us and I thought I would have some sheep and a few cows.'

'I have never heard of anything so outrageous in all my life,' Martin stormed. He placed his cup and saucer down none too gently and strode over to stand by the empty fireplace.

Annoyance flushed her face. 'Is it any more outrageous than living in a cellar? My God, Martin, you sound just like Rory did the day he left us.'

'I'm nothing like Rory. It's just you have no concept of what you are suggesting.'

'I beg your pardon? I am not a fool, neither do I wish you to treat me as one.'

'Martin. Kitty. Stop this, remember our guests,' Mary shushed, red-faced from embarrassment.

'Yes, yes, of course, I do apologize. Ingrid, Dan, forgive us. I am afraid we McKenzies are rather hot-headed.' Kitty smiled, trying to lighten the tension.

'Kitty, please, I implore you to think very wisely about this,' said Dan. 'Country living is very harsh. Every day hard, strong men simply walk away from their land. They leave everything behind, sometimes even wives and children. It's easier to do that than to scrape a living out of the earth year after year for no profit.'

Kitty added sugar to her tea. 'Some are successful, Dan.'

'Yes, mainly the wealthier sort. Those able to plough a lot of money into the property in the first instance and do not expect a return for some time.'

Ingrid placed her cup and saucer back on the tea tray. 'Is there some hope you may change your mind, Kitty? Dan and I will endeavour to help you in any way we can, but surely you would prefer to stay in Sydney?'

Kitty reached over and gripped Ingrid's hand. 'Actually, Sydney holds nothing for me now. But, thank you, Ingrid, you are a true friend.'

'Why not go to Melbourne or Hobart?' asked Dan. 'The cities there are just as good as Sydney and with a small amount of capital you might be able to go into trade again.'

'No, I think not. I need a change, buying another teashop is not a prospect favourable to me.'

Martin faced her. 'With my earnings, you can stay in Sydney and live in a cottage—'

'No, Martin.'

'You cannot be serious about doing such a thing?' he persisted. 'Have you thought about the others? Do you think they wish to endure those hardships again?'

Chin held high, Kitty rose from her seat. 'I am going, Martin, and those who wish to, can come with me. Those who wish to stay can live in the cottage you provide.'

'You are wrong to do this, Kitty!' Martin marched from the room, and seconds later, the front door slammed.

An embarrassed silence filled the room, until Dan placed his hand on Kitty's shoulder. 'You will need to do some research on what you must take with you and how much.'

'Come into the study, Dan. I have already started to plan and make a list. Ben has some books in the bookcases that are very helpful.'

Once Kitty and Dan left the room, Mary whirled on Connie. 'You have to talk her out of this craziness! She will listen to you.'

'Nay, Mary, it's not me who can tell that one what t'do. She's her own woman.'

Ingrid's mouth turned down. 'She is determined.'

'She is mad to think we can all live in the wild,' protested Mary. 'I will not go.'

The argument continued at breakfast the following morning. The minute Kitty sat at the table, Mary began. 'You are not seriously considering moving the family so far away, are you, Kitty?'

'I told you last night, Mary, there is land up north that I own. It makes sense to live there.' Kitty buttered a slice of toast.

'I do not agree. You are again making us change our lives. It is selfish.'

'Selfish? Selfish, you call it, trying to keep this family together?' She clenched her hands into fists to stop them from thumping the table.

Mary shoved her plate away, her breakfast unfinished. 'Why can we not simply stay in Sydney?'

'We cannot afford it. This house is fifty pounds a year to rent. Then, there are the food bills, clothing and wages. The list is endless. So, what do you suggest we do? Shall I go out and scrub floors? Or maybe, you could go into service at your friends the Richards' or Ascot's?'

'Now you are being ridiculous. I will not listen to you.'

'Why do I always have to have an argument with you over the important things? I am thinking of the whole family in this.'

'No, you are not thinking of the family, you are thinking only of yourself!' Mary jerked to her feet; anger radiated from her. 'You spent months wallowing in self-pity and thought nothing of us and now you expect us to simply give up our lives and follow you again.'

'How dare you?' Kitty stood so quickly her chair fell over backwards.

'I am going out.' Mary swished out of the room.

Kitty hurried after her. 'Where are you going?'

Mary collected her hat and pinned it on, next, she gathered her gloves and parasol. 'Gina Ascot has invited me to her house this morning. We are going to sketch in her garden. I will be home later.'

'I knew nothing of this.'

'Of course not, you were too busy planning our trip to Hell.'

Kitty gasped. 'That is enough.'

'The Ascots are fine, wealthy, socially acceptable people. The kind our mother would have been pleased to call friends. I will not go to some backwater and give up my life here.' Mary opened the door and walked out.

Chapter Six

The whole house was quiet, everyone finally asleep after a busy, but pleasant Christmas day.

'Happy Christmas, lass,' Connie said, exhausted, raising her glass of sherry to clink it against Kitty's.

'I was dreading this day, but was a lovely day,' Kitty mused.

'Aye, it was, but I'm glad it's over. Me feet are killin' me.'

'Another eventful year has gone. Next week we shall see in eighteen sixty-seven.'

'Aye. We crossed the oceans of t'world. If you had told me five years ago, that I'd be doin' such a thing, I'd have thought you were barmy.' Connie snorted. 'I tell you, with Dan buying this house and letting us live here rent free until we go north medd it really special. What a grand man he is.'

'Absolutely. I will forever treasure his kindness.'

'Well, he knows if you were married ter Ben, you wouldn't be goin' north.' Connie yawned. 'At least if summat goes wrong, there'll be this house to come home ter.'

'Nothing is going to go wrong, Mrs Spencer,' Kitty said in mock anger. Sighing, she relaxed in the chair. 'It was nice to have the whole family together, except for notable absentees.'

Connie stared at her glass; a wistful shadow passed over her face. "Tis days like these that mekk me miss Max all the more. The twins are growin' so fast an' he never even got t'see them.'

'I cannot believe he has been gone almost fifteen months.'

'Aye.'

Kitty put down her glass and fiddled with the black lace collar of her navy dress. The somber colours she continually wore since Ben's death in August did nothing to alleviate her depression.

Connie cocked an eyebrow as if reading her thoughts. 'When are you goin' t'wear some colour, lass?'

Kitty shrugged and, reaching up, she pulled the pins out of her hair and let it fall in heavy waves down her back. 'Soon.'

'This drabness doesn't suit you.'

'It's not meant to. Anyway, I am not out to attract anyone, ever.'

'Oh, stop that nonsense.'

Kitty yawned and rubbed her neck. 'I am worried about Mary.'

'Aye, she's not herself.'

'Last week, when Gina Ascot was here, she mentioned something about her cousin, who is becoming attentive to Mary, and it seems Mary reciprocates his feelings.'

'Nay, I never.' Connie stared at Kitty in amazement. 'Has our Mary said owt?'

'Not to me. She is barely civil to me now. She has changed so much since our arrival here and her new friends are not helping. She spends all her time at the Ascot's house. They encourage her to think and act above herself. I can barely keep up with her needs. My money does not stretch to new dresses and shoes every other week. Apparently, this Ascot cousin can give Mary everything she wants, but I do not want her marrying him just for money and an advantageous lifestyle. I want her to marry for love, for our lives can be tediously long when we are unhappy, as I should know.'

Connie placed her glass on the small table beside her chair and stood. 'The quicker we leave the better, I say. Though, Mary mentioned again this mornin' that she's not goin' north. With Dan buyin' this house, she seems ter think she can remain here once we've gone.'

'Well, she is not. I am tired of her attitude. Oh, I know she wants society and all I am offering is the bush, but I have to do what I think is right. If I had married Ben then our circumstances would have suited her, but I have little money, and at this moment I cannot give her the privileged life I wanted to. My wish is that the land will make us good profits and I can afford to give my family that life they were meant to lead.'

'Mary's young, but one day she'll understand what you doin' fer the family.'

'I hope so. I cannot believe she's become so self-centred. Who would have thought it of Mary?'

'Do you know the Ascots have asked her ter go away with them, t'their country house?'

'She has mentioned it, yes. I am not happy about it, but what can I do? The Ascots are nice people. Although, the interested cousin, I have yet to meet.'

'Is the date set to go north?'

'Dan thinks I am mad to go in the heat of summer, even so, I am impatient to get there and see for myself. Nevertheless, I think it will be about the beginning of March.'

'An' we're goin' by boat?'

Kitty hesitated, glancing uneasily at Connie. 'As you know, Dan and I have talked about this move until we are blue in the face, and each time, it becomes clearer that it would be best if I went first with Dan. Then, when I am settled, I will send for you all.'

'Why? Two days on a boat won't be too hard and we'll manage at the hut.'

'Connie, there is so much we do not know, such as the hut's condition. It has not been lived in for over a year. It will need a lot of work done on it to make it habitable.'

Connie gave Kitty a look that spoke volumes. 'I don't want t'be left 'ere, lass. Ever since we met, we've allus done everythin' together. I want t'be with you when you go, it's only right.'

'It will be very hard, Connie,' persisted Kitty.

'Nay, lass. When has hard work ever bothered me? Nay, lass, we're in it together.'

'I had thought you might stay here with the children, until I have it settled.'

'If you insist on it, I will, but it'll hurt ter be left behind.' Connie sniffed, a clear sign she was not happy.

'It shan't be for long. Dan has bought cattle ready to transport overland and the list of provisions is all but complete and ready to buy.'

'Cattle?' Connie raised her eyebrows in surprise. 'Isn't it sheep that everyone has out 'ere?'

Kitty grinned. 'Yes, mainly, but I want to be different and Dan seems to think cattle will do well up there, at least we are going to give it a try. Dan buys the cattle, I fatten them up and when they are sold, we share the profits, fifty-fifty.'

'How long will it be before we can come t'you, then?'

'I am not sure, a month or so.' Kitty rose, ready for bed. They faced each other, and then Kitty smiled sadly at the way their lives had turned out. 'Oh, Connie, it is madness, isn't it?'

Connie chuckled. 'Aye, lass, it is that, but it mekks life worth livin'.'

'It is a big undertaking, another journey for us to take. There will be many hardships to overcome.'

'We'll manage, lass, we're Yorkshire women after all.'

By the end of February, plans for the journey to the north were complete. A week before she was due to depart, Kitty sat perspiring in the sitting room trying to compose a letter to Dorothea. The summer sun baked the city in a heat so intense it withered the grass and plants. Hot, dry winds blew in from the west. They stirred up great dust clouds originally called brick fielders, because the dust borne on the wind from the brick making factories west of the city covered the town and its people in a thick, choking layou. The dust storms brought the city to a standstill and, combined with the heat, battered Kitty and the family as they experienced their first antipodean summer. There was no rest from the high temperatures, even at night. Irritability was rampant among the occupants of the house on Forbes Street as well as the population of the city.

The doorbell rang and as Hetta answered it, Kitty paused, wondering who called at this late evening hour.

'Is Miss McKenzie home?'

Hearing the stranger's voice, Kitty stood. In the hall, she faced the tall, thin gentleman. 'I am Kitty McKenzie. May I help you?'

He bowed. 'Timothy Ascot, Miss McKenzie. How do you do?'

'I am well, thank you, Mr Ascot.' She inclined her head stiffly to the man who had set Mary's heart aflutter and waved him towards the sitting room.

Once they both were seated, Kitty let him start the conversation, a decision she regretted as he talked of nothing but himself for ten minutes solid. She was grateful when Connie and Mary entered and sat with them.

Ascot crossed his legs and placed a hand on his raised knee. His thin lips lifted slightly in a pathetic smile. 'My dearest Miss Mary has drawn a likeness of me that flatters my features so much, I am sure to win a beauty contest.'

'Indeed?' Kitty hid her grimace by forcing a smile to her face.

'Oh, Mr Ascot, you are a delightful subject.' Mary trilled in such a way Kitty looked at her in surprise.

He smirked and fingered his black, narrow moustache. 'How charming you are, dear Miss Mary.'

Appalled at his obvious false charm, Kitty and Connie exchanged glances.

'I believe you live in the country, Mr Ascot?' Kitty asked, as Hetta brought in a tea tray.

'Hideous place, Miss McKenzie. I do my utmost to be away from there at every possible opportunity.' He sat straighter as she handed him his cup and saucer. 'Sydney, as primitive as it is, holds some semblance of society. Naturally, nothing will replace London in my affections.'

Kitty nodded. 'Naturally.'

He left them twenty minutes later, with the promise he would call again the following morning. It astonished and annoyed Kitty to find Mary transformed into a happy, twittering, silly girl in front of the fawning Ascot fellow.

'Did you not think he is so handsome, Kitty?' Mary gushed the minute he was out of the door. Her face, bright with vibrancy, reminded Kitty of their mother.

'He is acceptable enough, I suppose.' She considered his thin frame and sharp facial features unattractive herself. His pretentious manner and false banality did nothing to endear him to her.

'Did you like him, Connie?' persisted Mary.

'Aye, lass.' Connie quickly bade them all good night before she was questioned any more.

Kitty tidied her correspondence and put away her secretary. She glanced at Mary. 'You seem to like him a great deal.'

'I confess I do. What is there not to like?'

'What do you know about him?'

'Oh, Kitty! I have spent a great deal of time with him and all the Ascots. They are a good family, with position and wealth and standing in the community.'

'I know that already. I meant Mr Ascot, himself.'

Mary eyed her warily. 'Have you heard something about him?'

'No, should I have?'

'Not at all,' defended Mary. 'I want you to like him, please, for me.'

'Why? Why is it so important for me to like Mr Ascot?'

'Because I love him, and should he ask for your permission tomorrow, I will marry him.'

She was not entirely startled by her sister's words, but she still felt uncomfortable about the whole situation. 'I see.'

Mary rushed to grasp her hands. 'Please say yes. I want to be his wife.'

'I know nothing about him.' Kitty turned away from the earnest look in Mary's eyes. 'How can I be sure I am doing the correct thing by letting Mr Ascot marry you? He never came to me to ask permission to court you.'

'That is because I asked him not to because Ben had recently died.'

Kitty whirled back. 'This has been going on since August?'

'Oh, Kitty, I desperately want to marry Timothy. He can give me a good life.'

Kitty stepped away and leant against the sofa to gather her thoughts. Mary was proving to be as impulsive as their mother and it had to be curbed as soon as possible. 'I am unhappy that this has been organized behind my back, neither do I like that I am soon to go north, and this matter has only just come to light.'

'All you have to say is yes,' pleaded Mary. 'Please, that is all I ask. We will then be engaged, and we can marry when you come back. I thought all you wanted for me, Clara and Rosie are good marriages? I can have that now.'

Kitty sighed, unhappy at the way she had been deceived. 'I will think about it and decide in the morning. Good night, Mary.'

* * *

At the breakfast table, Kitty found Connie alone and mentioned her thoughts on a marriage between Mary and Mr Ascot. 'I have an uneasy feeling about him. He does not seem to be all he makes out.'

'I agree, lass. So, what you goin' t'do, then? If you say no, she'll never forgive you, an' it'll mekk her want him all the more.'

'Yes, I know. I am just so annoyed and disappointed in Mary for leaving this until I am ready to go north.'

'It was well planned. I'll give her that.' Connie sniffed and handed the mail over.

'I am left no choice but to say no. I will review the situation when I return.'

'She'll not like it.'

Mary didn't like it. She screamed and cried when Kitty told her of the decision. The magnitude of her tantrums astounded Kitty. This new Mary was one she did not like.

When Timothy arrived, Mary kept to her room so he wouldn't see her red and blotchy face. He formally asked for Mary's hand in marriage and seemed so certain he would not be refused that he was quite taken back when Kitty told him the opposite.

'I do not understand, Miss McKenzie.' His face waned. 'May I have a reason for your decision?'

'It is a simple one, Mr Ascot. I do not know you or your situation well enough to give permission to a question as important as the one you have put to me. You must understand I have to be certain Mary will be loved and cared for—'

'I assure you that she will, Miss McKenzie.'

'As you no doubt know, I leave to travel north next week. I shall be gone for a month or more. When I return, I may think differently. Until then, you may continue courting Mary under the guidance of Mrs Connie Spencer.'

A muscle above his eye twitched. 'Mary would much rather for us to be engaged before you leave.'

She raised her eyebrow at him. 'I am sorry, but Mary will have to wait. I need to be confident in my mind that I am making the right decision.'

'Miss McKenzie, I have everything to offer Mary. She will want for nothing.'

'My decision stands, Mr Ascot.'

'Then, I will bid you good day, madam!' He bowed stiffly and strode from the room.

Kitty sighed and sank into a nearby chair. The door opened and Connie entered, carrying Adelaide in her arms.

'How did it go, lass?'

'Not good.'

'I have some more news for you.' Connie grimaced.

'Oh, what is it?'

'A note was delivered while you were talking ter Ascot. It's from Ingrid. Dan was thrown from his horse yesterday. He's broken his leg.'

'No! That is terrible.'

'He'll not be able t'go north now.'

Kitty slumped. 'I am cursed.'

Connie put Adelaide down on the floor, where the little girl tottered around on shaky legs. 'You'll have t'put the trip off for a while, that's all.'

'No. Everything is arranged.' Kitty rose and wandered over to the window to stare blindly out of it. 'I shall go on my own.'

'You'll do no such thing! Ye Gods, lass. You can't do everythin' yourself. It won't kill you t'wait a couple of months.'

Kitty spun to face her. 'I hate it here. I hate this house! I still expect to see Benjamin sitting in the study whenever I enter it. I want to be free of the ghosts.'

Connie folded her arms across her flat chest. 'All right, lass, all right. Come next week, we'll be gone from here.'

'We?'

Connie grinned and bent down to scoop Adelaide into her arms. 'Aye, lass. We are all goin' now.'

'Connie—'

'Either we all go, or you wait for Dan.'

Kitty took a deep breath and smiled back at her dear friend. 'Well then, we had better start to pack.'

Hetta stuck her head around the study door. 'Miss, I don't want to disturb you...'

Kitty put her hand up to stop her until she finished counting. 'Yes?'

'It's about you going north, Miss.' Hetta fiddled with the ever-present apron she wore. 'You see, miss, I was wondering whether you'd mind if I didn't go.'

'Not go? Why?'

'I'm not as young as I like to think I am, Miss. I'd prefer to stay here an' tekk care of this house while you're gone, if I may?'

Kitty moved around the desk to stand before Hetta. 'Of course, you can stay. If that is what you want?'

'Aye, Miss. It is.' Hetta nodded, her shoulders relaxing a little.

Kitty smiled in reassurance. 'In fact, Hetta, I would be rather glad to have you here to keep an eye on things for Dan. I know, under your care, the house will be well looked after in case we come back to Sydney. Yes, I like the idea very well. What about Alice? Does she want to stay too?'

'No, Miss. She wants ter go with you, for she knows you'll need her.'

'All right, it is settled then.'

'Thank you, Miss. I'm so pleased. An' you can rest easy, miss, this house will be tekken care of like a palace.'

Later that afternoon, Ingrid visited as Kitty made some last-minute lists. 'I know it is a busy time for you, Kitty, but I had to leave the house before I lost my temper and I so hate losing my temper.' Ingrid laughed, accepting a cup of tea from Connie. 'Dan is driving me mad with his rantings of being bored. Sitting around all day, every day, with his leg up does not appeal to him.'

Kitty chuckled. 'I am sure poor Dan will find a way to make it to the office very soon, even if he has to be carried there.'

'No doubt,' agreed Ingrid. 'Though, I did want to tell you that we are still happy to have Joe on the weekends and during his holidays. I also thought that maybe Clara would wish to stay with us and continue her schooling at the ladies college?'

She gripped Ingrid's hand. 'Oh, Ingrid, you have enough to do without taking in Clara too.'

'Nonsense. My girls are with their nanny most of the time and Clara would be no problem with her. Clara enjoys our daughters' companionship, so she will not be lonely, and Joe is home at the weekends. Besides, she will keep me company when I can no longer go about my business. I am in the family way again. The baby is due in August.'

Kitty stifled a stab of pain. August. When Ben had died. It might have been she who was expecting a child if not for... 'I'm so happy for you, Ingrid.'

While she and Connie congratulated her, Martin arrived. After the hugs of welcome were over and Ingrid left to go home, they talked of his voyage until it was time for dinner.

As Martin helped the ladies to sit at the table, he mentioned the trip north. 'I am still not happy about the move, but, as it is my new boat taking you there, then at least I will know you have safely arrived.'

'We will be fine, Martin.' Kitty double-checked the lists she kept in her skirt pocket at all times. 'I hope I haven't forgotten anything.'

Martin carved the roast mutton. 'All the goods you ordered in the last few weeks have arrived at the dock, I checked. We leave in two days, on the evening tide. You need to be on the boat by two o'clock.'

'We will be.' Kitty sipped her wine. 'I am looking forward to the journey.'

'It'll be a bit different ter the one we had comin' over, I bet.' Connie raised her eyebrows and passed the tureen of potatoes around.

'Let us hope we have calm seas,' Martin grumbled. 'The last thing I want is damage to the boat. I have to prove to Dan his investment was worth it.'

Kitty sighed. 'Oh, Martin, do not be so dismal.'

'I cannot help worrying.'

'About us or your precious new boat?'

'That's not called for.' He dropped the knife. 'I worry incessantly over this family.'

Chastened, Kitty lowered her gaze. 'I know you do, and I am sorry, but at least you know Clara and Joe will be well looked after by the Freemans.'

Connie spooned peas onto her plate. 'Is Mary coming home tonight?'

'No. She is staying with the Ascots again.' Kitty played with her food and pondered the strained relationship that now existed between her and Mary. Mary refused to forgive her for saying no to Timothy. It seemed as though Mary was no longer a part of the family and it hurt.

'It is so unlike her to cause trouble.' Martin forked the sliced meat onto each plate. 'I'm not sure I like this new Mary. When did she grow up and become difficult? Has she packed yet?'

'Only one small case. Come tomorrow, she will be in a huff because she will be rushed.' Kitty refilled Connie's and Martin's glasses with wine.

'Are you going to see Joe?' he asked

'Yes, in the morning. Do you wish to come?'

'I will, thank you. Is he happy about you going?'

Kitty shrugged one shoulder. 'You will see for yourself in the morning.'

'It doesn't seem right. He and Clara should be with you, not the Freemans.' Martin drank the rest of his wine before filling his glass again. 'We are meant to be together.'

'Their education is important too. Ben paid for Joe's fees in total. I will not let it be wasted. I must think about Joe's future. He stands a better chance of being successful staying here at school, than he does coming with me.'

'And Clara?'

'Clara wishes to stay at the ladies' collage. She likes the Freemans and will be happy there. Oh, Martin, try to understand. It will be better for me to do what needs to be done on the land without worrying about the effect on them. It will be hard enough with four women and three babies. It won't be forever, only until we're settled and then they'll be with me again.'

'You were right, Kitty,' Martin said in the swaying hansom cab on their way home from Parramatta. 'Joe is happier than I've seen him for a long time.'

Kitty wiped her forehead with her white handkerchief. The midday heat sapped all energy. 'I think it is the routine and the discipline of the school he likes. He has never had it before, and it is doing him a great deal of good. He needs a firm hand, Martin, and I cannot always give him one. Yes, I believe Joe staying at school is the best decision. If he were not happy then I would bring him home, but you saw yourself that he wants to stay and going to the Freeman's house at the weekends is fine by him too.'

'I'm sorry, Kitty. I did not mean to criticize you.'

She squeezed his hand where it rested on the seat beside her sky-blue skirts. 'One day soon, we will all be together for good, Martin. I won't rest until we are. I promise.'

The cab rumbled to a halt in front of the house and Martin paid the driver while Kitty waited. On entering through the front door, Kitty took off her white, lace gloves and blue-feathered hat. The absence of wearing black helped to put her in a positive mood.

'Oh, Kitty, Martin!' Connie cried. 'Thank God, you're home!'

Kitty turned in alarm. 'What has happened?'

'It's Mary! She's gone.'

'Gone? Gone where?' Martin scowled. 'What do you mean?'

Connie's hand shook as she rubbed her forehead. 'When she came home, she went upstairs. She told me she were goin' ter pack. I saw her playin' wi't babbies and left her be. But later, she was nowhere ter be seen.' Connie grasped Kitty's hand. 'I looked in her room and all her clothes are gone.'

'She may have visited friends?' Martin suggested.

Connie's face flushed in anger. 'With all her clothes? Nay, lad, she's run off an' you don't need to have two heads t'figure out who she's run ter!'

'Now hold on a minute.' Martin paced the hall. 'Don't you think you are jumping to conclusions? She could have—'

'No, Martin. Connie is right.' Kitty wiped her hand across her eyes in weariness, then collected her gloves and pinned her hat on. 'Mary has gone to Timothy Ascot. I should have seen it coming.'

'Where you goin', lass?' Connie asked.

'To visit the Ascots. Although I believe it will be of no use.'

'I will come with you.' Martin kissed Connie's cheek for comfort. 'We'll find her.'

The Ascot's butler showed Kitty and Martin directly into the drawing room. Gina Ascot sat on the sofa quietly crying. Behind her stood her tall, imposing father James and on a small chintz chair sat his plump wife, Deirdre. The room, decorated in hues of deep red and gold, contained too much furniture and lacked style. A great many figurines covered numerous little occasional tables. Kitty hoped her crinoline skirt wouldn't knock something over. Large oil paintings, in thick gold-leafed frames, hung on brass chains along the walls. Potted ferns took up more floor space and the thick, dark damask curtains shut out the bright sunlight.

Kitty spoke no niceties and instead, plunged straight into the drama concerning their families. 'I believe you know the reason for my visit, Mr Ascot?'

James stood straighter still. 'Indeed, I do, Miss McKenzie. A most terrible business.'

'So, they have gone together as I thought?'

'Yes. It is beyond belief that my nephew has behaved so intolerably. This family and society itself have denounced him. How he could break such trust is quite incomprehensible.'

'I agree. My sister is young and obviously foolish to let him persuade her to do such a thing. He, being the elder and supposedly a gentleman, should have shown constraint.'

'He has never been one for patience, and young men usually act before they think,' he conceded.

'So, what is to be done? Does anyone know of their whereabouts?' Kitty peered at the sobbing Gina, showing no concern for the unhappy girl.

'I beg to assure you, Miss McKenzie,' Gina muffled through her crumbled handkerchief, 'I have no knowledge whatsoever of their plans.'

'You are as much to blame as they, Gina. You encouraged Mary to come here and be in his company and I was stupid enough to allow it.'

'Miss McKenzie, please! Gina is suffering enough,' Deirdre declared. 'She has no part to play in this. Mary and Timothy have made their own choices.'

Deirdre's self-righteous attitude irritated Kitty even more. She doubted they would be so calm if it was their daughter who had eloped.

Kitty ignored the other woman's outburst. 'Has Timothy any money, Mr Ascot?'

'Some. He has an allowance from his late father's trust. My brother bequeathed him a house as well. However, he may not go there.'

'Can he support my sister? For Mary has no money of her own, does he know that?'

'I'm not sure whether he knows of Mary's lack of dowry, but yes, he can support her. Though, their lives may not be swathed in opulence and riches. My nephew obviously loves your sister, Miss McKenzie, despite her low status, otherwise he would never have been so adamant to wed her. I truly believe that when the scandal has withered, they will be happy and make good this hasty marriage.'

'Well, let us pray he does marry her, Mr Ascot.'

'Of course, he will. He is a good man really, if maybe a little impetuous.' Ascot rocked slightly on his heels, smiling at Kitty with a hint of smugness. 'In fact, this coupling may be the best thing for your family. The Ascot name is well regarded in Sydney and in the country. The town of Goulburn is where my brother made his home and fortune. His property stands as testament to his good business sense. Yes, in the long run, your sister has done well for herself.'

'I very much doubt it, Mr Ascot.' Her gaze swept over them in utter contempt. She turned on her heel and left the room.

Martin hesitated, and then spoke to Mr Ascot. 'Should you hear word of my sister, please send a message to the house in Forbes Street. I will get it eventually.'

Kitty sat with Connie, sipping a refreshing cup of tea. Martin had left to go back to the wharf and the boat. Hetta and Alice, with Clara and Rosie, were taking the babies out for an evening walk in the perambulator. The house was quiet except for the soft tick-tock of the clock on the mantelpiece.

'How could she do this, Connie? She was always so reliable and trustworthy. Remember in the cellar? She was so wonderful in looking after the others. And at the tearooms she worked just as hard as anyone else. I just don't understand this.'

'Aye, lass. It's hard ter tekk in. I never would've thought it of her.'

'I don't think it is true love, more infatuation on her part, and for him, well, he is a mystery to me.'

'A right slimy toad, if you ask me.' Connie sniffed.

'I will not forgive her. She planned this because we are going north. I never knew she was so selfish or stubborn.'

'Nay, lass, don't tekk on so. She's young and mad silly with love or whatever. Besides, I'll put me life on it, that it was that ruddy Timothy promising her the world that med her go.'

'Why though? I do not understand his reasons. I really do not think he is so madly in love with her, otherwise he would not risk ruining her reputation with this elopement. Surely, he knows we are not wealthy? So, what is his game?'

Connie poured out some more tea. 'Are you sure he knows there's no money?'

'Maybe he doesn't?' Kitty's shoulders sagged in despair. 'But how could he think such a thing? Do we look as though we are extremely wealthy?'

'Nay, lass, I don't know, but he must have some plan. He must think there's money somewhere an' marryin' Mary is his way of gettin' it.'

Later that night, just as Kitty was going to bed, a knock sounded on her bedroom door. 'Come in.' She pulled her dressing gown back on.

Susie entered and gave her a letter. 'A message was delivered just now, Miss.'

'Thank you, Susie. Good night.' Kitty dismissed her. She still found Susie to be a lazy, gossipy type of servant and made a habit of not letting her know the family's business.

Walking to her desk by the window, Kitty turned up the lantern and read the letter.

Miss McKenzie.

Your sister and I were married by special licence today and the mar-riage has been consummated. You forced my hand with your refusal. So, no blame can be laid at my door.

Mary's dowry can be paid into my bank account in Sydney. I have enclosed the details. Should you feel the need to deny Mary her dowry, then you are putting her happiness in jeopardy. I believe you will want her to have all the comforts and benefits she desires.

I have informed the manager at the bank to contact me as soon as you have made the deposit.

Mary is unaware of this missive. I shall endeavour to preserve her innocence of this business.

Respectfully,

Timothy Ascot.

Kitty read the letter twice before she plunged the room into darkness and climbed into bed. Mary's dowry? It was so ridiculous she nearly laughed. Instead, she cried. She cried for Benjamin.

Chapter Seven

After a teeth-clenching, anxious ride through the treacherous heads where the river met the sea, they steamed up the Clarence River. It took all of Martin's confidence and ability to get them safely through. He and Kitty were relieved to enter the river's calmer waters. Snags and small islands filled the Clarence, and the broad expanse of water was, at times, difficult to negotiate. Martin's charts were unreliable due to the fact the whole northern area was newly populated. His maps showed the islands in the river, but not the obstructions of fallen trees floating on the tide or shifting sandbanks that could appear overnight.

Kitty slipped her arm through Martin's where he stood peering at the water in front of them. He had hardly slept during the three-day journey north to Grafton.

Martin scratched the stubble on his chin. 'How is Connie?'

'Better. Although she swears she will never travel by boat again.' Kitty grinned and gazed up at the cloudless blue sky. The summer heat silenced the birds in the thick dense bush lining both sides of the river.

'Seasickness is horrid indeed.' He checked his charts as his hand turned the wheel slightly. He sighed in relief. 'Grafton is just around that last island. I did it, Kitty. I navigated this boat through a river system I've not been on before.'

Kitty hugged him. His maturity astounded her. 'I am so proud of you. It was an enormous task and you did splendidly.'

Within the hour, the boat was safely tied to a dock. Martin and Kitty went in search of a warehouse to store her provisions. Walking into the town centre, they were surprised to see many large, ornate stone buildings. Most of the area was cleared of trees and lay flat and parched, burning in the hot sun.

Kitty took out a well-worn piece of newspaper from her reticule and read aloud to Martin. "Under thirty years old, Grafton grew primarily because of the large population of cedar trees that had first drawn the settlers. More industry came to the area. Sawmills, dairy farming, shipbuilding and farming brought prosperity to the region. The populace, grown over the years, swelled when gold was found in the eighteen-fifties further up the river. Now, long, wide streets are lined with all manner of shops and cottages. The town boasts a courthouse, police station and even has a newspaper, the Daily Examiner. The houses are simply made, mostly of timber, though some are of bricks, and all with the typical small verandas at the front to shade the front rooms from the sun."

'Remarkable.'

Kitty talked to several shopkeepers and found them to be friendly and helpful. Indeed, the town, shops, the little houses and its clear, wide streets impressed her.

She was also keen to explore South Grafton, a smaller town settled on the south side of the river. It would be from that side of the river they would leave for her land.

'We have to find a guide to take us to your holding, Kitty. Do you have any idea where it is situated?' Martin asked, as they walked back to the boat after securing a place for her goods.

'Southwest of Grafton, about thirty miles or so, I think.' Kitty winked. 'I was never taught to map read.'

Martin shook his head, frowning. 'For Lord's sake, will you be serious? This isn't a game. You need a guide.'

'Oh, Martin, calm down. I will acquire a guide and I do take this seriously but look at this place.' She swept her arms wide. 'It is a beautiful day and soon I will be walking on the land Ben left me. I want to laugh and smile and, for a little while longer, not have any worries to weigh me down. Can I have that, please?'

'I'm sorry, but I don't think you know what you have involved yourself in. This is the middle of nowhere.'

She lifted her chin and tossed her head. 'Ben bought the land and gave it to me.'

'As an investment. He bought it because it was going cheap. The owner was walking away from it. Doesn't that tell you anything? He would never have wanted you to come here.'

'I am not having this argument with you again.' Kitty marched on ahead, trying to cool her rising temper. How dare Martin? She was sure Ben planned to move to the land and make it into a fine estate like his family's one in York. Martin had no right to dismiss her dreams. Ben gave her something of value, she was sure. He would simply not give her a rundown piece of land for her wedding present. The groom's present was something special, something to be treasured.

'Well, you need to have it out with someone before you become more involved.' Martin stopped and put his hands on his hips. 'And what about Mary? You have just left her behind. You didn't even try to look for her.'

Kitty spun to face him, still hurt by Mary's actions. 'Mary made her choice. She is married. There is nothing I can do now. She is her husband's responsibility now, they have both made that clear.'

Martin sighed tiredly. 'I am going to find a load of cargo to take back to Sydney. I have to make this boat earn the repayments I owe Dan.'

'Martin, I am as unhappy as you in regards to Mary. I have sent Ascot all the money I can spare. I do not know what Mary told him to make him think I was wealthier than I am, but I can do no more for now. James Ascot sent a note before I left informing me that he'd accept her into his family. I must make my own life as she is obviously doing. And when I am settled, I will invite her to stay should she write me her details.'

Nodding, Martin stepped nearer and kissed her cheek. 'I know you worry; it was wrong of me to imply anything different.'

'Remember, one day, we will all be together. Please keep thinking that way.'

'If I ever get back into a cart again, I will make sure it has padded seats.' Kitty muttered. The jarring, bone-shaking ride over barely created tracks had completely made Kitty's posterior numb and she wondered if she had any teeth left or had they all been shaken out. The heat, which was intense, she could cope with, but not the jaw-rattling journey. However, they were nearly there now, so her guide told her. Her land lay roughly a mile away on the other side of the creek in front of them.

Her guide, Jim, a leathery-skinned old man tanned the colour of a native from years in the sun, stood in the middle of the shallow creek. With a stick, he gauged the depth of the water to find the best place to ford it. With a nod swamped by the large, black felt hat he wore, he indicated for Martin to bring the cart across. Jim walked in front, directing him.

Kitty held on tightly as the horse crossed the water and then strained to pull the cart up the dusty rocky bank.

Jim climbed onto the front seat beside Martin and signalled which direction to steer the horses. A narrow traveling path had been hacked out of the virgin bush at one time.

Kitty gazed around her and breathed in the warm scented air. Tall eucalyptus trees, squat tea trees, thick native bushes and undergrowth caused some trouble as it slowly reclaimed the track. In the distance to the west, great mountains dominated the horizon.

'Eh, miss, your border starts 'ere.' Jim's deep, rumbling voice broke into her reverie.

Martin stopped the cart and Jim climbed down and tied a red strip of material around the tree trunk. Then, looking at the map in his hands, he walked back to the cart.

'Your land starts 'ere, see?' He jabbed a dirty finger at a spot on the map. Turning, he pointed over to the west. 'It goes for five hundred yards to the west and seven hundred yards to the east. Then, it fans southwards for about a mile or so, understand?'

'Yes.' She studied the map and then peered into the dense bush around her. 'Where is the hut?'

'Not far, another hundred yards or so. You have a trickle of a creek fifty yards from the hut, but it usually dries up in summer and only runs in the winter if there's rain.'

'What about the creek we just crossed?'

'It's not yours.' Jim shook his head at her and climbed back into the cart.

'But I can use it?'

'Depends on the owner,' Jim mumbled, and Kitty only just managed to hear him.

As Martin drove through the bush, obvious signs of trees having been felled earlier appeared, making a rough path for them to reach the hut. After a short time, a cleared space of about one hundred yards long by two hundred yards wide opened before them. A shabby, wooden hut with a bark roof reigned supreme in the middle.

A mob of kangaroos stood poised by the hut, watching the progress of the cart. Abruptly, they moved as one, bounding away into the trees. The noise they made sounded like rumbling thunder. High above their heads a flock of white cockatoos flew up in alarm. Their screeching cry shattered the stillness and hurt Kitty's ears.

Amazed and excited, she scrambled down without waiting for Martin to help her and stared at her new home. Her brain refused to function, but tingles of exhilaration mixed with apprehension ran along her skin.

The hut, made of tree trunks cut in half lengthways, appeared solid. Each length of timber slotted into the corner posts of the structure. A door, in the middle of the wall, faced her. On each side of it were square, windowless spaces. The roof was made of sapling tree trunks and placed across the beams were long sheets of bark cut from the huge eucalyptus trees. Sapling trunks weighted down the sheets of bark to stop them from blowing off in the wind. All this was tied down and strapped together with crude bits of rope and long strings of toughened hide. To the left was a large, railed holding yard.

'You cannot do it, Kitty,' Martin said behind her.

'Do not start harping at me, Martin.' The dust floated about Kitty's ankles as she strode to the hut, and she lifted the hem of her brown skirt to Try and avoid the worst of it.

The door creaked open at her push and she timidly stepped inside the dim, musty interior. She waited for her eyes to adjust. When they did, she closed them in sheer despair. The scene before her made her weary just looking at it. Dirt and dust covered every surface. The hut was one big room with a basic stone fireplace and chimney in one corner. The rest of the room was empty, except for a rusty iron double bed against the far wall and a wooden plank shelf above it. In many places along the walls, Kitty could look through gaps to the outside. She stared at the roof and the ugly patches of rotted, peeling bark. Judging by the water stains, it let in rain.

She took a deep breath and then straightened her shoulders. 'All it needs is a bit of repair work and cleaning,' she whispered to herself. It was another challenge, and hadn't she always accepted challenges? Summoning a smile, she headed back out into the sunshine.

Around the back of the hut, a wooden water barrel stood beside the wall. Further away, a small chicken pen, built of planks from a shipping crate, leant drunkenly. Kitty, hands on hips, surveyed the rest of the cleared land around her. Some twelve yards away, a large plot of earth, once cultivated, now reverted back to native grasses. On the far side of the clearing, the thick bush showed signs of previous human presence. Tree stumps were frequent, and, in parts, trees had been felled but not sawn up.

'I've found a few traps laid in the bush,' Jim said walking towards her. 'Two once held possums in them, but only bits of carcasses remained so I reset them.'

'I know nothing about traps, Jim.'

'I thought as much, so I've tied the red material around the trees directly beside the traps. Watch out for them. You'll need the traps to catch fresh meat. Can you shoot?'

'Shoot?' Her eyes widened.

'Aye, you'll need to shoot for fresh meat too.' Jim looked at her as though she were a simpleton.

She wiped the sweat from her brow with her handkerchief. The sun was merciless. 'I shall acquire a rifle.'

'On the other side of that belt of trees and scrub, there is a few miles of part swamp land. It's not the best for your cattle but it's better than thick bush. At least, they will be able to eat some of the grasses there. I reckon you'll need to clear a lot of land and sow grass before you increase the size of your herd. That marsh area will not hold many cows, though it is surrounded by dense growth and it forms a natural barrier to the swamp so your cattle may be easier to keep an eye on while in there.'

'Well, that is good, isn't it?' Kitty asked hopefully.

Jim rolled his eyes. 'Now there's a large cattle station further south. The owner picked the right spot because it's all rich grass plains. You don't have that here. You don't have enough cleared land to run cattle and crops and you'll need to do both to make a decent living.'

'It doesn't have to be on a grand scale, Jim, just enough to live a good life. If I wanted it easy, I would have stayed in Sydney.' Kitty raised her eyebrows, daring him to comment further.

Jim headed for the cart. 'We best get going back to town, it'll be past dark before we even get to the nearest road.'

It was close to midnight when Kitty and Martin finally made it back to the hotel, exhausted and dirty.

Connie had waited up for them in their hotel room. 'Well, what was it like?' she asked the minute they entered the room.

'Is there anything to drink? I think my throat has a ton of dust in it. I can barely swallow,' Kitty gasped, unpinning her grime-covered hat.

'Aye, lass, there's cool lemon water in the jug. I'll get you both a glass.' Connie went to a small side table by the wall.

'I need a bath. I am caked in dirt.' Kitty sighed.

'You'll have t'wait until mornin'.' Connie handed her and Martin their drinks. 'So, what's it like?'

'Awful!' Martin got in first, staring at Kitty.

She frowned at him. 'It's not that bad. It is very dry. The hut is made up of one room and it needs repairing. I'll need to employ a man, or even two, to do all the work that needs to be done. The soil needs to be ploughed over and Jim said I need a fence around the vegetable plot to keep the wildlife out.' Kitty suddenly grinned. 'Oh, Connie, it will be hard, but so rewarding.'

Martin snorted. 'Good Lord, Kitty. You must be insane. It'll kill you.'

Kitty waved her hand at him and smiled even more. She was tired and dirty but fired up with enthusiasm.

By the end of the week, Kitty's supplies were on the other side of the Clarence River and loaded onto a large wagon, along with a milk cow tied to the end. Kitty hired a bullocky and his team. The bullocks, although slow, awkward-looking beasts, could pull enormous weights. The bullocky and his team left a full day before them due to the team's slowness.

With Dan's money, Kitty bought two huge, chestnut draught horses and a drop-sided cart to be driven by the two workmen she had hired. The family would travel on the cart, packed with blankets to sit on. Finally, after three days of planning, Kitty and her small party said goodbye to Martin and left South Grafton behind to take up residence at the hut.

'You'll have to give the property a name, Miss McKenzie,' Jessup, one of the hired men, said as they drove along the winding path through the bush. He was short, of thin build, and cheery with a ready smile. Next to him sat the other hired man, Holby, a little older, taller and taciturn. He said little and always wore his wide brimmed hat pulled low over his brow.

'Give it a name?' Kitty repeated over his shoulder from her position in the back of the cart.

'Aye, miss, landholders always give their places a name. It makes it easier for us fellas. We tell people our names and the name of the property we work for.'

'Oh well, in that case, we must think of a name.' Kitty winked at Connie and Alice.

Connie frowned and leaned closer to Kitty. 'Some people should know their place. He has no right talkin' t'you like that. Don't let them tekk advantage. Start as you mean to go on.'

Kitty smiled and nudged her. 'I promise I will show them who is boss. Remember, I am now an owner of a rifle.' Kitty chuckled. Nothing would displease her this day.

Connie shook her head and raised her eyebrows. 'Aye, but can you use the blessed thing?'

Towards sunset they caught up with the bullock wagon at the wide creek near the property boundary.

Jessup and Holby climbed from the cart and went to aid the bullocky. With much cursing, yelling and cracking of whips, the bullocky got his team across. Kitty shuddered to think what would have happened if the creek had been running high from any recent rains. Connie's twins hollered in delight when it was the cart's turn to be driven over. The rocks on the bottom jostled the cart, causing the twins to peer over the side and watch the water rush by. Alice stared wide-eyed, even though the water came only halfway up the cart's wheels. She held onto Little Rory with grim fear as they lurched up the bank and onto level ground again. Kitty hugged Rosie to her and pointed out the beginning of the boundary as they drove on.

At last, the cart rumbled to a halt amidst a cloud of dust. When it cleared, Connie and Alice looked at each other in horror. They sat rooted to their seats and stared at their new home. With disbelieving eyes, they slowly climbed down, holding the babies in their arms.

'Come inside,' Kitty called to them, standing by the door.

Their shock did not diminish once inside the hut. Its interior made them shudder.

'Nay, lass...' Connie swallowed.

Tears shimmered in Alice's eyes.

Rosie stuck her finger in her mouth. 'I want to go home to Clara and Mary.'

'Oh, it's not that bad.' Kitty glowered at them. 'We will soon have it nice. Come, Rosie, you can help me.' She left them to look around while she supervised the unloading of the cart and bullock wagon.

After some initial hesitation, Alice lit a fire in the stone fireplace. Jessup and Holby collected water from the trickling creek near the hut. While armed with old cleaning rags, Connie and Kitty rolled up their sleeves before donning aprons. Once it was generally swept and wiped down, the men brought in the babies' cots and the extra trundle bed for Alice. Connie, Rosie and Kitty were to share the old iron bed left behind by the previous owner.

Boxes, mattresses, crates of provisions and trunks of clothing soon filled the hut. Alice found the sacks of vegetables, plus other food and started to make a stew before they lost daylight. She threw the vegetable peel and other scraps into the crate of hens Kitty bought from a farmer in Grafton, and they sent up an awful clamour in desperate need to be released from their tiny cage.

Kitty fashioned a makeshift table with a tea chest, while Connie made up the beds and nailed thick curtains at the glassless windows.

With the last of the sun's rays slowly sinking behind the distant mountains, Kitty lit two lanterns and they ate tasty stew from a dainty China service balanced precariously on top of the tea chest. Washed and then put to bed, Rosie and the babies were soon asleep. The day's journey and exploring their new surroundings had worn them out well. Too tired to achieve any more, Connie and Alice scrambled into bed also.

Kitty leant against the open door and gazed out over her land. The men had lit a fire and rolled out their bedding. Thin columns of wood smoke drifted up without hindrance of a breeze. The low bellowing of the bullocks serenaded them to sleep as most of the bush sounds became quiet as darkness fell. A bird called once and then was silent. The chirping of the insects in the undergrowth remained the only sounds of the night. The stars shone brightly in the Milky Way and the full moon enveloped the land in long silver shadows.

She breathed in deeply. For the first time in a long time, peace and serenity entered her heart and mind. She thought of Ben and smiled. The land wasn't perfect, but it was hers. 'Thank you, my darling, for guiding me here. I will make you proud.'

The loud racket of the kookaburras, or the Laughing Jackasses as they were nicknamed, chorusing from high in the trees, woke everyone just before dawn. The array of birds heralding the new day was deafening, as magpies joined sulphur-crested cockatoos, and other native birds in trilling high and clear. Mosquitoes had taken their fill from the women and children during the night. Red bumps and lumps covered their faces and hands. The children grumbled over their itchy bites and Connie applied cold night cream to their flushed, angry spots.

Soon after breakfast, Alice and Connie began sorting out the hut to make more room. Kitty left them to it and went to pay the bullocky. He led his team out of the clearing and disappeared into the bush, but the crack of his whip could still be heard for some time after.

Kitty turned to Jessup. 'Repairing the roof is the first priority.'

'No worries, Miss McKenzie. There's a special type of eucalyptus tree that produces the bark we can easily strip off in sheets. I'll go and look for some now.'

Holby held an axe and a saw in his hands. 'Do you want a room added on?'

'Absolutely, Holby.' She grinned. 'You read my mind.' They would find it impossible to live in one room for any length of time.

Alice met Kitty at the front of the hut, carrying a bucket of dirty water. She started to speak but the cow's bellow drowned her words.

'I think it needs attention.' Kitty grimaced in the cow's direction. 'Can you milk it, Alice?'

'Heavens no!' Alice stepped back in horror.

'I'm sure it cannot be so bad.'

Laughing, Kitty and Alice tried unsuccessfully to milk the poor animal.

Jessup, on his way past, paused. 'No, Miss McKenzie, you'll never do it that way.' He proceeded to show her and Alice how to pull the udder's teats in long, slow movements.

Eventually, after a few lessons from him, they were able to get enough milk to make the cow comfortable. Kitty covered the pail of milk with a wet linen cloth to keep out the flies and secured it with rocks in a shallow and shady part of the house creek. The ripples of water came a third of the way up the sides, helping to keep the milk cool and safe from spoiling.

After some minor repairs, the hens and rooster were turned out into the old chicken pen behind the hut. Connie dug a small patch of soil for them to scratch in and feast on the worms and insects. Fresh eggs would be a staple part of the family's diet and Kitty wanted the chickens made safe.

Just on dusk, Holby finished making much-needed shelves. With many thanks from the women, he nailed four of them to the wall of the hut. They were sanded to a smooth finish, enabling Connie to place more items, like the lanterns, out of reach of the children. Holby promised to make a proper table and chairs. He didn't talk much, but his natural carpentry skills more than made up for any of his other shortfalls.

Slowly the sun slid down behind the horizon at the end of their second day. Weariness cloaked them all like a heavy coat.

'We have worked hard, and I am pleased with the day's progress,' Kitty said, after a meal of salted beef and potatoes roasted in the fire.

'Aye, and I'm ready fer me bed.' Connie looked over to where all four children lay sleeping.

Kitty chuckled. 'It is barely eight o'clock.'

The women's work was as arduous as the men's in the heat and the dust. Kitty was so thankful to have Jessup, who was a complete Godsend. He always thought ahead, tackled every task with a smile on his face and chatted all the time. He told Kitty of his experiences of working and living on big sheep stations in the Bathurst area, situated west of Sydney and over the Blue Mountains. He showed her little things Kitty would never have realized. He taught her to set traps, how to skin the small animals they caught and read the tracks of different creatures living in the bush around them.

He educated Alice about bush food, or bush tucker as he called it, and showed her which natural fruits could be eaten and which were poisonous. If he shot a wallaby, a small type of kangaroo, he insisted she learn how to skin it and cook it in the ashes of a large smouldering fire made in a slight hollow at the back of the hut. The skins would then be strung out and left to dry, to be eventually made into a rug or blanket. Wallaby was not something the women tasted before and were hesitant to try it at first. However, they soon learned the meat, cooked fresh upon being killed, was a welcome relief to salted mutton or beef.

Alice cooked damper, an easily made flat bread, on the hut's cooking fire. It was vastly different to making dainty pastries, but she reassured Kitty that as soon as they bought a proper cooking range, she would be back to creating her mouth-watering delights.

Holby marked out the area for the new room and prepared the foundations. He worked non-stop and was more comfortable being left alone to get on with his job.

On the fourth morning after their arrival, Kitty asked Jessup to show her how to use the rifle bought in Grafton.

He took off his hat and scratched his head. 'No offense, Miss McKenzie, but you're a small woman and you've no need to use it as Holby or me can shoot all you want.'

Kitty bristled. 'What has being small got to do with it?'

'It'll give you a kick, Miss.'

She straightened and raised her chin. 'I am sure I can handle it, thank you, Jessup.'

They walked a good distance away from the hut and stood at the edge of the swampy grass plain. Jessup set the rifle into her shoulder.

The weapon's weight surprised her.

'Look down the barrel, see that small notch at the end?'

'Yes.'

Suddenly, Jessup moved Kitty's hand and swung the rifle to their right. 'Kangaroos,' he whispered close to her ear, pointing to a small mob further into the long grass some fifty yards away. 'Try and aim at one.'

Kitty tried to keep herself as steady as possible, but the rifle became heavier with each second. Closing one eye, she spied a huge grey. The kangaroo turned its head slightly and saw them. It stilled. Kitty swallowed, trying not to think of it as an animal just an object, and slowly pulled the trigger. The blast rang in her head. She stumbled from the rifle's kick. Jessup put his hands up to steady her, while the mob bounded off in the other direction.

'Did I get it?'

Jessup grinned at her. He took his battered hat off and wiped the sweat from his sandy brown hair. 'No, miss, you didn't, but that was all right for your first attempt.'

She rubbed the sore spot on her shoulder. 'What shall we shoot at now?'

'I think it best if we did some practice work, yes?' Jessup chuckled, taking the weapon.

They spent the afternoon shooting at different objects and walking around the property. Jessup showed Kitty the holes dug in the ground by the round, fat wombats, a native animal that lived in burrows. He taught her how to read the signs of the bush, and so that she wouldn't get lost within a mile radius of the hut, he marked trees with a KM cut deep into the bark.

'If you should become lost, watch the birds, for they like to be close to water. If you find a creek, stay with it and follow it the way it is flowing. Eventually, you will reach a hut of some sort or a larger river, as its common knowledge people build near to water.'

Kitty nodded and listened intently to all his advice as they strolled back to the hut. Another wonderful sunset turned the sky amber gold. On nearing the clearing, the amount of work completed by Holby surprised her. The new room now had corner supports and half the front wall.

Connie came out of the hut and closed the door behind her so the children couldn't escape 'The whole bush rang with the noise you medd. How did it go?'

'Good, although I still need a lot of practice.' Kitty smiled. 'I am tired and sore.' She walked towards Holby as he stood sawing a sapling trunk. 'This is a grand effort, Holby. Well done.'

'I'll get on and help him,' said Jessup. 'There's still half an hour of daylight left.'

Kitty aided Connie in gathering the clean washing hanging along a rope strung between two trees at the edge of the clearing. Washing the clothes was an arduous task, requiring stamina and tolerance. With so much clothing and bedding to wash, it meant a whole day was allocated for it. On arrival, Connie and Alice had put away all of Kitty's fine clothes; now the women wore light muslin and linen dresses which were easier to wash and cooler to wear in the heat.

A slight breeze rustled the leaves of the trees. Above their heads flew a screeching flock of cockatoos. Unexpectedly, a man on horseback came thundering through the trees from the south.

He pulled his poor, sweat-lathered horse to a stop and dismounted in a swirl of dust stirred up by its hooves. He was a rough-looking chap, wearing dirty, dusty clothes and a large, brimmed hat pulled low over his brow. Scowling at the two women, he then turned to stare at Jessup and Holby who came to stand a short distance away. Alice glanced out of the window space with interest.

'Who's in charge here?' the newcomer grumbled, spitting dust onto the ground at his feet.

'I am. What business is it of yours?' Kitty scowled.

'You've no right to be here on this land.' The man's eyes narrowed at Jessup and Holby as if waiting for them to deny the fact.

Kitty raised an eyebrow. 'I have every right as this is my property. Who may you be?'

'This land belongs to Blue Water Station.'

'I believe you are mistaken. This place is mine and I have the relevant documents to prove it. Now please leave.' Kitty stood straighter and raised her chin, daring him to defy her.

The man mounted his horse roughly, making it roll its eyes and turn around on the spot. The dust rose once more. 'You'll be sorry,' he growled and rode away in a rumble of hooves.

'He was right friendly, wasn't he?' Alice called through the window.

'Excuse me, miss?' Jessup came to them with Holby just behind him.

'Yes?'

'Are you sure your papers are right? I mean that this is the right property?'

'Yes, Jessup, they are correct. I went to the surveyor's office in Grafton. They knew of this property and the surveyor gave me a guide to direct me here. The maps from the surveyor confirm mine. Do you know where that man came from?'

'Blue Water Station. It's Grayson's property southwest of this one.'

Confused, Kitty frowned. 'Why would he send one of his men here? This place has nothing to do with him.'

'He's most probably been running his stock on this land when it was green after the last rains. That's why it's now down to dust because of him overgrazing his cattle or sheep on it. He obviously ain't happy about having thousands and thousands of his own acres but wants yours too.'

'The nerve. My cattle will have nothing to eat because he stole my grass!' Her temper rose as quickly as the heat on a hot summer's day. 'I will prosecute him for this.'

'Now, lass, calm down, we've got no proof as yet.' Connie sent Jessup a sharp look. 'You don't want ter say or do owt that you might regret later.'

'Let's hope we get rain before your cattle arrives, miss,' Jessup said.

'Indeed.' Kitty stormed into the hut.

Connie twisted round to Jessup. 'She's got a temper, she doesn't use it often but when she does it can lead to all sorts of trouble. So, don't stir it up without good cause.'

Soberly, Jessup folded his arms. 'You need to be full of fire to last out here, our dependence on her being tough in this harsh land is what is important. She can't afford to be dainty and fragile on the land. If she's got a temper to match her red hair, then all the better I say.'

Chapter Eight

The Kookaburras, alarm clocks of the bush, rang out their call through the early dawn. Kitty woke, washed and dressed before stoking the fire. Alice too, awoke and dressed, then began making the significant amount of porridge needed for breakfast.

Suddenly, Alice gave a scream that rent the air.

'Good God, Alice! Whatever is the matter?' Kitty hurried to her side.

'Oh, miss, look.' Alice pointed to the sack of sugar she was about to dip a cup into.

Kitty slowly pulled back the top of the sack and recoiled. A black, scrambling mass swarmed over the sugar blocks. Ants! Black ants of a size Kitty had never seen. She quickly threw the cover over and stepped back.

'What's up, lass?' Connie asked from the bed.

'Ants got into the sugar. It is ruined.' Kitty sighed, eyeing the sack with distaste.

Alice shivered. 'We'll have to get it out of the hut.'

'I will go for Jessup. Those ants may be poisonous.' Kitty shuddered and left the hut.

The sky turned from pink to blue and the rising sun showed no rain clouds. Kitty stared up into the wide expanse and prayed rain would come soon. It was the middle of April now and autumn in the Southern Hemisphere. Only, nature had decided otherwise and still sent the summer heat.

Jessup rounded the side of the hut. 'Morning, Miss.'

'Good morning, Jessup.'

'Holby and I were talking last night, and we think it would be best for you to buy a plough and start turning over the ground. The soil needs to be picked over for stones and rocks, but we can still get some winter vegetables planted. What do you think, miss?'

'Yes, good idea. Maybe you can take the cart and buy one for me? I don't feel like making the trip today.' She trusted him completely, although he would not be carrying money. Everything bought would go on the accounts she acquired with the Grafton storekeepers.

'I'll get the cart ready.'

'Oh, before you do, there are ants in the sugar sack. Can you deal with it?'

'Yes, I'll see to it now.' He followed her into the hut and deftly removed the sack without many of the ants escaping. 'You can still use some of this once it's sorted. These blighters can give a nasty bite, but that's all.'

Kitty grimaced at the thought. 'Before you leave, collect the list I have made. We may as well purchase all of it together. Let us hope the store owners don't send their bills all at once.'

After Jessup left for town, Holby secured more logs along the walls of the new room. He worked steadily until noon, and then told Kitty he was going into the bush to cut down more trees. He took his midday meal of bread and a cold hunk of meat with him.

'Let us take the children down to the other larger creek,' Kitty suggested to Connie. The heat made everyone uncomfortable.

'I've sewin' ter do, lass. An' then there's—'

'Oh, come on, Connie. The little ones will enjoy it so. They can play in the water under that big overhanging tree. They will be cool there out of the sun. I might even try my hand at fishing.'

'Aye, all right, lass. The poor little loves are cooped up in this hut too much as it is.'

In the short time it took to reach the large creek their dresses clung to them from sweat. They took it in turns carrying Little Rory, who seemed heavier with each step. Unlike the narrow house stream, this wider creek had a deep, steady flow.

Alice hitched Little Rory higher on her hip. 'None of us can swim.'

'It will be fine.' Kitty skidded down the bank to the water's edge. 'Jim, the guide, stood in the middle and the water only came to his waist. However, he said there are deeper parts further down.'

They walked along the bank, stumbling over tree roots and rocks until they reached the overhanging tree. Kitty impulsively removed her and Rosie's dresses and stockings and, laughing, they played in the shallows.

'Come, Rosie, it is wonderful.' She held her sister's hand until they were waist deep.

Connie sat in the shade on the edge of the grassy bank watching the twins as they splashed and frolicked at the water's edge.

Taking off her stockings, Alice kicked at the water with Little Rory, until Kitty came and took him into her arms. She walked further into the creek and bobbed up and down in the water, making him gurgle and laugh.

In turn, she took Charles and Adelaide out with her before going out alone and, with some soap, washed her long, sweat and dust-coated hair. She ducked under to rinse, but when she surfaced a cold tingle rose over her skin. Something or someone watched her. Her stomach clenched in fear. Afraid, she forced herself to peer into the surrounding bush. Nothing moved.

Ever so slowly, Kitty waded, as casually as she could, back towards the bank and the others. She stubbed her toe on a half-submerged rock and staggered. On the bank, to her right, a twig snapped. She froze.

'Lass?' Connie rose, the smile leaving her face. 'What's up?'

'Gather the children,' Kitty whispered, edging closer to her.

'There is no need to be frightened.' A voice echoed around the bush as a man on horseback crashed into view. 'I will not hurt you.'

Alice screamed and hugged Little Rory to her while Connie swept up the twins in one movement.

Kitty struggled to the bank and realized her wet chemise and petticoats were now see-through. Frantic, she grabbed a towel and covered herself. Panic and anger made her yell. 'How dare you come here! Who are you?'

'The more important question is, who are you?'

'Get off my land,' Kitty spat, forgetting for the moment that the creek didn't belong to her.

'Now there, you happen to be wrong, madam.' The man's voice held an educated and superior tone. He talked as though each word was important and chosen carefully to neither waste time nor make him look a fool. 'This creek runs throughout my land. You may finish your bathing and stay at the hut tonight. However, by dawn I want you gone.'

Kitty glared up at him. He wore a brown, wide-brimmed hat, but his dark grey hair showed where it touched the collar of his fresh, clean, white shirt. The shade thrown by the brim of his hat shadowed the contours of his face so she couldn't make out his features clearly. Nevertheless, his highhanded manner and haughty demeanour made her blood boil. He sat arrogantly on his ebony horse with one hand holding the reins and the other resting on his moleskin clad hip. Strapped onto the saddle was an expensive looking rifle and a silver water bottle. He was a man in control and demanded obedience.

Kitty's voice shook with controlled rage. 'This creek may not be mine, but the property behind you is! So, you have no right whatsoever to tell me what to do.'

'Have you heard of Squatter's Law, madam?'

She raised her chin. 'I know enough that you can't take over someone's property. Squatters take crown land. My property is bought and paid in full.'

He smirked. 'You have the relevant papers to prove this?'

'Indeed, I have.' She wanted to hit him, hard. 'Not that it is any business of yours.'

'Oh, it has a lot to do with me, since I have been the one maintaining this place.'

'Maintaining it?' She laughed mockingly. 'More like letting your animals strip it bare of all vegetation.'

'Nonsense.' The man's upper lip curled. 'If there is no grass then you can thank the lack of rain and kangaroos for that. I would not allow my stock anywhere near this place.'

Rory cried and Kitty glanced at him.

'Where is your husband?' The stranger peered at her as if challenging her to lie to him, which she promptly did.

'Away.' She dared not look at Alice or Connie though out of the corner of her eye, she noticed Alice pull Rosie closer to her in case the little girl said something she shouldn't.

'When he gets back, tell him to come to me at Blue Water Station.'

Kitty snorted. 'I do not think so.'

The man sighed and fixed her with another direct gaze. 'It is in your own best interests.'

'We want no business with you.'

'Listen to me. Life out here is hard, and farming is unforgiving of mistakes. I will give your husband a good price for this property. I recommend you pay attention to what I have to offer.'

His patronizing tone flared Kitty's anger. 'Never!'

He inclined his head and his narrowed gaze never wavered from hers. 'I am a patient man. One day you will come to me.' With the slightest of movements, he turned his horse and disappeared into the dense bush.

Kitty heaved a shaky sigh.

They gathered their things quietly. Kitty was deeply troubled by the encounter but said nothing to the others. Back at the hut, they felt safer, and they shuddered to think what it would be like here without Jessup and Holby to safeguard them from harm. It surprised the women how quickly they had come to depend on the two men.

Alice quickly went about her tasks preparing the evening meal, secure in doing mundane chores second nature to her. Connie attended to the wet children, while Kitty fed the chickens some grain and collected wood for the fire. They went about their work subdued and a little nervous. The encounter with the horseman reaffirmed the isolation they felt.

Kitty threw her armload of wood into a pile by the door. The imposing stranger dominated her thoughts. Jessup said his name was Miles Grayson and Blue Water was a rich and well-developed station. 'Well, if he thinks he can buy me out then he can think again.'

Kitty's back ached. She stooped once more to pull another weed from around the tiny vegetable seedlings. Sweat trickled inside her clothes and dust coated her russet skirts. Throughout March, April and into May, no rain descended from the azure sky to saturate the property's dry, crusty earth. The parched, brown grass shrivelled and gaping cracks appeared in the ground.

With a lot of hard work, they had ploughed a plot twenty yards long by ten yards wide at the side of the hut and enclosed it in wooden panelling. Holby told her they would never have vegetables if a fence wasn't built to stop the kangaroos, wallabies, wombats and the like from eating the seedlings the minute they popped out of the ground.

Watering the garden was a hated and exhausting chore to them all. The house creek no longer flowed so they had to carry up buckets from the larger of the two creeks. Kitty stayed on tenterhooks as she did this job, expecting Grayson on his ebony horse to charge out of the bush and declare the water his. No one had seen him or his men since his first visit, but Jessup warned them that Grayson's men would be keeping an eye on them. Kitty detested the very thought but pushed it from her mind.

The hot May sun shone down fiercely, and she glared up at it. 'Don't you know it is now autumn here?' she grumbled at the yellow-orange orb sitting high in the clear blue sky. 'Can you not be so harsh on us?'

She paused to stare at her new home. Much had been achieved despite a few setbacks.

The new room was completed; a bedroom for Connie, Kitty and the children, while Alice still slept on the trundle bed in the main room. This improvement to the hut made it safer for the children to move without having so much clutter to trip them. Holby then built a small lean-to onto the back of the hut for storage with a connecting door for direct access. His next project was building a hut for himself and Jessup. He was certain that when the rains came, they would continue a good while, and he had no wish to spend the coming winter in the open. Besides, they worked hard, and Kitty wanted them to have somewhere more private and comfortable than the ground to sleep on each night.

The hut was still primitive by anyone's standards and not very relaxing. Kitty missed the niceties of the house in Forbes Street and she missed those she left behind, especially Mary. Ingrid's last letter told Kitty the gossip was Timothy and Mary lived at his Goulburn home, but no one was sure. Nothing more on the subject was mentioned.

The sound of cattle bellowing made Kitty raise her head and stare in that direction. The cattle Dan bought had appeared after twelve weeks of overland trekking. The beasts arrived in poor condition with bones protruding beneath their slack hides. Many had sores, split feet and all were underfed. Kitty was certain the drovers had not given them adequate rest and feeding spells. The herd was three dozen beasts short of its original total. Jessup muttered something about the drovers selling some off to make extra money along the way, nearly causing a fight to break out.

Kitty refused to pay the drovers their full wages and ended up having to get her rifle to force them from the property when they became violent. They scampered off into the bush and, despite her worrying they would return later to raid the herd, nothing more was seen of them.

Jessup and Holby shot five distressed cows, releasing them from their misery. The rifle's blasts killing the poor defenceless animals angered and frustrated her. She wrote a long letter to Dan explaining what happened to the cattle and the action she took.

The land possessed little grass after the drought of summer and autumn and the two men moved the cattle daily from one spot to another about the property. At the furthest parts, they took it in turns to watch the cattle overnight, in case of attacks by dogs, natives or bushrangers. Kitty put the plan to fatten the cattle for market and the breeding program on hold until the rains came.

'Miss McKenzie?'

Kitty, lost in her thoughts, jumped at the sound of Jessup's voice. 'Yes?' She wiped the moisture from her brow.

'Two more of the cattle are dead. That makes it eight this week. We have no need for any more salted beef so Holby is burying them. We still have two full barrels buried deep in the ground from the last lot we shot. The meat won't keep in this heat for the journey to Grafton to sell it. The cattle have to be moved somewhere better, miss, before they all die.'

Walking over to where he stood resting his elbows on the fence, Kitty adjusted her wide-brimmed straw hat and sighed. 'How am I to do that? You know as well as I do that my property contains no more grass and I have spent more than enough on bought feed too.'

'As I see it, you're going to have to rent pasture from someone. Otherwise the cattle will be dead by the end of the month.'

'Damn it!' Kitty banged the fence with her fist and kicked at it with her boots.

'Miss, I know you might not want to hear this, but you really should think about selling up. This is no life for a lady. Grayson will give you a good price, I'm sure.'

'Never!' Kitty roared at him. 'Do not dare mention his name or the subject of selling again, do you hear me?' Tearing off her sweat-dampened hat, she stormed into the bush.

She walked for some time in the cool shade before wandering down to the big creek. The water level was lower than last month. It still flowed though, albeit very slowly. Kitty looked at the water longingly, she was hot, dirty and sweaty. She gazed around the bush on both sides of the creek. Satisfied she was alone, she removed her clothes except her chemise. Running into the water, she then waded deeper and unpinned her hair. She dunked her head and let the cold refreshing water wash away her grime.

'I am going to teach myself to swim,' she whispered to the aged trees on the banks.

Making sweeping movements with her arms, she lifted her legs and kicked foolishly about. She giggled as she sank beneath the water. Spluttering, Kitty chuckled and tried again. Once more she sank. Determined, she frowned and tried harder, making smaller movements with her hands and kicking furiously out behind her. She propelled a small distance.

'I did it! I swam.' Scrambling onto the edge of the bank, she flopped onto the ground and lay there panting with her legs still in the water. Her chemise stuck to her like a second skin. She couldn't stop smiling at her achievement.

'Very well done.' The voice of her nightmares came quietly from above.

A scream died in her throat. Her heart skipped a beat, and then thumped in a rapid tattoo. Her clothes were out of reach. Frantically, she clambered back into the water and knelt to cover herself from his prying eyes. Heat flushed her face. She forced herself to glare up at him. 'How...how dare you?' Kitty flung at him, finally finding her voice. 'Have you no common decency?'

Grayson lounged in his saddle; his hat pulled low. 'I could say the same for you, madam. No decent lady would swim nearly naked for all to see.'

His mocking stiffened her spine. 'I believed myself to be alone. I forgot that you make a habit of spying on people.'

'On the contrary, spying on people is the least of my habits.'

'I care nothing of you or your habits. Will you please leave? I would like to go back to my family.'

'You may come out whenever you wish.' His voice deepened to a gravelly, yet subtle velvety sound. 'It's not like I haven't seen your body before.'

Her eyes narrowed as her stomach flipped. 'You are no gentleman.'

He chuckled, then, after pinning her with another stare, turned his horse and disappeared into the trees.

Kitty swore a filthy word the men said when they thought she wasn't close by. That man! That insolent, awful, insufferable man! He irritated her so much she wanted to shriek. Oh, the shame of it, for him to see her near naked. No man had seen her like that ever. And for him to do so made her skin crawl with embarrassment. She hated him.

In June, the rains came and stayed on and off, as Holby had predicted, for four weeks. The larger creek flowed so fast and had risen so high it was impassable. Having finished the building of their hut, the men built a pigpen, but the purchase and transportation of the pigs, supplies and the mail would have to wait.

Inches deep in thick mud and puddles, the yard turned into a quagmire. To drain the water away they dug channels around the hut and vegetable plot. The horses stood dejectedly under sopping trees, while the milk cow bellowed mournfully. They lost two chickens due to the wet conditions but having chicken on the menu was a welcome change. Kitty hoped they would lose no more since they needed eggs and broody hens to raise chicks.

In a break between showers, the men checked the stock, while Connie washed clothes and Alice swept the hut floor.

Kitty donned her boots. 'I will take the children out for a walk. They have been cooped up for too long.'

Rosie clapped her hands. 'Can I take my ball?'

'Yes, pet.' Kitty sat Little Rory on the table and put on his shoes. 'Charles, you hold my hand, please.' She raised her eyebrow at him in warning, for he was a terror and liked to run off.

Outside, she paused to sniff the fresh clean air of winter. Grinning at the children, she ran with them across the clearing. Their hoots and shouts echoed. A green haze of new growth covered the ground. Magpies warbled and called out their greetings. The colours of the trees seemed brighter, cleaner and each of their particular scents' sharper. Some eucalyptus even broke out into late flowering, while the Wattle trees burst into yellow blossom. The wildlife descended in abundance. Kangaroos bounded out of the scrub.

The moisture in the ground raised the humidity. Sweat beaded Kitty's forehead as she and the children explored the creeks and hollows, and the swamp.

'Oh look!' Rosie pointed to the fluttering butterflies, all the colours of the rainbow, and chased a few.

'Watch where you tread, pet.' Kitty smiled, and then laughed as Charles caught a slimy green frog. Little Rory stumbled and fell many times, as he tried out his new ability, walking. When he grew tired, she gathered him up and kissed his cheek.

Holding Adelaide's hand, Kitty strolled. She loved the bush in all its diversity. Amongst the tall trunks and lush undergrowth, her worries left her. It fascinated her to see rain forest and bush scrub combine and wanted to learn about the land she had grown to love. A wonderful sensation of everlasting prevailed when surrounded by the continuous growth of the land. The significance of building a future here was obvious to her in the bush. She wanted to send roots, family roots, deep down into the earth like the huge cedar and eucalyptus trees had done for thousands of years. This land, this earth, this tiny piece of the world she owned flowed through her veins. Australia had been her destiny, her fate. She would not fail it.

Spots of rain hit them.

'Come, it is going to rain again.' Kitty made a game of beating the rain as they ran for home. Once inside, they fell into a heap laughing and squealing.

Connie grinned. 'Right then, let's get you dry and ready fer you dinner.' She bundled the children into the bedroom.

Alice set out the plates and served their meal as the rain fell harder. From the leaks in the roof, drops pinged into the collecting buckets.

Jessup knocked and then stuck his head around the back door leading into the lean-to. 'We've just brought half the herd into the holding yard, Miss.'

'Oh?' Kitty looked up from unlacing her boots. 'Have the weeks of rain affected them?'

'No, Miss. In fact, there some ready for market now. They've feasted on the new grass and some of the better beasts are in good shape.'

'Excellent.' Kitty smiled.

'If we sort out the healthier ones to go to market and we can fatten them up some more with the last of the feed until the creek has gone down a bit.'

'Yes, good. Thank you, Jessup.'

Alice passed him a tray of food covered with a towel. 'Take your dinner now, that'll save you from coming back out in this weather.'

He winked and grinned at her. 'Thanks, Alice. By the way, is there some of your rice pudding left?'

Alice slapped him with her cloth. 'What, with you around?'

Jessup closed the door as Connie brought in the children. They ate the beef stew and tried to talk against the deafening roar of rain hitting the roof.

Banging on the front door stilled Kitty's hands on cutting up a piece of meat for Charles. She frowned, not certain she had heard correctly. The hammering came again. Alarm filled her. She, Alice and Connie looked stupidly at each other.

Connie lowered her fork. 'Jessup and Holby use the back door,' she whispered.

Kitty reached for her rifle. She nodded to Connie and Alice to take the children into the bedroom. 'Who is there?'

'It is Grayson.'

She waited until Connie had closed the bedroom door. 'What do you want?'

'To talk.'

Kitty slowly slid back the wooden plank; the door's bolting device. She opened the door a foot wide, her gaze wary.

'May I come in? It is raining.' He stepped towards her.

'No.' Her grip tightened on the door. The weapon rested against her skirts. She had not seen him up close before and she frowned at the tingling that ran along her skin. He was tall, well over six feet, and Kitty had to crane her neck to look up at him. It was another time in her life when she hated being short.

'May I speak to your husband?'

'H-he is not here,' Kitty stammered under the intensity of his steely gaze. She frowned at his dark grey hair peeking out under his hat, strange for a man only in his late thirties. Two deep lines went down from his straight nose to the corners of his well-shaped month. His silver- grey eyes drew and held her captive.

He regarded her with cool contempt, which did nothing to soften the harsh lines of his face. 'When will he be back?'

'Soon.' She swallowed.

'He must take you to higher ground should this rain continue.'

His gaze travelled over her and she blushed, remembering the naked scene by the water. 'Why?'

He muttered something under his breath, as though fed up with her silly replies. 'Because this plain will flood shortly, if the rain continues.'

'Thank you for letting me know. Goodbye.' She moved to close the door, wanting to block him from her sight and mind. He made her feel exposed, uncertain.

He shot out his foot to stop her. 'I am still willing to buy you out. Tell your husband.'

Kitty raised her chin, even though she didn't reach his shoulders. 'We are not selling. I made that clear.'

He stepped back and stood proud. 'I have yet to speak to your husband. I believe he will feel differently once I have put forward my offer.' He folded his arms and smirked. 'It is quite generous.'

'Go to hell!' Kitty slammed the door in his face and leant her back on it. She heard him walk away and his horse snort.

Connie and Alice came out with the children and they all began talking at once. Kitty said little as Connie poured her a cup of tea. 'You can't keep pretending that you're married, lass.'

'I will if I have to. Hopefully, he will become bored with us and forget we even exist after a while.'

A knock on the back door made them jump. Jessup appeared again. 'I thought I would check everything is all right, Miss. We saw Grayson leaving.'

'Everything is fine.' Kitty sighed. 'However, will we flood do you think, if the rain does not stop soon?'

Jessup scratched his head. 'There may be a chance. Though, it'll take several days of this before it gets close to the hut. Holby and I will keep an eye on the creek level.'

Kitty gave a ghost of a smile. 'Thank you, Jessup.'

In the golden light of early evening, Kitty sat on a large boulder and waited anxiously for Jessup's return. A lot depended on this first cattle sale and she was terrified they might not reach a decent price. There were bills to pay and accounts to settle, and she wanted to send word to Dan telling him how well they were coping. They could endure the harsh conditions and lack of comforts if it eventually meant they would be successful. She held visions of a grand house full of every comfort for her family, and acres and acres of fat healthy cows. It could be done. She would do it.

With a bit of luck, Jessup would also bring home mail. It was many weeks since they last collected the mail and she longed for some contact with those left behind. She hoped Mary had written.

Kitty gave a deep sigh and absently watched a little brown-feathered bird come to drink at the creek's edge. The evening had lost its heat and it was restful to sit by the calming sound of the flowing water. With the rains gone, the creek had fallen a little, but it was still deep. Lizards and insects moved freely around her. She thought how much Benjamin would have enjoyed sitting here with her watching the sun go down. In quiet times like these, she ached for him. It frightened her to think she may be alone for the rest of her life. Indeed, the very thought of being romantic with another man was unthinkable. She liked men and she took pleasure in their company and wit. Only, the one man she wanted was gone and sometimes the sadness was too much to bear.

Twigs crunched in the undergrowth. 'So, we meet again?'

His voice sent shivers of apprehension down her spine. She sat up straighter, though didn't turn around. The saddle leather creaked as Grayson dismounted. She held her breath while he walked the short distance to her.

'You seem to have an affinity with this creek.' He stood a few feet away.

'I know this is your land, but we have to pass through it to reach the main road. If there was another way to go, we would.' Kitty refused to look at him. She despised the fact they must use anything of his.

'I do not mind you crossing through my land.'

'My deepest gratitude to you. Though I was told there were droving rights where people can cross other properties to reach main roads, or something like that... I shall instruct my solicitor to—'

'There's no need, really.' Grayson cut her short.

Silence stretched between them for a moment. Kitty stared out over the water and into the bush beyond, begging for Jessup to reappear. She had no wish to converse with the awful, arrogant man. His presence made her stomach knot.

'You were lucky the rain stopped when it did.'

'Yes.'

'Do you always talk to people without looking at them? It is most rude.'

'Then I am rude.'

He sighed heavily. 'It would be advisable to move further away from both creeks.'

'We will manage.'

'It will flood one day. You have this creek to your north, a smaller creek to the east of you and swampland to the south. In the course of many weeks of torrential rain, the swamp will become an inland sea. It makes sense to—'

'I do not believe I have asked for your advice. So, please keep it to yourself.' How dare he presume to tell her how to run her life? 'You may be the wealthiest man in this part of the district, and you may have the largest property. Nevertheless, I will not let you treat me like some subordinate. Do I make myself plain?'

From the corner of her eye, she saw Grayson step back. 'Forgive me. I was merely trying to save you from disaster. I apologize.' He bowed stiffly and turned away.

Angered by his conceit, Kitty leaped up and quickly followed him. 'Nothing you can say will induce me to sell to you,' she hurled at his retreating back. 'Can you, with your smugness and pride, understand that?'

Grayson spun to her. His broad chest blanketed her vision. 'I have concluded that I no longer want or need your land, madam! It is an accident waiting to happen, and I can do without that.'

Kitty stumbled back. His scent of soap and fresh linen tickled her nose. 'G-good. Then there is no need for you and I to see each other again. Is there?' She raised one eyebrow haughtily.

'None whatsoever.' He nodded once and went back to his horse.

'Loathsome man,' Kitty mumbled, watching him ride away.

'Miss Kitty!' Alice's call came from the track leading back to the hut. Soon she came into view, holding a lantern high above her head.

'I am here, Alice.' Kitty hadn't realized how dark it had become. She still found it difficult to fathom the sudden darkness that descended quickly in this country. There was very little twilight in the evenings and after the last of the sun's rays disappeared, there was nearly total blackness. With the next month heralding deep winter, the days were shorter and the nights cooler. Not that she minded this, for it was a pleasant relief after the heat.

'Miss McKenzie!'

At Jessup's sudden shout, Kitty and Alice peered into the bush on the other side of the creek. It was now completely dark with only a half moon.

'We're here!' Kitty cupped her hands to her mouth. 'Do you think you can make it across?'

'Yes, Miss. Stand back from the edge. Cluster won't like the lantern in his face as he comes up the bank.'

Kitty and Alice walked back to the edge of the bush, trying to make out any movement in the water. Jessup encouraged Cluster to get on, and with a swish of water, they lumbered up onto the bank.

'Did everything go well?' Kitty asked immediately.

'Yes, miss, I've a large parcel of letters for you. The Post Mistress said she was getting worried you were never coming to claim them.' Jessup smiled and patted the large pack slung over his back.

'No, the sale?' Kitty near snapped in frustration.

Jessup grinned, his white teeth gleaming in the lantern light. 'They did you proud, miss, not as good a price as some of the others were fetching, but considering their condition a few months ago, they did good. Your money is in the bank.'

Kitty let out a pent-up breath. Tears welled. She nodded and swallowed the lump in her throat.

At the hut, Connie and Holby stood smiling outside the door. Jessup, tired after such a long ride, bade them all good night and took his dinner tray to his hut. Holby turned the horse out into the railed yard and gave it grain, and then he too went into the men's hut.

With the children asleep, the three women huddled around the lantern and poured out the contents of the pack onto their makeshift table. They gasped at the amount of letters and small parcels spilling over the surface. Kitty grinned in the dim light. She took a moment to sort them into piles and dates. The bills and cattle-sale papers were pushed to one side to be read in the morning. The more important items, the letters from the family, were gazed at tenderly.

'There are two letters from Dorothea in York, two letters from Joe, three letters from Clara and three letters from Ingrid and two from Dan.' Kitty opened another larger envelope. 'Alice, this has been forwarded on by Hetta, it is for you.'

'Oh!' Alice hugged the letter to her chest. 'It is from my family.'

'Oh, the joy of it, lass.' Connie beamed.

Kitty opened one brown paper wrapped parcel, revealing a leather-bound book. 'This is a new book I ordered back in Sydney.' She laughed.

'Which one is it?' Connie scanned it. 'I enjoy those adventure stories as much as the children. You'll have ter read it ter us in the mornin'.'

'It is Charles Dickens, A Mutual Friend.' Kitty picked up another parcel and unwrapped it. Inside was another leather-bound book. 'This is for Rosie. Lewis Carroll's, *Alice in Wonderland*.'

'This was worth the wait.' Alice beamed at the pile of letters in the dim light.

'Pour the tea, Alice. I will start to read them now. It has been so long since I have heard from Dorothea.' Kitty sat on a padded wooden crate used as a bench seat.

Dorothea's shock and pain on hearing of Ben's death was evident in her letter. Georgina nearly had a stroke from such devastating news, and together, mother and daughter were inconsolable. Dorothea's handwriting, usually so beautiful, was shaky, a clear sign of her distress and growing age.

Kitty sighed and opened Dorothea's second letter. She read it quickly, impatient for her news, but soon realized it was not written by Dorothea. In fact, she was ill. A trusted friend had written the letter under Dorothea's instructions. Kitty slumped in sadness at the thought of her dear friend not being her robust self. She missed her dreadfully.

Kitty sipped her tea and waved Dan's letter at Connie. 'It is a relief to know everyone in Sydney is well, especially Clara and Joe. Dan wants to journey here, but Ingrid's pregnancy is not going well, and she needs him home. Although, once the baby is born, he promises to come with Clara and Joe.'

'I miss them.' Connie sniffed.

'There is no mention of Mary. I am desperate for news of her.' The worry of Mary and the continuing disappearance of Rory kept her in a flux of emotions. Sometimes, their selfishness made her want to scream in frustration. Then, at other times, she would do anything to hold them close again.

Kitty remembered the promise she made to herself on the day of her parents' funeral to always keep the family together. It had not been so easy. Forces beyond her control conspired to split her family apart. Did I try hard enough to keep us together?

Later, lying in bed beside Rosie, staring up at the bark roof, she watched, mesmerized, as a small black spider hung suspended by its web. She observed it until her eyes grew heavy and in the shadows of the roof, she saw Benjamin's face appear and smile at her. His beautiful blue eyes sent her his love and Kitty ached for just a minute more with him, but his face faded to be replaced by another. A face with cool, grey eyes, hard lines and an arrogant sneer.

Chapter Nine

Kitty plodded away from the swamp; the rifle slung over her back. She had spent the last few hours trying to shoot wild ducks for dinner. However, all she accomplished was a sore shoulder from the rifle and aching muscles from crouching low in the reeds for hours.

When the notion came into her head to go north, she did not think for one moment about failure. The very idea did not even take root in her mind. She knew it would be hard. She knew life in the bush away from the comforts and necessities of a town would be difficult at first, but never in all her dreams did she think it would be like this.

As cold August winds buffeted the land, small hardships became harder to overcome. Spirits dropped. The isolation taxed them. They were sickening a little of each other's company. Kitty had risen to the challenge of being a farmer in the bush, but the realities drained her stamina. Six months in the bush without seeing her family and friends, with no relief from the constant worry of succeeding, lowered her self-esteem and courage.

The weather played havoc with every decision made. Whereas before the heat played a role in their lives, now so did the cold. Winter showed them it could be equally uncomfortable as the heat of summer. No matter how many blankets they put on their beds they still shivered. Despite their attempts to properly insulate the hut, cracks let the iciness creep in.

However, if the nights were cold, the days were not. For most of the time, the heat returned once the sun was high. The combination of the dust, dirt and the flies nearly drove the women mad. They constantly improvised when they ran out of supplies from town. Just the simple tasks of washing and cleaning were a challenge to even those strong of heart. No amount of boiling would get some stains out of their garments and the children's clothes were becoming outgrown and in some cases beyond repair. Connie spent hours sewing the rips and tears for the bush was not kind to any material.

In addition, there was the problem of cooking. The hut's fire never cooked the food correctly. It was either raw in the middle or so burnt on the outside the middle couldn't be reached unless a hammer was taken to it. Kitty longed for something fresh, like strawberries or a delicate pastry. Poor Alice tried to use her many talents, but the inadequate cooking equipment proved to be an obstacle too great to overcome.

Tedious amounts of time were wasted doing things normally achieved much quicker back in the city. Collecting water, gathering wood and the catching of fish took time and patience. Small mundane jobs grew monotonous, such as the boiling down of candle stubs and reduced blobs of soap. The weeding and watering of the vegetables, plus the upkeep of the fence to keep out the wildlife, grew tiresome.

However, the prospect of the children becoming lost was their biggest fear. Kitty tried to instill in them the wisdom of not straying too far, but the slightest thing would capture their interest.

Jessup and Holby worked hard and without them Kitty knew they would never have survived. Even so, the life of a farmer was made up of long days full of work that was back breaking, repetitive and soul destroying. Should the slightest thing go wrong, the consequences were usually enormous.

A toothache for one of the babies meant hours of crying in the confines of the small hut, driving everyone to despair. Connie's anxiety grew over someone becoming sick or injured and there was no doctor readily available. At first, they'd overlooked these matters, as it was all new and exciting. Now though, the pressure rose and failure haunted Kitty.

No further rain fell, and the August gales dried out the land once more. They moved the cattle to other pastures much further away from the property. Kitty neither knew nor cared who owned this grazing land, she believed it to be crown land, but if it wasn't then so be it. Her main concern was fattening the cows in readiness for breeding. There was not enough grass for them on her land and she was again losing cows by the day due to diseases from insects, their poor diet or from them simply escaping and being lost.

It annoyed her when reports from Jessup told her that just half an hour's ride away, Grayson's Blue Water Station thrived as an independent small village. His animals and beef cattle were fat and well, the grass green and plentiful from pumped creek water. He even had gardens around his prodigious house bigger than the clearing in which the hut stood. Grayson had everything she herself wanted for her family, but the present situation showed no promise of her obtaining it. Kitty hated no one more than Miles Grayson.

'Miss Kitty!' Alice hurried along the track at the edge of the bush to meet her.

Her heart thumped. 'What is wrong?'

'Grayson's here.'

A shiver ran down her spine. 'He's not been near for months. Why is he here now?'

'He didn't say. He arrived about five minutes ago and has been talking to Jessup near the holding yard. Connie is keeping an eye on him.'

Kitty marched along the track, continuing straight on when it came out of the bush near the hut. She was not going to be intimidated by Grayson. His absence during the last few months was a great relief for her.

Jessup stepped back, as though to give them both room.

Grayson studied Kitty at she strode towards him. His eyes narrowed as his gaze roamed over her. She was hot, dirty and sweaty, and still a good-looking woman. He watched as she raised her small chin and held her head at an angle ready to do battle with him. He admired her pluck and, despite being angry at her for lying to him, his loins ached in wanting. 'Good day, Miss McKenzie.'

Her face flamed. 'You wish to see me?'

'Yes. Can you spare me a minute, please?' He raised his eyebrows at her and gave a ghost of a smile. He was annoyed over her lack of response to him. He was not used to being disregarded by anyone, especially a woman. Usually his every word was listened to with respect. Everyone who knew him gave him their instant attention. He was not a man to be slighted. Only, this tiny woman before him had done it on each occasion they met. She infuriated and intrigued him all at the same time.

'I am busy.'

'I understand that.'

'We have nothing to say to each other.'

'I believe differently.' He was doing his best to remain calm. He did not understand why she was the only person he knew who made him want to lose his patience the minute he looked at her. He always considered himself to be a tolerant man, unless confronted by a fool and then as such they should be treated like one. Even so, this pint-sized woman with the glorious copper hair drove him nearly mad every time he was in her presence and he could find no reason for it. He knew, by the tone of her voice, her natural grace and poise, she was not born into the lower classes. This observation had made him curious. His lack of knowledge about her sent him to Sydney to make inquires. The answers he received brought him here now.

'Shall we walk a little?' His manner was everything correct.

She sighed dramatically, handed the weapon to Jessup and flashed a quick look at the older woman. 'Very well.'

His jaw tightened in annoyance.

They walked to the larger creek. At the top of the bank, he stopped and glowered down at the water. He was usually a man at ease in all he did. Always sure of himself in any environment and, as an intelligent and wealthy man born to the upper class, he never doubted anything he did. This assurance bred superiority and haughtiness. He was not ashamed of his pride and arrogance. From infancy he learnt his role as a gentleman and therefore demanded respect from all. In turn, he honoured his position by adding to his intellect, his wealth and his social position in the community. Nevertheless, the mark of a true gentleman was never to abuse such a position. For all his conceit, he knew he was kind and thoughtful to those he thought deserving of his friendship and tolerance. He had never once, in all his privileged life, had it thrown back in his face.

'What do you want?' She did not look at him.

'Why did you lie to me?'

'Pardon?'

'You have no husband. Why did you tell me that you did?' He gazed at her profile, thankful for the opportunity to study her.

'I...' She bit her lip. 'It was my protection.'

This saddened him. 'It was not my desire to frighten you.'

She rubbed her forehead wearily. 'Well, you could have fooled me. From the start, you frightened and intimidated me.'

'Shall we start again?' He held out his hand. 'Miles Grayson. Pleased to meet you.'

Slowly, she turned. Stubbornness etched her heart-shaped face and her emerald eyes blazed. She touched his fingertips lightly, as though he repulsed her. 'Katherine McKenzie.'

'Will you come to my home for dinner one evening next week?' His question widened her eyes. Indeed, it surprised him, but he meant it. He had never needed to appeal to a woman before. In fact, most women happily surrendered to any ordeal just to be by his side. Nonetheless, no woman as yet had sufficiently captivated him to require offering his heart. Only, somehow this little spitfire was already under his skin. He needed to eradicate her before he was lost. Dinner in his home would soon show him whether she was a genuine lady of class or a great pretender. It would show him if she was suitable, or not, to be a member of his society. It would decide for him whether he liked her enough to become better acquainted.

'I think not.' She moved away, heading back to the track.

Grayson did not expect her refusal and frowned in surprise. His station, Blue Water, was known throughout the district as a place of beauty and everything fine. Many people were desperate to become part of his social scene and be invited to his magnificent home. Obviously, Miss McKenzie was not most people. 'I would enjoy it very much if you did come.'

She turned to him, honesty written clearly on her face. 'I do not think I would.'

'Why not try it and see?'

'I could think of nothing worse than to sit across a dining table with you for an hour or two.'

'You do not mince your words, do you?'

'And why not? Why should I say the words you want to hear just because you are a wealthy landowner? I will not humble myself to you. You have done nothing to induce me to like you. I will not pretend to be what I am not.'

Her words cut into him like sharp chips of ice. No one ever talked to him in such a way. It shocked him, but only for a second. Then his temper, which was swift, ignited and his lips curled in contempt. An overwhelming desire to hit something hard or to pick her up and shake her until her teeth rattled consumed him. He did not trust himself to speak. As he walked past her, he gave her a look of utter loathing.

When he had gone, Kitty collapsed on the ground in a dazed state.

Connie found her some minutes later. 'Lass? Oh, lass!' Connie knelt beside her and placed comforting arms around Kitty's shoulders. 'What 'appened?'

Kitty shook her head, remaining silent. She sat like someone made of stone unable to speak. She could not explain herself or even understand why she behaved as she did. Purposely, she had taunted him to hate her and succeeded. His visits would be no more and it gladdened her. His brooding looks or cutting remarks were too difficult to deal with. He disturbed her mind when she was trying so hard to be brave and tough in this harsh land. 'Do you know what day it is today?' she finally whispered.

'Aye, Saturday.'

'The date?'

'Er...'tis easy ter lose track of dates out 'ere in the middle of nowhere.' Connie frowned. 'Er... August the—'

'A year this day since Ben's death.'

'Oh, me lass.' Connie hugged her tighter.

'How did I survive a year without him?'

'You did because you strong an' courageous.'

'I do not feel strong or courageous. I feel sick at heart.'

'Tomorrow, we're goin' into Grafton, all of us,' Connie spoke tenderly, taking control. 'You've taken too much upon yousen an' if you continue this way, then trouble will strike. 'Tis time ter 'ave a change of scenery, lass. We need ter relax fer a bit.'

Kitty did not argue.

They arrived in South Grafton after midday on the following day. Winter winds blew fierce, but for the first time in months, the four adults unwound and let their worries fade away. Holby volunteered to stay behind and watch the animals, and Kitty promised him a week's break after they returned, grateful she could depart the property and know it would be cared for. Without the reliable Holby, she would never have been able to leave the animals and take this much-needed break. The last six months had been harder than she thought and meeting her arrogant neighbour, Grayson, had not helped.

They stayed in the same hotel of their previous visit. After washing and dining, they strolled along the main road to the small variety of shops. Kitty spoiled the children; buying them bags of sweets, chocolates and toys. Next, she bought perfumed soaps, ribbons, stationery, new shoes and clothes. Finally, they walked down to the river munching on toffee apples and watched the river crafts ply up and down the water.

Dinner consisted of leek soup followed by a crisp salad, cold meats of ham and tongue. Dessert of fruit tart and fresh cream finished the meal with coffee and cheese. It was wonderful to be served such a meal at a real table with a snow-white tablecloth. The women hadn't needed to cook, serve or clean up afterwards. It was heaven. Kitty slept well that night, alone in a soft bed between stiff clean white sheets.

On their second morning, Connie tidied the twin's clothes. 'What we're doin' today?'

'I am going to post these letters while you get the children ready. I shan't be long, and then we might buy some material for a few new dresses. I will arrange for them to be made while we are here. Hopefully, they will be ready before we go back.'

'An' when is that to be?'

'Next week maybe.' Kitty lifted one shoulder. She wasn't too keen to go back to the toil just yet. Her property, such as it was, made her proud and she didn't wish to return to Sydney, but she was enjoying this little bit of relaxation before she must endure the hard work again.

'You look nice, lass, although you've lost weight. You worry too much. You're as tiny as a sparrow.'

'Oh well, at least it is a pleasant change to wear light colours again after six months of brown and grey service dresses.' She took pleasure in swishing her pale lemon linen dress. Ruffles of white lace edged the bottom and frothed at her sleeves. A new, wide-brimmed straw hat sat at an angle on her head. Lemon-coloured ribbons trailed down onto her shoulders.

'You look sixteen not nearly twenty-four.'

'I feel a hundred.' Kitty grinned. 'I will return in an hour.'

She strolled along the street, but as thunder rolled, she quickened. Heavy clouds blotted out the sun. Great fat raindrops landed in the dust. Kitty gathered her skirts and ran the last few yards to the post office just as the downpour hit.

'Come in, come in, my dear,' the postmistress called out from behind the counter.

Kitty laughed, wiping the moisture from the letters she held. So much for her dress!

'Wind first and now the rain.' The elderly woman chuckled. 'Once it starts it never knows when to stop, does it, Mr Grayson?'

Kitty's smile died. Her stomach clenched and her heart banged in her chest. He stood in the corner of the shop, a newspaper under his arm. She closed her eyes, weary of being near him again.

'I think Miss McKenzie is aware of how much rain we get here,' he said to the postmistress, all the while looking at Kitty.

'Miss McKenzie? Why, it is you who receives so much mail.' The woman hurried into a back room and returned with a wrapped parcel tied with twine. 'It is nice to put a face to the name at last.'

'Thank you.' Kitty took the parcel from the counter. 'We are unable to come to town often. I am sorry if my mail collects too much. May I post these letters, please?' she asked with a tight smile. She wanted to leave immediately as she sensed Grayson's gaze boring into her back.

Thunder rumbled overhead, but Kitty ignored it as she opened the door.

'You seriously are not going out in that, are you?' Grayson was suddenly close, dominating the very air around her.

'I must get back to the hotel,' she told him through clenched teeth.

'And ruin that pretty dress which so becomes you?' His lips twitched.

She fumed inside. 'Is there a need for you to talk to me?'

'I would like us to be friends. Is it possible?' Grayson stared at her long and hard. The antagonism abruptly left his face to be replaced with something Kitty could not name. 'Please.'

'Why?'

'Well, we are neighbours for one thing—'

'Unfortunately.'

'But a fact all the same. In the country, neighbours help each other in times of need.'

'Help each other? Do not make me laugh.' Kitty kept her voice low so that the postmistress wouldn't hear. 'Besides, I am not in need. And should I be, then you would be the last person I would call.'

'Can you not overcome our...regrettable beginning?' A pulse throbbed along his jaw as it tightened.

'Oh, come now.' Kitty mocked him. 'It has gone well beyond that.'

'Nevertheless, I would like us to be friends. Is that so hard to believe?'

'Yes, yes, it is.'

'I have apologized for my behaviour over your property. What more do you want?'

'Apologized? No, you have not!' Kitty struggled to control her temper.

An angry flush stained his cheeks. 'I will not embroil myself in another slanging match with you. It is beneath me to do so.' He took a deep breath. 'I invited you to dine at Blue Water.'

'And you thought that was all you needed to do? That I would fall at your feet in gratitude for such an honour?' Kitty gave a false laugh and went out into the rain. The man was quite insufferable.

The timely break in Grafton had been a blessing. They felt renewed and full of vigour again. However, now it was time to go back. Supplies and a few comforts for the hut filled the wagon. Kitty wondered anxiously how Holby fared without them and was enthusiastic to put into practice new plans for the land.

Thick mud and deep holes in the road slowed them down. The recent bad weather played havoc with the bush roads and the horses strained to pull a full wagon along the deeply rutted tracks.

When they were only halfway home, the wind and rain returned in a wild storm. Jessup cursed and stopped the horses to erect a canvas awning over the family and goods. 'Miss?'

'Yes?' Kitty stuck her head out and a blast of rain slapped her.

'The mud is too thick in this part, we're bogged. We need to lighten the load for the horses to pull it out.'

'Yes, of course. We shall get out, but can we leave the children in?'

Jessup nodded and took hold of the horses' bridles. Kitty helped Connie and Alice down and they waited. In vain, Jessup coaxed and tugged the horses' bridles, but the wheels sank deeper.

'It is not working,' Kitty called out through the squalling rain.

'We'll have to take some of the crates and sacks off.'

The wind rose and drove the rain horizontally. Above their heads the trees tossed wildly and creaked under the elements. Together, the women unloaded the wagon with Jessup, while the storm grew ferocious. Jessup again tried to lead the horses out of the bog. After a few jerks, the wagon wheels jolted free and, with a cheer, the women hurriedly re-packed the wagon and climbed aboard.

A mile further down the track, a creek bed, usually dry, was now a swirling torrent.

'This area must have received more rain than we did in Grafton,' Jessup said, getting down from the wagon once more.

Kitty joined him and they inspected the creek. 'How deep is it?'

Jessup wiped the rain off his face. 'It's a shallow bed, not more than three foot at its deepest.'

'Can we cross it?'

'Yes, I think so, but I'll just check to make certain.' He took off his boots, socks, rolled up his trousers and waded into the middle. The water only reached his thighs. 'I think we'll be fine, Miss.'

'Shall we unpack the wagon and make two trips?'

'Oh yes. I wouldn't want us to get bogged in the middle fully loaded.' Jessup pulled his boots back on but tucked his socks into his pocket.

Ten minutes later, Kitty, Alice and Connie stood amidst half of the wagon's load. Jessup held the horse's heads once more and led them across the creek. The children's pitiful faces peeked out from under the awning. Connie waved to reassure them. Rosie smiled, holding on tightly to Charles and Adelaide. They made it across easily. Jessup placed the children safely under a tree, instructing them not to move.

'He will have to make three trips,' Alice said, holding Little Rory in her arms. 'All of us together with the rest of the supplies will be too much to take across in one go.'

Kitty nodded. 'You and Little Rory can go next with the supplies. Connie and I will wade across. It is not deep.'

'Gee, speak fer yourself.' Connie knocked Kitty on the arm in protest. 'I'm not wadin' across. Let him mekk another trip.'

'Don't be silly. We are already wet.'

'I'm not wading across.' Connie sniffed and folded her arms.

Jessup came back and helped Alice and Little Rory onto the wagon. 'Shall I take the supplies this trip or you and Mrs Connie?' Jessup asked Kitty.

'Take Connie, then come back for the supplies.'

He helped Connie up and then led the horses back into the water. Within seconds, the wheels became stuck in mud on the creek bottom. The horses strained and managed to haul them out and reach the other side, but on the return journey the same thing happened. Jessup had a devil of a time getting them across. Finally, he made it back to Kitty.

'It will be touch and go this time, Miss.' He lifted the last crate of goods onto the wagon.

'I will wade across, that will make it a little lighter.'

'I'll have to try another route across, the wheels have churned up the mud good and proper.'

A roar of wind tore through the trees so strong it nearly knocked Kitty off her feet. A few yards away a tremendous crack split the air and a tall, thin eucalyptus tree crashed down through the other trees. The horses pulled at the harness, trying to bolt. The whites of their eyes showed in their terror.

Thunder pounded behind them on the track. A small buggy bounded around the bend with Grayson in the driver's seat. Kitty groaned when he stopped and climbed out.

'Is everything all right?' Grayson was just as wet as they were, but somehow, he still appeared smart, handsome and masterful.

'We are managing quite well, thank you.' Kitty dismissed him.

Grayson ignored her and turned to Jessup. 'How deep is it?'

'Not very, Mr Grayson. It's only difficult because of the bottom. The wheels and the horses get stuck in the mud and rocks.'

'I will help you.' Grayson and Jessup turned to the wagon.

Kitty went to speak but decided against it. She was cold, wet and knew without a doubt she looked frightful. She had no wish to converse with Grayson while at such a disadvantage.

In the torrential rain, she watched the two men lead the horses into the water. They nearly reached the other side, before the wind in the trees spooked the already nervous horses and they backed away, tossing their heads in fright. It took all Grayson's and Jessup's combined strength to hold them. At last, they steered the horses to safer ground and Kitty sighed with relief. Grayson and Jessup stood talking and gesturing towards the creek.

'Miss?' Jessup called through cupped hands. 'We think it best not to take the horse across again. So, Mr Grayson is going to bring you home while I take the others.' Jessup waved and went back to the wagon to help Connie and Alice put the children on board.

Stunned, Kitty blinked away the raindrops as the wagon rolled away. 'No! Wait.' She stumbled into the water, but the weight of her skirts slowed her down. Disheartened, she watched the wagon roll away without her.

Grayson waded back towards her. 'Come.' He held out his hand to assist her.

Lifting her chin, she spurned his outstretched hand, gathered her drenched skirts and tried to walk through the water.

'Get in the buggy.'

'I will walk, thank you,' Kitty threw back over her shoulder, and nearing the other bank, she trudged into the thick mud. It squelched over her boots and she stumbled, trying to pull each foot out of the gooey muck.

'For pity's sake,' Grayson growled. Rain dripped off his hat brim. He went across, gripped his horse's bridle and walked back into the water. 'You are the most stubborn woman I have ever had the misfortune to meet.'

'Did it occur to you that I did not want your help? You sent Jessup and the wagon on when they could have easily waited for me. You told him to go!' Kitty was so angry she barely stopped herself from screaming in frustration. She swung to face him and quickly realized it was a mistake. She swayed as her body went one way, but her boots remained stuck facing the other. Letting out a startled cry, she hit the water with a splash. The shock of being submerged in the cold water made her cry out again. She struggled to get up in a tangle of heavy wet skirts.

His deep laughter infuriated her. She strove to stand with dignity. However, the more she tried the worse her situation became. Her boots weighed her down as she tried to rise and, overbalancing, she toppled forward onto her face. The jolt of going under again left her spluttering and coughing.

His laughter continued while she wrestled, red-faced, to gain control of her feet. 'I hate you!' she screamed, squatting in the water to manually lift her feet out of the mud. 'You might at least help me, you...you!' Her temper flared as his mirth rang out through the trees over the noise of the storm.

'What was it that you said to me in the post office?' He tapped his chin in thought, his eyes bright with humour. 'Oh yes, that if you were in any trouble, I would be the last person you would call.' He laughed again at her furious scowl. Her hair fell free of its chignon and clung in untidy strands about her face.

Kitty could not speak such was her fury. In her mind, all the swear words she ever heard were hurled silently in his direction along with ferocious glares. He was a swine of the first order! She hated him with every ounce of strength in her body.

All at once, the fight went out of her. She simply gave up and knelt in the cold water, shivering.

His laughter subsided to a chuckle on seeing her sitting there defeated. Chortling to himself, he splashed his way to her and bent down. Quick as a flash, Kitty pushed him with all her might. He collapsed into the water flat on his back. He came up spluttering and cursing. Now, it was Kitty's turn to laugh, and she did, unrestrainedly as her mind repeatedly played the scene of surprised shock on his face as he went into the water. She hugged her sides as her amusement grew and shook her body. It was a wonderful release.

'You little minx!' With a hoot of laughter, he lunged for her and pulled her down with him. The attack was unexpected, and Kitty swallowed a mouthful of water as she went under. Her choking brought him to his senses. His face changed to concern and he took her arms. She grinned through the coughing and pushed at him again. This time he was prepared and grabbed her hands, drawing her against him.

Her merriment died instantly. Somehow, raw emotion charged the atmosphere between them. Grayson's cloudy- grey eyes stared intensely into her own. Her breath caught in her throat. His mouth lowered towards hers and she welcomed it like someone starved. They kissed hungrily, straining and tugging at each other in a desperate need for more. Kitty raked her fingers through his wet hair, pulling at him. Grayson gripped her hips, arching her body along his.

'God, I want you more than I want to breathe,' he murmured against her mouth before plunging into it with his tongue. His hand cupped her breast through the soaking material. Kitty ached for him to release her from her corset. She strained against him, her mind spinning out of control. She wanted to taste him, touch him everywhere, do anything to ease the throbbing throughout her body.

Abruptly, icy air slapped her as he wrenched himself away.

Kitty shivered. The freezing water lapped at her, but it was impossible to stand. It seemed as though she had no bones in her body, only floppy muscles refusing to hold her up.

Grayson effortlessly hauled her out of the mud and into his arms. He carried her to the opposite bank, then went back into the water and brought his horse and buggy across.

'You are cold,' Grayson stated, picking her up. He deposited her onto the buggy's seat.

Kitty nodded, unable to form anything coherent. She shook with cold and the shock of actually kissing him. Guilt ripped her apart as Ben's image came to mind. What had she done? Tears welled and, exhausted, she surrendered easily when Grayson brought out an oilskin coat and placed it around her shoulders. Silently, he drove her home.

Chapter Ten

Kitty's struggling property rent apart her dreams of living a grand life. Four weeks after their return from Grafton, conditions went from bad to worse, sapping her newfound eagerness and energy. Twenty-five breeding cows out of the herd were lost or stolen. All four children came down with chest colds so bad that, at one stage, it seemed they might lose one or all of them. The women alternated between crying and praying. Holby returned after his few days' break with his nose broken and cracked ribs. He refused to say how it happened and they nursed him along with the children.

From then on, the downward slide gained in momentum. Jessup, tired from all the extra work, slipped when cutting wood and the axe blade went into his foot. Alice cleaned it up and even sewed the few stitches the cut required. While Connie and Alice cared for the men as well as the sick children, all the outdoor work fell on Kitty. The sow and her piglets arrived from Grafton causing more labour besides splitting firewood, hoeing and watering the vegetables, milking the cow, feeding the chickens and collecting eggs. She also had to move the horses to other pastures, monitor the herd, collect water, set traps and shoot game. Fear of failure forced her to continue when her body cried out for rest.

Now, as Kitty stalked through the bush with the rifle over her arm, she fought to keep the depression from settling on her once more. The September sunshine hardly warmed her. White, fluffy clouds raced across the azure sky and the trees swayed in unison. The cold blustery day even kept the birds and animals silent.

Placing each foot carefully, she searched the scrub for any movement. She needed to shoot some sort of animal. Since Jessup's accident, they had not eaten any fresh meat. The traps revealed nothing every time she checked them. The garden produced few fresh vegetables at this time of year, and she refused to kill the chickens, for many sat on eggs.

Ahead, she saw a flash of fur. She cocked the rifle with caution, wincing at the sound it made, though she hoped the noise of the wind would drown it out. Slowly she took aim, closing one eye until she had the large kangaroo's chest in her sights. He paused, ears pricked, and she held her breath. Her finger tightened on the trigger and the deafening blast rang in her ears. The rifle kicked and she winced as it struck her shoulder, knowing she would suffer for it again tonight. To make it worse the animal mocked her with a glance and bounded away. Tears of frustration burned her throat. 'Damn and blast!' she yelled, rubbing her aching shoulder. Why couldn't something be easy—just once!

She weighed up the options for going on but decided against it. Tonight, it would be another meal of vegetable stew or damper and potatoes roasted in the fire. Their low supplies meant she would have to journey into Grafton. Only, the thought daunted her for the weather had been tempestuous of late with rain periods and gale force winds. She did not want to have to cross any flooded creeks by herself.

Unbidden, thoughts of Grayson filled her mind. She had not seen him since the day of the creek fiasco. Her faced reddened at the remembrance of their kiss. Never in her life had she been kissed with such a passion and wanting before. He had reached into her soul and consumed her, as if she were his life force—and she responded with wanton abandon. It shamed her now to think of it. She threw away her pride and self-respect so easily it disgusted her. She did not even like the man. So, what did that tell her? She was no better than a common whore.

All the kisses she had shared with Benjamin had been sweet and loving. He, being a complete gentleman, never took more than she was willing to give. Between them they shared a tender loving of hearts, with no soiling of hungry lust to ruin it. They knew the act of loving would be something they could do at length in the privacy of their bedroom once married. Only, they didn't know their time together would be so short.

Kitty plodded on. Her dream for this land was not working as planned. It was a harsh lesson and she still refused to admit defeat, but it was becoming increasingly difficult to keep a brave face. She was ploughing money into it faster than she had expected, and she really couldn't see a vast difference in what that money made. The herd's condition and the supply of grass were still not great. She tossed around the idea of moving them to someone else's land and pay rent on it. Again, it was an expense not allowed for. She knew, without a doubt, if Dan had not given her some shares in the business he and Ben founded, she would never have lasted this long.

On reaching the hut, she went straight to the lean-to and scooped grain into a bucket for the chickens. She opened the back door and asked Alice for any food scraps. In another bucket, she made a slop mixture of food scraps, grain and water for the sow and her piglets. Carrying both buckets, she first went to the sow's pen and poured the slops into the trough. The sow and her squealing piglets charged for the trough, jostling for the best position. Kitty fed the chickens their grain and checked for eggs.

'So, this is what stops you from giving us a welcome.' Dan's voice was just heard over the din from the pigs.

Dan, Clara and Joe stood at the corner of the hut. Goose bumps rose on her skins as she ran to kiss and hug them. 'Oh! How wonderful!' She kissed each of them again and hugged Clara and Joe tight, not wanting to let them go. 'I've missed you so.'

It seemed like a whole lifetime ago since she'd seen their beloved faces. She grinned through her tears. Together, they walked around to the front of the hut and went inside to surprise Connie and Alice.

'I would never have encouraged you, Kitty, if I had known what you were to endure. It is too much for you,' Dan spoke quietly as was his way. 'You must come back to Sydney and either sell up or employ a manager. I am adamant about this.'

They walked through the bush and Dan held the rifle. As he was a better shot than her, Kitty hoped he could shoot a kangaroo for dinner. Dan, Clara and Joe had been at the property for two days, and despite the cramped conditions, no one complained. Their happiness was too much at being together again. Ingrid's baby boy, born two weeks ago, was well. Therefore, Ingrid told Dan to take the children north to see her.

'It is not too bad. I am managing.'

'But you don't have to.' Dan stopped and faced her. 'It is not working, Kitty. You have to accept it.'

His thoughts ran similar to hers, but stubbornly she couldn't give in yet. 'It has only been seven months. These things take years. Once the cattle are in a better condition, I will begin a breeding program. In the meantime, we can live on what we grow and the money I get from our investments will pay the wages and buy the few things we need for the place. I will get by. I have no alternative.'

'Come back to Sydney.'

'No.' Kitty walked on, ending the discussion. Besides, there was no chance of them shooting any kangaroos while they talked non-stop.

With more luck than skill, they shot a kangaroo and hauled it back to the hut for cooking. The younger children, now over their chest colds, were allowed outside with the group. The weather was warmer, as spring finally made an appearance.

At the side of the hut, they dug a pit and set a fire into it. When a good bed of embers was established, Jessup placed the kangaroo on it and raked the coals over the carcass. The natives had used this method of cooking for hundreds of years. Joe and Clara were full of wonder as they watched the process. They eagerly helped place the potatoes in the embers at the edge of the pit. Alice showed them how to make damper in a flat pan over the fire, while Dan talked to Jessup and Holby.

'It does me the power of good ter have those two darlin's 'ere,' Connie said to Kitty, smiling in the direction of Joe and Clara sitting around the fire.

'You and me both.' Kitty sipped her glass of red wine. Dan brought a variety of treats for them from Sydney. New material for dresses, wine, fruit and chocolates. He also brought ladies magazines, recent editions of Sydney newspapers, a few books and stationery.

'How they've grown. Why Joe is nearly a man already, an' Clara grows more beautiful every day.' Connie drained her third glass of wine.

Kitty smiled to see her with glowing cherry cheeks and starry eyes. 'Yes, they certainly look older.' She nodded, watching her brother and sister.

Joe had grown so tall, at thirteen his body was changing into a young man with wider shoulders and stronger facial features. He reminded Kitty of Rory for they were much alike in looks. Her stomach fluttered at the thought of Rory being somewhere in the country and missing out on seeing his son grow.

At that moment, Little Rory wobbled towards her and she put out her hands for him and settled him on her lap. Rory did not see his son take his first steps or hear his first words. It saddened her that he might not see him ever.

Clara sat beside Kitty and played with young Rory. 'He is so big.' She laughed, clapping Little Rory's little hands inside her own.

'He has a good appetite.' Kitty chuckled, then looked keenly at Clara. She was a pretty girl of nearly twelve and showed promise of becoming a beautiful woman. 'How are you, my pet? Tell me if you have any concerns about anything. I want to know if you are all right.'

Clara dimpled and her lovely blue eyes shone with youth and vigour. 'I am happy. The Freemans are lovely, and I like living with them. At first, I was a little sad, but Joe came home every weekend and I felt better after a few weeks. Now, I love it. Aunt Ingrid—'

'Aunt Ingrid?' Kitty said amused.

'Yes. She asked me to call her that, instead of always Mrs Freeman, I like it too.' Clara giggled.

'So, what do you and Aunt Ingrid do?'

'Well, she was so ill with the baby we didn't go into town much at all, but she taught me to play the piano very well. We sing, paint in the garden, we embroider and then there is school. Sometimes, Aunt Ingrid receives callers and I help with the tea things, but not lately since little Andrew was born.'

'Is he a lovely baby?' Kitty asked, relieved that leaving Clara at the Freemans had not been a bad thing to do. Indeed, it spared Clara the harshness of living in the bush.

'Oh, he is so sweet and so good. I love him, and the others, but mainly him.'

'Good, I am glad.' Kitty leant over and kissed Clara's cheek.

Movement to the left made Kitty pause in pegging a petticoat on the line. She dropped it back into the basket and turned. Grayson rode up the track from the direction of the swamp and dismounted close by. His steel grey eyes never wavered from her.

Kitty's stomach twisted. Her throat went dry.

'I am sorry to disturb you.' His jaw clenched and unclenched.

'It is quite all right.' She put a hand up to tidy her hair and hoped to appear sophisticated and worldly, but while the dark forest-green stripe of her dress matched her eyes and complemented her copper hair, it was much worn and showed age. She wanted to die of shame.

His gaze seemed to absorb her every detail. His eyes softened, as though imparting a message all their own, one she couldn't read.

'Kitty. Kitty! Little Rory has put a stone in his mouth and will not spit it out!' Clara's distressed call interrupted Grayson's intense study of her and they both turned as one towards the hut.

Connie came out and dealt with Little Rory. 'Good day, Mr Grayson.' She nodded to him.

'Good day, Mrs Spencer.'

'We have family staying with us,' Kitty said. His eyes widened and she realized it was the first sentence she had said to him in a conversational tone.

'You must be extremely pleased.'

'Indeed, yes.' Kitty paused, as Dan joined them. 'Dan, you must meet my neighbour, Mr Miles Grayson. Mr Grayson, this is my business partner and more importantly my dear friend, Mr Dan Freeman.'

Dan shook Grayson's hand. 'I am led to believe that you have a sizeable property, Mr Grayson?'

'Blue Water is of good size, yes. However, as a man of business, you would understand that because of the size, it brings its own problems.'

'I do understand that.' Dan nodded.

'In fact, I came here today to invite Miss McKenzie to a picnic on my property the day after tomorrow. Of course, you are now all invited. It is to honour the arrival of my parents and brother. They are here for a short stay.'

This news startled Kitty and she stared at Grayson, comprehending just how little she knew of him. She didn't expect to hear him speak of his family. Indeed, she never gave it a thought he would even have one. He always gave her the impression that he was one man alone, solitary and aloof. Someone reserved and detached from all family love. Suddenly another thought entered her head. Was he married? There was no mention of a wife at any time.

'Thank you, sir. That is most decent of you. Is it not, Kitty?'

She forced a quiver of a smile. 'Um, well, there is a great deal to do here, Dan. I am not sure whether it is possible for me to go, but you must accept.'

'Come now, Miss McKenzie. One day away from here would not see it go to ruin. The day will be an enjoyable one, I promise you,' Grayson told her, but Kitty caught something in his voice that sent shivers along her skin.

'I agree, Kitty. You work too hard and a little pleasure is sure to do you good.'

'Very well...' she acknowledged with a small nod. Though, she was not happy about it and refused to look at Grayson. 'If you will excuse me, gentlemen, I must be about my business.' As she walked away, she knew his pewter grey eyes watched her. Never had one person been able to unnerve her like he did.

With each turn of the cart's wheels, Kitty's stomach churned. She stared straight ahead determined to control her strung nerves. She had no wish to know Grayson better nor did she want to visit his beautiful home. Obviously, no one understood how much this day would cost her. They did not appreciate that a day surrounded by wealth and style would destroy the fragile grip she held on her emotions. Did they not know how humiliating it would be for her to be back into the lifestyle she had been born into but had lost, first by her parents' death and then for a second time by Benjamin's? She could not do it. She did not want to be shown what she could not achieve.

Her own property would never be grand. In fact, Kitty wondered whether they could even last another year. She couldn't expect Dan to spend more money on cattle and improvements to the property without guarantee of a profit. The land was dreadful. She admitted that now. The soil was not good for cattle or crops. It was too swampy, and they would always need more, better grazing land to keep the cattle in good condition. It would take time to clear her whole property of trees for grazing. Kitty was fighting a losing battle to keep positive about her future. It hurt to think Ben's last gift was not a very viable one.

'It's not much further, miss, just over that last rise.' Jessup broke into her thoughts.

The well-formed road carved through the bush most successfully. No ruts or holes dominated this track unlike the one to her hut. It seemed that a bevy of workers spent endless hours filling holes in the road after the rains. Behind her came the excited voices of Joe and Clara. Dan talked quietly to Rosie. Alice and Connie had stayed behind with the babies, for they knew the invitation was not for them. They were working class. No matter how much Kitty argued the point she was friendly with the Freemans, Connie still refused to attend.

Jessup slowed the cart on the summit of a large hill. There was an opening through the trees and for a spellbinding moment, spread out before her, lay the huge expanse of Blue Water Station. About a mile away stood the main buildings of the homestead. Winding through the valley bottom some distance from the house was the Orara River, from which the homestead derived its name.

'My, that is a grand sight,' Dan said, leaning over to Kitty.

'Yes, it is,' Kitty replied, smitten by the vision below.

Jessup flicked the reins, moving the horses on. Kitty concentrated on the scene peeking between the trees. At the bottom of the hill, open flat fields stretched out around them.

Traveling nearer to the main hub of the station, they passed many buildings, windmills and holding yards. Closer still, they passed farm buildings, workmen and cottages with women and children going back and forth. Then, they turned off the dirt roadway and travelled along a white, gravel driveway. Large pine trees lined its route like sentry soldiers. The shade they gave was a wonderful relief from the spring sunshine.

Kitty's party grew quiet as they absorbed such splendour. The long drive weaved through beautifully landscaped gardens. The flowerbeds, neatly trimmed, each held a magnificent array of roses, gardenias and azaleas. Lush green lawns swept through the gardens and away out of view, glimpses of stone statues and fountains tantalized Kitty, making her want to investigate this garden of Eden.

The prestigious house made of sandstone blocks loomed before them. It simply took Kitty's breath away. Dormer windows punctuated the roofline. A wide, deep veranda with wrought iron lace work, the same as on the upper floor, surrounded all sides of the house. At intervals along it, opened cedar French doors led out from individual rooms. Fine, white lace curtains billowed gently in the slight breeze. Chairs and small tables lined the walls with each tabletop holding a pot of vibrant geraniums.

Four wide steps made of the same sandstone as the house swept down from the veranda in line with the central dark, wooden double doors. In front of them, Jessup pulled the horses to a halt. An elderly servant, dressed in a service uniform of dark blue, stood at the bottom of the steps. She wore no mobcap or apron.

'Welcome to Blue Water Station. I am Mrs Morris, the housekeeper. Mr Grayson has informed me to tell you that the party is being held down by the river. If you care to follow me inside, refreshments await you. I will let Mr Grayson know you are here.' She was a small woman, like Kitty, only Mrs Morris was plump and motherly. Kitty smiled at her as she climbed the steps.

At that moment, Grayson walked out onto the veranda. 'Welcome.'

'Thank you for your invitation.' Kitty felt tongue-tied and gauche. Again, he looked at her intensely as he was wont to do whenever they met. She blushed.

'Your home is most splendid, Mr Grayson,' Dan spoke, shaking Grayson's hand.

'Thank you, Mr Freeman. Please, come inside. You must wish to freshen up before joining the others.'

Grayson took them through the hall and into a large sitting room on the left. The highly polished timber floor reflected their movements and Grayson told them it was locally milled cedar, as were all the timber features throughout the house. The English, French and Italian furniture in the hall and sitting room were of a superior quality. Oil paintings by Constable, Turner and colonial artist Conrad Martens amongst others lined the subdued painted walls in colours of pale blue and white. It was a beautiful room and Kitty loved it.

'If the ladies would like to follow Mrs Morris, she will take care of you,' Grayson mentioned, giving Clara and Rosie an encouraging smile.

This side of the man was new to Kitty. Her gaze lingered on his mouth. The same mouth that kissed her so passionately, so hungrily. It had not been the action of a gentleman, but at the time Kitty had wanted it more than air. I must not think of that day or his kiss. He was a neighbour and an arrogant one at that. She didn't even like him. Shaking her head to clear her thoughts, Kitty quickly left the room and followed the young maid Mrs Morris had summoned to take them upstairs.

The upper floor was decorated and furnished in the same style as below, only the colours changed from room to room. Nothing was ostentatious, but the rooms Kitty saw, as they passed along the upper hall, enchanted. Whoever decorated the house possessed sublime taste.

'Is it not beautiful, Kitty?' Clara asked, in awe of the surroundings of the powder room.

'Yes,' Kitty answered, trying desperately to tidy her hair, which escaped from the combs and ribbons Connie used to put it up. Giving up on the task, Kitty tucked the mass of hair under her straw hat. She worried at her appearance. The sun had streaked her normally copper hair a lighter shade and her skin was no longer white but tanned. She wore a new pale lilac dress, made in Grafton on their last visit. It was embroidered over the bodice with fine silver thread in the design of swirls. Silver satin edged the short sleeves and the skirt flared out majestically over the crinoline cage not used since coming north.

'Can we swim?' Rosie giggled, jumping up and down. Her newly curled hair slowly slipped out of its ribbons.

'Keep still, Rosie, and behave,' Kitty scolded. 'You are to be the best of girls today, understand?'

Rosie nodded and stood near Clara. Kitty sighed and took Rosie's hand. She prayed ardently nothing would go wrong.

Downstairs, Grayson, Dan and Joe waited for them. With a smile to all, Kitty and the girls fell in with the group. They walked down the hall and into another splendid room, more like a library, and out through a set of French doors and down the steps onto the lawn. Beautiful landscaped gardens with white, snaking, gravelled paths invited them to stroll. At intervals they stopped to admire a water fountain or some particularly lovely and unusual plant. The gardens were designed to fill the senses and enhance the house, and they performed the job admirably. Grayson led them across the lawn's lush green expanse towards tall eucalyptus trees edging the banks of the gentle flowing river. Soft laughter and chatter filtered to them.

Kitty's stomach tightened. She held Rosie's hand tighter. Her legs threatened to give way and she took a deep breath to quell her nerves. It annoyed her to feel this way, for she had so many

times before spent numerous hours in the presence of the afflu-
ent. Indeed, the parties her own parents hosted were legendary
for their wealthy and influential guests. Yet, today in the middle
of the Australian bush on a picnic given by her arrogant neighbour, she suffered like a naïve and unsophisticated girl no older
than Clara. It was a mistake to come.

They rounded a bend in the path through the trees and came
into a clearing situated above the bank of the river. Standing in
a small group, holding drinks in their hands, a few men stopped
talking to smile in their direction. The ladies of the party sat either on blankets on the grass or on chairs by small square tables.
It was a setting worthy of a painting. The pale pastel colours of
the women's dresses contrasted brightly against the backdrop of
the dark trees and river behind them.

Grayson led them to the others. 'Everyone, please let me introduce you, Miss Katherine McKenzie, her business partner, Mr
Freeman and her brother and sisters.' Grayson turned to Kitty
and her party. 'My father, Ronald Grayson. My mother, Blanche
Grayson.' Grayson paused to let Kitty and Dan shake hands with
his parents.

Kitty's exhaled in relief as Ronald and Blanche Grayson smiled
warmly with genuine pleasure. Ronald was a tall man, an older
version of Grayson, except his eyes were a soft blue, his hair
white. Kitty liked him immediately. Blanche Grayson exuded the
graceful air of a dainty woman. She was not a lot taller than
Kitty, but she possessed a fragility about her. Blanche's kind,
golden-brown eyes smiled. Kitty imagined that in Mrs Grayson's
younger days, she would have been a great beauty.

'Miss McKenzie, this is my brother, Campbell,' Grayson said.

Campbell Grayson was as tall as his brother if not a little
more, but the major difference was his young, good-natured
face and wavy brown hair. There was no evidence of premature
greyness. He took Kitty's hand and kissed it like a chivalrous

knight. She grinned up at him. He was devilishly handsome like Grayson, only Campbell seemed to have a softer edge and was much friendlier. Instinctively, Kitty sensed that, unlike his elder brother, he was never angry, arrogant or superior.

'I hope we will be good friends, Miss McKenzie. Good friends are so rare to find do you not agree?' Campbell's laughter reached his light blue eyes.

Kitty smiled at his affability. 'I would like to be your friend, Mr Grayson. One can never have enough.'

It was Campbell who introduced her to the other couples of the party and then to Blue Water's resident doctor, Len Saunders, and last of all to a willowy, slender young woman about her own age with jet-black hair and dark brown, expressive eyes.

'Miss McKenzie, this is a dear friend of ours and my mother's goddaughter, Miss Serena Feldon. Serena, Miss McKenzie.' Campbell smiled, and added, 'I shall go and acquire refreshments for you both.'

'Pleased to meet you, Miss Feldon,' Kitty acknowledged warmly after Campbell left them.

'Indeed.' Her gaze roamed Kitty's dress and, aware that Miss Feldon wore a new style, Kitty blushed in embarrassment. Even though it was newly made, her dress was outdated by Sydney's fashion, which eventually followed the styles of London and Paris. The magazines brought by Dan had confirmed this.

'I am told you live on a...farm?' Serena Feldon's beauty stopped the minute she opened her mouth to speak. Acid toned; her dark eyes narrowed as haughtiness cloaked her manner. She grimaced as though Kitty was something repulsive.

Kitty bristled at the slight. 'I do have a property, yes.'

'And you live there alone?'

'I have my family.'

'But no husband I'm told.' Serena's voice was like dripped venom. 'How odd.'

'I find nothing odd about it.' She lifted her chin.

Serena twitched her silk skirts, shaped flat against her stomach and trailed out behind her over a bustle at the back. 'I am hopeful that the union between Miles and myself will take place next spring. It is my destiny to be his wife and mistress of Blue Water.'

Kitty inclined her head and forced a smile. 'I-I wish you much happiness.'

'Miles told me your farm is nothing more than a rundown shack and you live in the most appalling conditions. How dreadful. You have my sympathies.'

Her malice is not even subtle. Anger rose in Kitty like a flood. She searched for some witty retort, but her mind went blank. The slender woman smiled like a contented cat and drifted away, pleased to have won the first round.

Temper ignited; Kitty breathed deeply. Inherent common-sense came to the fore. Jealousy ate away at Serena like gangrene. It was obvious Serena disliked having to compete with another single woman for Grayson's attention. Kitty chuckled. Serena was welcome to him. She watched the other woman sidle up to Grayson and simper at him. Shaking her head, Kitty sighed. The poor woman did little to hide her feelings as she gripped Grayson's arm and smiled at his comments.

Kitty looked around for her family. Serena's scathing remarks did little to boost her flagging confidence. She needed to leave this place. It was paradise with a serpent and Kitty wanted to be home. Dan was talking easily to Ronald Grayson, while Joe stood on the bank with a guest. Clara and Rosie sat chatting to Blanche and the two other ladies. She would look a fool if she told them they must leave, but she had no alternative. The thought of staying here another minute longer was appalling. Sudden tears blurred her vision and she groaned. What was wrong with her? Crying solved nothing and the last thing she wanted was an awkward emotional scene.

'Is everything all right, Miss McKenzie?' Campbell asked, suddenly beside her.

'Yes.' She blinked away moisture. 'Yes, of course.'

'Here, Miss McKenzie, this will cool you.' He handed her a tall glass of wine. 'Would you care to accompany me on a short walk along the river?'

Grateful for his attentiveness, Kitty smiled. 'Thank you, I would like that very much.'

They walked past the others and Kitty nodded in reply to Blanche's assurance the girls would be well looked after. As they strolled, Campbell talked a little of the history of Blue Water Station, and as maddening as the owner was, Kitty couldn't but help taking an interest in Campbell's narrative.

'Miles bought this place when nothing was here but a small timber house. With his inheritance from our grandfather, he built the main house as it is now and also spent most of his money on buying more land and cattle. It really was a win or lose situation. He could have easily lost everything and had no money at all until our own father dies. However, just about everything Miles touches turns to gold, literally! He found a small amount of gold here in the fifties. Though, with all the gold fields in Victoria attracting people from around the world, Miles was able to keep a lid on his own findings. Besides, he owns all the land around the spot where the gold was found so no one could get to it anyway.'

'So, the gold made him rich?' Kitty asked despite herself.

'Well, he was already wealthy.' Campbell reddened in embarrassment. 'The gold just added to it and let him build Blue Water Station into a thriving community. Here, there is a blacksmith, a tannery, a small flour mill, a dairy, a stores shop for the wives of the workmen to buy supplies from, a doctor lives here and so much more.'

'The station would be mostly self-sufficient then?' Kitty's anger diminished, leaving her deflated. Grayson had everything. His station was all Kitty dreamed for her own. Only, she knew hers would never compare to the likes of this one. It would not be possible. For an instant, she wondered whether her land contained gold, but dismissed the idea just as quickly, with her luck it would be fool's gold.

'Yes, very nearly so. I must say to Miles's credit, he worked very hard for many years to make this property what it is. He laboured with his workers on all the constructions and many a time we have visited only to find him camping out in the hills with the men who watch the cattle.'

Kitty stopped to stare out over the river. 'You do not live here permanently?'

'No, my parents and I live near Bathurst in the west. We have a station of our own there. Do you know of Bathurst?' Campbell bent to pick a wildflower and gave it to her.

Kitty thanked him and walked on. 'No, not really. I only know it is over the Blue Mountains. I remember now, my man, Jessup, mentioned your property.'

'It is a beautiful homestead.'

A thought puzzled her. 'If your family has a station, then why did Grayson decide to have one of his own?'

Campbell gave a soft laugh. 'You do not know my brother well enough yet, Miss McKenzie, or you would not have asked that question.'

'Oh?'

'Miles didn't want to run a station already profitable and secure, there's no challenge in that. No, he needed to test himself and prove he could do it too. My brother is a complicated man. I do not think there is a person alive who can understand him.'

Campbell's words did nothing to help order her thoughts on the man either. Grayson was a paradox.

Soon after, they turned back and spoke of other things. Kitty told him a little about her early life before her parents died. In turn, he told her about his home near Bathurst. When they reached the others, they found there was one more to the party and before Kitty saw him properly, Clara happily told her that Parson Sims, a fellow passenger from the Ira Jayne, was here.

With a smile, Kitty greeted the new guest. 'Parson Sims.'

'My dear Miss McKenzie. I cannot believe my luck. What joy it is to find you and your family safe and well.'

'I did not know you were in these parts?' Meeting the parson again reminded her of the journey out to Australia. It was a time when she had been in love and on her way to Benjamin. Her smile faded.

'I am simply passing through. I met Mr Grayson while in Sydney and he invited me to visit anytime I journeyed this way.'

'Are you staying long?'

'Only a day or two, I'm afraid.'

'If you have the time tomorrow, do you think you might call on us at my home? Connie and Alice would so much want to see you too.' The two minutes spent talking to the Parson relaxed her more than the whole two hours she had been at Blue Water.

'Oh, I would like that enormously. Tell me, did you marry your fiancé?' Parson Sims's question had the others present turning their heads to listen to this piece of news about their new friend.

Kitty swallowed, wanting to escape the question. Dan's face clouded and Grayson's eyes narrowed while a pulse thumped along his jaw as he waited for her to answer.

'No, I did not marry,' she murmured.

The Parson was sensitive enough to drop the question. 'I am sorry to hear that. Now tell me, how are those lovely babies of Mrs Spencer's?'

Surrounded by Parson Sims, Campbell and Dan, Kitty spent an agreeable afternoon. She and Parson Sims reminisced about their voyage, telling funny tales to the guests, making them all laugh. She even enjoyed a pleasant conversation with Ronald Grayson, but all along she was aware of Miles staring at her from the other side of the tables. The purring Serena kept him busy and Kitty dismissed them from her mind.

At five o'clock, the party wandered back to the house. All the guests were staying the night except Kitty's party. The whole group came out to the front steps to wave them off. She let Dan thank Miles for his hospitality while she said good-bye to Ronald and Blanche before Campbell helped her into the cart. 'It was a very great pleasure to meet you, Miss McKenzie. I hope we meet again soon.'

'I hope so too. Besides, we have to, we are friends now.'

'Of course, we are! Ours will be a friendship of a lifetime.' Campbell's laugh rang out, causing Blanche and Ronald to look at each other. Ronald winked at his wife in understanding, but Miles stiffened.

For the next three weeks, Kitty saw a lot of Campbell and together they went for walks through the bush. He soon became friendly with Connie and Alice and played with the children. When Dan, Joe and Clara returned home to Sydney, Campbell arranged to meet her and Connie in Grafton and took them out for high tea to cheer them up. Several times, he invited her to Blue Water for dinner and morning tea. Thankfully, Grayson was not present on all of the occasions due to his need to be on different parts of the station. Whether that was accidental or on purpose Kitty didn't know.

Campbell was a perfect gentleman and would talk for hours about his home and the places he had visited on his European tour. The three women adored him.

On a cool October day, Kitty read a farming digest before the fire. In the bedroom, Alice sat cutting out paper dolls and animals for the children to play with.

Connie knitted socks opposite her. 'Yer know he's in love with you?'

Kitty glanced up and chuckled. 'Campbell? That is silly. He is not in love with me. We are just good friends.'

'Oh, lass, are you blind? The poor man's in torture every time he looks at you.' Connie shook her head. 'Besides, you need ter be married. It's unnatural fer a young woman as pretty as you ter waste away out here. You're ripe for loving, 'tis time you were wed.'

Annoyed that Connie should say such a thing, Kitty lowered her book. 'I believe you are wrong. You are seeing things not there.'

'Ask yourself why he's always 'ere.'

'I have given him no encouragement. I have no feelings for him in that way. My heart belongs to Ben and it always will. I will not fall in love with Campbell Grayson or anyone else. Please, do not bring it up again.' Kitty threw her book down on the table and stormed outside.

The day was fresh and crisp and without her shawl, goose bumps rose on her skin. She walked towards the creek, frowning as Connie's words echoed in her mind. The very thought of falling in love again was so abhorrent to her she shuddered. She liked Campbell Grayson very well. He was a charming and attentive young man. Even so, the thought of him as a husband was quite absurd. No one could take Ben's place and to think otherwise seemed unfaithful.

Kitty looked down at her ring-less hand and gently rubbed the spot on her finger where Ben's engagement ring had been. She'd taken it off on moving north, for she did not want to lose it when digging in the soil planting vegetables. She missed feeling the band on her finger. Though, more than that, she missed Ben. Her bad dreams of drowning in his bright red blood had faded somewhat, due mainly to her being so tired from hard work that she fell into bed exhausted each night. But still, some days she thought she would die without seeing his loving smile again, or his soft tender gazes. She ached to be held, pained to be loved.

A hollow void, a black pit of despair, engulfed her. She tried to fight it, tried to become angry at it, but it was too strong. Connie's innocent words triggered off a pain so acute Kitty wanted to die. Her mind swirled with images of Ben's loving face mixed with Miles Grayson's eyes. Ben's gentle laughter turned into Grayson's wry smile and she felt helpless against it. The tears splashed over her lashes. For too long she kept her tears from falling. She was tired of being brave.

On reaching the creek, she stumbled onto her favourite rock and hugged her knees to her chest; sobs rocked her. The ache she carried around in her heart seemed to squeeze the very life from her. This was not what she imagined for herself when younger. She didn't expect so much misery and grief in her life. It was one thing after another, and she was worn-out from carrying it all on her shoulders. She couldn't do it anymore and simply didn't want to. Just for once she wanted someone to say she could lean on them and they would take the worry from her. Just for once she wanted a strong man to hold her and wipe the stress from her life.

'Kit?'

She barely heard his voice over her sobbing. When her crazed mind realized who stood beside her, she groaned in anguish and pain. 'Go away!' She buried her face into her hands. It was the ultimate insult to have him, of all people, see her this way. Her abhorrence of him burned in her chest like a simmering volcano.

'Are you hurt?' Grayson's voice was soft.

She didn't want his pity or his so-called chivalry. A seething anger consumed her, and she welcomed it. Anything was better than this devouring misery. She spun to him in hatred. 'Leave me alone. Can you not understand that I despise you?' Every time she saw him, it was a betrayal of Ben and a reminder of a lost life together. The concern etching Grayson's face only increased her guilt and self-loathing. 'Get out of my sight!' She lunged at him with her nails ready to tear at his face. The one thought in her mind was to do him damage. He had to hurt like she was hurting! Why should she suffer alone? He had everything she did not, he deserved to be wounded and to bleed from the heart.

He was not prepared for her pounce. She knocked him backwards off the large boulder. They both hurtled onto the ground. Kitty landed on top of him and fisted him hard in the face and chest. She used her nails, and such was her anger and hurt it made her stronger than normal.

'Kit! For God's sake! Stop it! Stop it, damn you!' Eventually, Miles grabbed her wrists and wrestled her over until he pinned her beneath him.

'Get off me, you bastard! I hate you!' Kitty's cursing and yelling was punctuated by jerking attempts to free her hands from his grip of steel. 'I hate you. You are nothing. Do you hear me? Nothing.'

'Stop it, Kit. What is the matter with you?' He struggled to calm her, but it only infuriated her more. Abruptly, and with a curse of the damned, he crushed her lips beneath his own. It was not a loving kiss or even a kiss of passion. They both tried to subdue the other's will in a fight for supremacy and a need to win.

She tore her mouth from his to spit in his face. 'Get your filthy hands off me.'

Miles wiped his face on her bodice. Kitty squirmed to get out from under him. Getting a hand free, she tore at his hair, but he whipped his head away and she ripped his shirt. Her nails raked his chest leaving pinpricks of blood. Surging with power, she ripped the shirt further and bit him.

'Christ, Kit.' Miles groaned.

Heat throbbed between her legs; an astonishing awareness so strong she moaned. She bit him again, but not as hard, and then licked the spot. When Miles grunted, she grinned like a she-devil. This new power delighted her. He moved over her and she felt his need stiff against her thigh. The heat now circled her belly, urging her on. She moved her hips instinctively, knowing she wanted what only he could give her.

'Kit...' Desire flared in his eyes before he closed them. 'Sweetheart, you must stop this.'

'Kiss me, damn you.'

He looked at her and shook his head. 'No, this is not what you want.'

'You know nothing about me!' She bit his bottom lip and thrust her tongue into his mouth. He freed her other hand and she tore the rest of his shirt from him and dragged her nails across his broad back.

He reared away; torment imprinted into his strong face. 'I must go. You are distraught, not thinking—'

'Aren't you man enough to take me?' She reached up and pulled him to her. He was the only one who could take this need from her. She had to be loved or go mad. Crazed, she tore at his belt and trousers. His groan made her work faster. 'Help me, damn you,' she demanded in fury-ridden lust.

He was not tender in stripping her clothes from her. Indeed, in places the material tore though neither of them cared in their task to dominate the other. They forgot the cold air and decency as they came together as savagely as animals. Miles's body completely covered her. There was no gentleness in either of them. It was as though her mind could not function properly until the deed was done.

Miles plunged into her deeply, repeatedly, and she bit back her gasps as the sensations flowed through her. He waited for her release and then shuddered to a final eruption.

Slowly, the red mist cleared from Kitty's eyes. They stared at each other in mutual horror.

He groaned deep in his chest as if in pain and rolled off her. He sat with his back to her, his knees drawn up and head bowed.

Somewhere in the trees above their heads, a kookaburra rang out its mocking laugh and Miles shivered. He took a deep breath as though to clear his head.

'It was my fault.' She spoke to his back and with no emotion. In fact, she felt numb all over. Dead to all feeling inside and out.

He half-turned. 'No, Kit, please—'

'I attacked you. I...I...wanted to hurt you or someone. It's no excuse, I know.' She scrambled to her knees and pulled the clothing about her. Kitty felt herself sway, but she stubbornly concentrated on Miles profile, refusing to give in to the blackness ready to consume her. 'I cannot see you again, ever. I have betrayed the man I love, and myself, in the worst possible way by committing such an act. What...just occurred...should be a loving act between two people who...l-love each other. I wanted to punish someone, most probably you, I don't know. I am sorry.' Kitty gulped back a sob. 'Try not to think too badly of me.' She turned away.

'Kit! Kit, please, it doesn't have to be this way...'

Miles's begging followed her as she ran, stumbling through the bush. Tears clouded her vision. Blind, she tripped, fell and staggered to her feet again. Her life was over. Nothing ever again would matter or be normal. She had killed every vestige of self-respect.

A sob broke from her throat as Ben's handsome face appeared in the shadows. 'Ben? Ben, help me...' Her whisper lingered in the growing darkness. She reached out to the shimmering image before her, but it vanished at her fingertips and she fell to the ground. 'Please, Ben, my love, forgive me...' Her cries echoed around, bouncing off the trees, taunting her.

'I'm so sorry, Ben. It should have been you. It is you I love. Oh, Ben.' Kitty's cries died to whimpers and she sat hugging herself. 'Why did you leave me? I cannot do it without you.'

Later, Connie found her. She brought a thick woollen shawl, which she quickly wrapped about Kitty's shoulders before gathering the shredded bodice together, the corset gone. 'Nay, my lass, what am I ter do with you?' Connie hugged her tight.

Kitty hiccupped and stared out into space. 'I did the most awful thing.' She looked up in anguish at Connie. 'I am so ashamed.'

'Nay, lass. Sometimes nature 'as a way of tekken control an' there's nowt you can do about it.'

'I acted worse than a whore—' Hastily, Kitty jerked away and vomited into the grass. Connie held her hair back from her face and made soothing sounds. Finally, unable to retch any more, she leant back against Connie and wept quietly in her arms.

'That's better, lass. You're best t'cry an' get it done with. You keep things bottled up inside yourself for too long. Let it out, lass, let it out. It'll do you good.'

Chapter Eleven

Miles stared into the flames, swirling the golden contents of his brandy glass. It was late and his family had retired. Outside, the rain lashed at the windows, matching his mood. He was being pathetic he knew, but he couldn't help himself. The more he dwelled on what happened that dreadful day by the creek the worse he felt. For three weeks, he had wanted, ached, to go to her and tell her he was sorry, but he simply could not.

For the first time in his life, he was running away from something.

He had never thought of himself as a coward, but to see the condemnation on her face would be a blow to his very soul. Why hadn't he kept a cool head? Why hadn't he just held her and helped her? No, not he, Miles Grayson. He took what he wanted because he knew she would never give it normally, would never ask anything from him. Now, he was ashamed of his actions.

Miles groaned and took another swallow of his drink. Images of her, wild, untamed and demanding, tormented him. The thought of her taut body, silken skin and the searing heat of her kisses all conspired to damn him. His body responded to his wayward thoughts and he groaned again. He suffered the torments of Hell, and knew he deserved it. With a heavy sigh, he swallowed the last of his brandy and resisted the urge to throw the glass into the fireplace.

'Want another one?' Ronald stepped into the room. 'I came for a book, but you look as though you need company.'

'I will, thank you. A large one.'

Ronald poured brandy into two balloon glasses and gave one to Miles before sitting on a leather wing-backed chair opposite. 'Do you want to share what is on your mind, son?'

'What makes you think I have something on my mind?'

'Because I have known you all your life and I know when you are troubled. Besides, something has been making you get drunk every night for the last few weeks.'

'It is nothing, Father.'

'Very well.' Ronald shrugged. 'Of course, it could be a woman?'

'It is nothing.'

'Miles, a blind man can see both of my sons are after the same woman. Campbell spends nearly all his time over at the McKenzie property and waxes lyrical about the charms of the lovely Miss Kitty, and every time he does so, you look fit to kill.'

At that moment, Campbell strode into the room. 'There you are. I thought everyone had gone to bed.' He plopped onto the sofa between the two chairs.

Ronald frowned. 'Where did you get to today? You missed dinner. You know how your mother likes everyone to be around the dinner table.'

'I spent the afternoon at the McKenzie property. I got caught in the rain and Kitty made me stay for tea.' Campbell smiled, his high regard for Kitty very evident.

'It's Kitty now, is it?' Miles slurred at his brother. 'What happened to Miss McKenzie?' A slow maddening anger eroded Mile's senses at the idea of his brother spending more and more time in Kitty's company when he was unable to.

'She gave me permission to call her by her first name.'

'Did you tell her that we are leaving at the weekend?' Ronald interrupted.

'Yes, Father, I did. Though, I did ask her to come to Bathurst and visit us when she has the time. She said she would.' Campbell beamed at them.

'That will be nice, son. Your mother thinks greatly of Miss McKenzie. Best go up to bed now, yes?'

Miles stood, waving his glass at his brother. 'You should not be taking her away from her duties. Her property needs a great deal of attention and she cannot give it if she is away all the time.'

'Rubbish man. She's a lady not a farmhand,' Campbell scoffed. 'She has two good men to work it. She needs to be able to get away from the demands and pressure of the place once in a while.'

'How would you bloody know? You have never done a hard day's work in your life! You would rather give the orders and sit back and watch the work being done.'

Campbell jumped to his feet. 'What the hell would you know about what I do back home? You are never there. You left us years ago. It doesn't make a man, a man, just because he gets dirty alongside his workers. You think you are so great because you have done well here, but you don't impress everyone. A great house does not make the man, Miles, because this house is as empty of love as you are.' Campbell shook his head in pity.

The gesture angered Miles beyond reason. With a roar, he flung himself at Campbell and they both fell to the floor. Envy and pent-up frustration on both sides had them trading blows for blows.

Cold water thrown in his face jerked Miles's head up. His father held a dripping jug and quickly grabbed Campbell by the collar. Miles shook his head to clear his mind.

His father glowered at them both. 'What on earth has got into the pair of you?'

Miles glanced at Campbell, who was wiping blood off his mouth.

The library door opened, and Blanche stood there in her dressing robe. 'Good heavens above. What has happened?' She walked into the room, shocked at the state of her warring sons.

'Go back to bed, dearest. It is finished now,' Ronald said.

'I think not. I demand to know what you were fighting about.'

Miles shrugged off his father's hand and walked over to the drink tray to pour a brandy. 'I apologize, Mother.' He tipped his head back and emptied the glass in one gulp.

'I shall be leaving in the morning,' Campbell spoke in a tightly controlled voice.

Miles turned and sought his brother's gaze. 'No, Campbell, I do not wish you to go. I apologize for my behaviour. I have no right to take my bad temper out on you. You are my brother. Please stay.' Miles nodded once to Campbell and strode from the room.

'What is wrong with him?' Blanche scowled.

Ronald sighed. 'I will talk to him in the morning.'

'I am sorry too, Mother.'

Blanche glared at her youngest son. 'And so, you should be! Why I thought you had both outgrown that sort of actions. It is no way for gentlemen to behave, I am ashamed of you.' She stormed from the room.

Campbell sat down again and hung his hands between his knees. 'What is the matter with him, Father? He has everything a man could want, yet he still acts like the arrogant, hard-hearted swine like he always was.'

'Does he have everything a man can have? Think about it, Campbell. Miles has all this,' Ronald spread his arms out, encompassing the beautiful room, 'but no one to share it with. You hit a raw nerve when you said this house is empty. He is thirty-nine years old and has spent the last twenty years building this grand place, for what? He was always a deep thinker and a loner, but now he has turned into a cold and unapproachable man who I do not understand anymore.'

'He has no one to share it with because he is joyless and emotionless,' Campbell scorned. 'What woman could fall in love with a man who is incapable of loving back?'

'That is a bit harsh, son.'

'It is the truth, Father. Miles likes perfection in everything he does and every possession he has. No woman is good enough for him, how can they be?'

The return of warm weather in November lifted Kitty's spirit a little. She rose early with the men each morning, and while Jessup guided the plough behind Cluster, she and Holby planted the seed potatoes behind him. After they planted an acre of corn and half an acre of potatoes, Kitty asked the two men to chop down a strip of the bush west of the hut. She wanted more land cleared and another room and a veranda added. She was determined to make something of the property or die in the attempt.

The unrelenting work kept her busy from dawn to dusk. Toiling beside the men, she would not let them baby her. She worked harder than she ever had in her life and was thankful to fall into bed at night and sleep the dreamless sleep of the exhausted.

Kitty knew she pushed everyone hard. Every now and then, it would prick her conscience that she was punishing them as well as herself. Only, at the end of each day, when she saw how much they'd accomplished she knew it was worth it. She would endure the blisters on her hands, and her back aching so much she could barely stand straight, just as long as another day passed without her thoughts drifting towards a certain insufferable man.

By the end of November, Kitty felt as though she was a woman of great age. Every muscle in her body protested when she moved, and her features no longer held claim to beauty. Some days, her tiredness made her physically sick, much to her disgust at her own fragility. The work stripped the weight from her. Days would go by without her even smiling. No longer did she read delightful stories to the children or talk around the fire at night with Connie and Alice.

She turned from being a carefree spirit with dreams and a gentle soul into a scowling, demanding and cold-hearted wench. The property started to prosper, but she did not.

'It's 'ard to believe it's December tomorrow,' Connie said to Alice as she cleared away the breakfast dishes and watched the children play.

'My, the year's gone fast, hasn't it?' Alice shook her head in wonder.

'When Jessup goes to Grafton in a day or two, I'll arrange for him to buy supplies for Christmas,' Kitty mentioned, glancing up from her account books.

'I thought he was going today, miss?' Alice asked.

'No, not today. There is too much work to be done. Holby needs a hand with building the veranda.'

'May...I go with him when he does go?' Alice wrung her hands in the towel she held.

'Of course, is there something you want?' Kitty studied her row of figures.

'Well, actually...Paul has asked me to marry him and I said yes. We need to see the reverend.' Alice's lips quirked, waiting for Kitty and Connie's reaction.

Kitty's eyes widened. 'Jessup asked you to marry him?'

'Why, lass! That's grand news,' Connie cried, hugging Alice to her.

Kitty rose. 'I am very pleased for you both, though a little surprised. I did not realize you were romantically involved.'

'It has been a gradual thing, Miss.'

'You are good people and I am sure you will be happy together.' Kitty summoned a smile, but for some reason an overwhelming sense of loss filled her.

Alice was a practical woman but was clearly delighted her news was finally told and accepted. 'If it is all right with you, miss, Paul and I would like to live in the men's hut. Holby said he would sleep in a tent.'

'Yes, that is fine.' Kitty nodded, going back to her books.

'I can't get used t'you callin' Jessup, Paul.' Connie chuckled. 'He'll always be Jessup ter me.'

Kitty closed her books. 'Tell him to hitch the wagon, Alice. You can both go to Grafton today and see the reverend. The veranda can wait. Stay overnight if you wish. You may need to do some shopping. Whatever you buy put it on my account.' She averted her gaze. Alice's innocent happiness cut through the barrier she had erected around her own heart.

Alice touched her arm. 'You are so good, miss. Thank you.'

'Enjoy yourselves,' she mumbled.

Once Alice left the hut, Connie looked at her. 'You all right, me lass?'

'Yes, Connie.' She put the books away and picked up the rifle. 'There is a list on the table for Jessup. I am going to check the traps and the cattle. Holby said he thinks the bull has finished servicing, but I want to check myself. I shan't be long.'

'Can I come with you, Kitty?' Rosie asked, coming out of the bedroom holding her doll.

'No, pet. Stay and do your numbers for me and help Connie with the little ones.' She turned away from the disappointed look on Rosie's face.

Two days before Christmas, on a bright summer's day, the whole family congregated in a small timber church in Grafton for Alice and Jessup's wedding. Afterwards, Kitty arranged for the wedding party to go back to the hotel and celebrate in a private room. It was a wonderful day made all the more special by the attendance of Martin, who gave the bride away, and the Freemans who brought Joe and Clara. Alice cried on seeing them, for she was close to them as any older sister after spending nearly three years working and living with them.

Holby remained at the property, letting everyone stay in Grafton for Christmas. The day following the wedding they enjoyed a picnic by the river and that night attended a parody of the Shakespearean play, Taming of The Shrew performed by a touring dramatic society. Kitty pretended to be happy successfully enough to convince Dan. She even laughed with Ingrid at the antics of the play's actors.

At breakfast, the morning after Christmas, Kitty slept late. Martin remained alone at the table when Kitty entered the dining room. He ordered her a large breakfast of bacon, eggs, mushrooms, kidneys and toast, before pouring her a cup of tea.

'I cannot eat all that, Martin,' she remarked.

'Yes, you will. I cannot believe how much weight you have lost.'

'There is a lot to do at the property.'

'And Connie tells me that you insist on doing nearly all of it by yourself.'

Kitty put a lump of sugar in her tea and stirred it. 'Tell me about your voyages. It has been too long since I saw you.' She smiled, effectively changing the subject.

They ate their breakfast and afterwards went for a stroll down by the river. It was another fine day and the promise of a hot summer was evident. Blossoms graced the trees, and cottage gardens exploded with roses and other flowers. They walked in silence for a while, content to watch the boats and the coming and going of the town's people.

'Will you come back to Sydney, Kitty?' Martin broke the stillness with his heartfelt plea.

She paused to gaze out over the river. 'I admit the thought has crossed my mind.'

'Then why don't you? You could live in the house in Forbes Street comfortably enough. You have income from the shares Dan gave you, and you will have the money from the sale of the property and livestock. It makes sense, Kitty.'

'I will think about it some more.'

'What is there to think about? You have proved yourself with the property.'

'No, I have not.' Kitty sighed. 'It is doing a little better, but it is hardly a profitable business and it will not be for many years.'

'Then why stay?' Martin asked in desperation.

Kitty shrugged. 'I like it. I like walking through the bush and hearing nothing but the birds. There is a silence there that is strangely comforting.'

'There is nothing there except hard work, and years of it,' he scoffed.

'I do not mind that really.'

'Will you please give it serious consideration?'

'Yes, I promise.'

They turned back and went to join the others, but before reaching the hotel, Kitty placed her hand on his arm, halting him. 'Have you heard anything of Rory?'

Martin shook his head. 'No, I haven't. I've told a few people to keep a look out for him, but nothing so far.'

'I still pay for the advertisement to go in the newspaper.' She took a step and then faltered. Ahead, talking to another man at the entrance of the hotel, stood Miles Grayson. Before Kitty turned away, he looked across and saw her. The expression on his face changed to one of surprise before he quickly masked it.

'Kitty! Martin!' Clara called out to them, running down the street ahead of the others. 'Look what we bought.'

'Heavens above, Clara, do the ladies at your college teach you anything about manners?' Martin tried to be stern.

'Oh, Martin, Kitty, look.' Clara pointed to Joe. In his arms wriggled a small brown and white puppy.

'Where did you get that?' Martin asked in amazement.

'Dan bought two of them from a woman further up the street. She has a whole litter for sale. Dan is picking out the other one now.' Joe held the puppy up for Martin to see.

Kitty looked past them to Miles. He still stared at her and her stomach churned. She fought a wave of nausea. He stood tall, important and ruggedly handsome. He wore no hat today and his dark grey hair glistened in the sunlight. She bit her bottom lip and hated how her heart thumped so wildly. Did he think about her at all?

Joe interrupted her thoughts. 'Dan bought the puppies for Kitty.'

She spun to her brother. 'He bought them for me?'

'Yes. He said you need dogs for the property. And he bought two so they would keep each other company.' Joe laughed as the puppy licked him.

'I don't want dogs.' The extra responsibility was unwelcome.

Martin frowned. 'You cannot refuse them, Kitty. They are a gift.'

She sighed. 'Oh, I suppose so.' Seeing Grayson spoiled her mood. She had done so well in the last couple of days to keep her depression at bay. Now, because of him, she was reminded of the act she committed and how she tainted the sweet love she and Ben shared by behaving in such a deplorable way.

When she next looked across the street, Miles was gone.

Connie awoke early. The pinkish light in the room told her it was dawn. She looked across at the cots, the twins and Little Rory still slept. Rosie slept in the small bed against the wall. Connie dressed and left the room. She noticed the kitchen fire was out and frowned, wondering why Kitty hadn't lit it before she left to do her chores. Walking out of the back door and into the lean-to, Connie collected pieces of wood and tied bunches of dry grass for the fire. On hearing a cough, she paused. When the sound came again, she dropped the wood and rounded the corner to find Kitty retching into a bucket.

'Lass! What's up with you?' She held Kitty's shoulders as she retched again. 'Did you eat somethin' that didn't agree with you?'

Kitty straightened, wiping a shaking hand over her eyes. 'Oh, Connie.'

'Come inside lass, an' into bed. I'll get you a cup of tea.'

'No, the noise will wake the children. I'll just sit in the fresh air on the veranda.'

Kitty sat on a bench Holby had made along with a small square table. Every day Rosie gathered wildflowers to put on it and yesterday's flowers drooped in the warmth. It was going to be another hot, dry day. The fiery month of January had started.

'Feeling better?' Connie studied her pale face.

'Yes, thank you.'

"Ave you been sick like that before?'

'Some.'

'When?'

'Just the odd times.'

'Oh, lass.'

'I know.'

'What you goin' to do?'

'No idea.' Kitty gave a false laugh. Her chin trembled only a little. 'I cannot have his baby,' she whispered.

'No.'

Kitty pushed up from the bench. 'I shall start in the vegetable garden before it gets too hot.'

'Lass...'

'Leave it, Connie. We will talk later.'

'Grayson would marry you for the babby, lass. Think about it, its father is the wealthiest man in the district. The bairn would want for nowt.'

'I would never even consider it. I would not sell my child for luxuries gained.'

'Oh, stuff an' nonsense!'

'This child is mine. No one else's.'

'I'm thinkin' of the bairn.'

'What about me? I barely like the man.'

'Then you foolin' yourself an' you a hypocrite.' Connie turned away.

As the day wore on, the sun burnt through Kitty's clothes. The band around her Mackinaw straw sundowner grew damp with sweat, but she continued down the line, hoeing at the vigorous weeds that seemed to pop up overnight. She stopped, stretched her aching back and surveyed her day's work. Rows of vegetables straight and neat. The soil was much better than it was ten months ago when they'd first arrived. Plenty of manure dug regularly into the soil had improved it immensely. The vegetables grew plump and fast in the heat.

'I have brought you a drink, Miss.' Alice carried a tray that held an earthenware jug of a cool lemon drink, a glass and a plate of oatmeal biscuits.

'Thank you.' Kitty placed her hoe against the garden fence and poured out a drink while Alice held the tray.

'May I ask you something, miss?'

Kitty eyed her warily. She didn't have the energy for anything difficult today. 'Yes?'

'May Paul and Holby build an extra room onto our hut? It would be done only in their own time, of course.'

'Um...yes, I do not see why not.' Kitty was thankful the question was an easy one.

'Thank you, Miss. It is for a bedroom, then we can have more room—'

A loud piercing scream rent the air. Both Kitty and Alice jumped at the sound. In seconds, Kitty was running out of the vegetable garden with Alice placing the tray none too gently on the ground and following.

In the clearing at the front of the hut, Rosie stood whimpering and crying, holding a bunch of wildflowers in her hand. Connie raced out of the front door. As they neared Rosie, a repulsive, long, brown snake slithered through the grass towards them.

'Oh my God.' Connie grabbed Kitty, who stood frozen in terror. Rosie fell to the ground, moaning.

'I'm coming, Rosie,' Kitty called, swallowing her panic. The snake was obviously looking for somewhere to hide and the hut was the closest place. 'Get back into the hut and shut the door. Put a towel in the gap under it. Hurry!' She pushed Connie in the direction of the hut and ran to the side, giving the snake a wide berth.

Eyeing a stick close by, Kitty picked it up and threw it at the reptile. The stick landed a short distance from its head, but it was enough to make the snake dart to the left and head for the bush.

She ran to Rosie, who lay groaning on the ground, the fallen wildflowers scattered about her. 'Rosie, sweetheart. You are all right now. I have you.' She clutched Rosie tight, trying to soothe her. 'Where are you hurt?'

'M-my...l-leg,' Rosie mumbled between her sobs.

Alice joined them and while Alice held the little girl, Kitty inspected Rosie's legs. Two sets of puncture wounds, one at the ankle the other on the calf, filled Kitty with mind-numbing horror.

Tears ran down Alice's cheeks. 'We must get her inside, Miss. Send Paul for the doctor!'

Spinning on her heels, Kitty yelled for Connie.

At once, Connie was out the door and running towards them. They gently lifted Rosie up and carried her to the hut. Inside, they placed her on the double bed. Rosie grew fevered and her moaning became stilted.

'Alice, get Jessup and Holby. They should know more about snake bites than we do.' Kitty wetted a handkerchief in a basin by the bed and placed the damp handkerchief on Rosie's forehead. 'Help me, Connie, what do we do?'

The suffering child tossed and turned as the poison moved its way through her body.

'I don't know, lass, I'm sorry, I don't know.' Connie glanced at Rosie and then to the twins and Little Rory. 'I'll tekk them into the other room.'

Kitty gripped Rosie's hand, and with the other hand, she wiped her sweating forehead and flushed face. 'Darling, everything will be fine.' Her dear little sister needed help, only she had no notion how to assist her. Everyone knew snakes were in the country, but Kitty never saw any, and she didn't know how to minister to a snake's bite.

She rose from her knees as Jessup and Holby arrived. 'What can we do?'

'Was she bitten on the leg?' Jessup bent down by the bed.

'Yes. Twice I think.'

'Twice? Good God!' Jessup and Holby looked at each other. Holby muttered something about a doctor and ran out of the room.

'Miss, give her a drink while I try and get the poison out of her leg.' Jessup's grave face sent Kitty's heart into somersaults.

Rosie's moaning grew. Connie came in to hold her hand, trying to offer comfort. Her leg was now a ghastly purple hue and so swollen it was twice its normal size. Rosie gave a sudden, wrenching jerk and then was still. Connie whimpered and Alice's cry filled the room.

Kitty stood as though paralyzed at the side of the bed with a glass of water in her hand. The glass hit the floor and shattered. The water seeped into the cracks between the wooden floor planks.

Rosie was dead, where only twenty minutes before she had been picking wildflowers.

'Adelaide, lass, don't be playin' with that.' Connie retrieved the clinging insect from her daughter's petticoats and threw it away in disgust. Little Rory played on the ground by her feet with some wooden animals Holby fashioned for him from bits of wood. Further away, Charles threw a ball for the two little puppies Dan bought for Kitty.

'Charles, don't stray too far, pet,' Connie called. Though she resumed her needlework, she always kept one eye on her son, for he was at the age where he wanted to wander. Since Rosie's death a week ago, the adults were even more vigilant on watching the children now. They were never allowed to go further than a few yards from the hut.

No gentle breeze allayed the shimmering heat from the land. Connie sighed and brushed her hair out of her eyes. She scanned the clearing for Kitty but knew she would be far into the bush.

A small wooden cross, over to the right at the edge of the scrub, drew her gaze. Pain clutched at Connie's heart. She had loved little Rosie from the first moment, had taken care of her when Kitty first started to search for work in York, and then continued to look after her when Kitty worked the clothes stall. Rosie became the sweet child Connie and Max were never granted until the twins came. Now, she joined Max in Heaven above, which gave Connie the only bit of comfort achievable from such a senseless waste of life.

'Horsey, Ma?' Charles said, stumbling up the step onto the veranda.

'No, pet. Jessup is workin' with them now. We'll see them later.' Connie kissed his small hand and returned to her sewing.

'Horsey, Ma!' Charles jiggled in excitement.

'Later, love.' Connie glanced up as Charles ran off. 'Charles, lad.' She stood and then paused. Miles Grayson mounted on his large ebony horse trotted down the track.

Connie placed her needlework on the small table and walked to the top step.

Grayson dismounted. Taking off his hat, he inclined his head. 'Good day, Mrs Spencer.'

'Good day.'

'Is Miss McKenzie available?'

'She is away seein' t'cattle. She'll not be back before sunset.'

'I have just returned from Sydney and heard your distressing news from the doctor at Blue Water. I came to offer my condolences.'

'That's mighty kind of you, Mr Grayson. Dr Saunders was a great help to us even though he arrived too late ter save our Rosie. I'll let Kitty know you came.'

'Is she coping?'

'She's doin' best she can.'

Grayson hesitated as though he wanted to say something else but refrained. He donned his hat again and mounted. He gazed at Connie for some time and then sighed deeply. 'Please, tell Miss McKenzie if there is anything, I can do for her, then I would only be too happy.'

'I will, an' thank you for your kindness.'

He looked at the children gathered around Connie's shirts. 'You seem to have your hands full.'

'Aye, I have.'

Grayson's gaze rested on Charles who, bigger and more adventurous than his sister, stood away from Connie and stared back at him. 'You have a fine family. Good day, madam.' He turned his horse and rode away.

Kitty returned home later that afternoon, hot and tired. She gulped a drink and then gathered her towel and some clean clothes. 'I am going to the creek for a wash, Connie.'

'Grayson came today.' Connie forestalled her from going out the door.

Kitty paled. 'What did he want?'

'Ter give us 'is condolences for our Rosie.'

'Is that all? Did he say anything else?'

'No.' Connie touched her shoulder. 'Lass, what you goin' ter do? He's goin' ter come one day an' see you big with child.'

'Leave it, Connie. I cannot deal with it right now.' She hated to be reminded that she carried Grayson's child. She ignored the situation as best as she could.

Leaving the hut, she walked down to the creek. The evening sun still blasted the countryside like a furnace. Kitty went to her favourite secluded spot around the bend of the creek and stripped off her dress and untied her boots, throwing them to one side. She waded into the water and at the deepest part, dived under. She came up quickly, gasping at the coldness.

Kitty swam for a while, watching the sky turn from blue to orange as the sun slid behind the distant mountains. It was so peaceful to let the water carry her and she allowed her tortured mind to go blank for a while. She drifted down the creek on her back, staring up into the tree canopies hanging over the water and the birds flying overhead. *If only I could fly away from my problems and grief.*

Goose bumps rose over her cool skin. The sun hung low. Kitty looked around; she'd travelled further than she thought. Slowly, she began swimming upstream. However, tired after a hard day she couldn't manage it and, with a sigh, made her way to the bank. She sat to catch her breath. Her chemise and petticoat clung to her and she glanced down at her flat stomach. It was hard to believe a child grew inside her. She didn't allow any sentiment to surface; it couldn't become important to her. She needed time.

'Kit.'

Kitty twirled at the soft voice and closed her eyes. Grayson stood just beyond the line of trees on the bank.

'I will not come any nearer if you do not want me to.'

She shrugged and, ignoring her violently beating heart, scrambled to her feet and picked her way along the bank back to her clothes. 'I must go back. It is late.'

'I am sorry about your sister. It was a dreadful thing to happen.'

She stared at him. 'I did not know how to help her.' The words fell out of her mouth, surprising her.

'There is not a lot anyone can do in those situations. Brown snakes are deadly, and to receive two bites on such a small body, well, no one could have saved her.'

'I should have been watching her. I never gave snakes a thought, I should have though. Jessup and Holby both told me they would be about in the hot weather. Holby said they would be able to smell the chickens...and...I should never...have...' Her throat became thick with emotion, but she was determined not to let him see. She walked on, tripping in her haste to put space between them.

'Kit, let me help you.' He clambered down the bank, sending pebbles and dirt cascading down to meet her. Taking her elbow, he guided her around a large rock jutting out of the bank.

'I am fine, thank you.' She pulled her arm out of his grip. His touch made her skin tingle.

'I want to help you.'

'I do not need your help,' Kitty rasped. Her wet hair hung untidily about her face and shoulders, but she cared little. She stomped away.

'Oh, your independence is maddening.'

She turned on him, her heart thudding with temper. 'It is my independence that has kept me and my family alive. So, I will thank you to keep a still tongue in your head!'

'You are the most frustrating woman ever born,' he growled between clenched teeth. 'I only wanted to help you, for God's sake.'

'Help me? You are a little too late for that! Where was your help when my cattle arrived and were falling dead at my feet? You knew they needed good pastures to feed on and you knew I did not have any. But did you offer to give up a small area of your immense land? No. You watched my cattle die, one by one, day after day. I would not take your help now, if my life depended on it.'

'I am sorry.' His quiet words halted her headlong rush to get away from him.

Kitty sagged before slowly looking into his clear, silver eyes. The fight left her. 'I was going to give you first refusal for my property a few weeks ago.'

'I will buy it. You see, I have land on the other side of your boundaries and your property is in the way from reaching it from the homestead. I have always wanted the land you own. It would give me straight access across all my property.'

'How ironic. I want to sell it but cannot.' She shook her head. 'I am tied to it forever now. I could never leave Rosie.'

'Then let me help you make the place pay its way,' he pleaded.

'Why?'

'To repay for my awful manners when you needed a friend you could rely on, plus the...the other thing.' Grayson frowned.

Kitty stiffened and fought the urge to lay a hand over her stomach. She turned and trudged away up the bank.

'Will you and your family come and have dinner with me at Blue Water?'

She stopped at the top and shook her head. 'No, thank you.'

Sweat trickled down Kitty's back as she swept the veranda, while listening to Alice softly sing a ditty about York as she cooked their midday meal. The words of it brought a little smile to her face. Some days she longed to walk through the narrow-cobbled streets of York, smell the smutty air from the burning coal fires and feel the icy sting of snowflakes hitting her face. Fond images slid into her mind of her and Rory making a snowman and of reading some interesting book by her bedroom fireside while a blizzard raged outside the window. The memories were bitter-sweet.

Had there been a time when she was completely happy and carefree? She barely remembered now. It seemed so long ago since she lived at her lovely old home in a leafy street in York surrounded by all of her family. Listening to her mother instruct the housekeeper of her plan to host another party, and her father telling them tales of the sick. They died over three years ago, and yet sometimes it was like they'd never existed, only in her dreams.

She was twenty-four years old and soon to be a mother of a bastard child. The thought chilled her. For weeks she shied away from making any decisions, but the situation would not go away just because she ignored it. What would she do? Return to Sydney and lie to people? Saying she was married and widowed within months, or stay in the bush and be ridiculed by the local town's people for being a loose woman?

A clap of thunder in the distance broke into Kitty's thoughts and Alice came out to stand with her on the veranda. Angry, dark clouds skidded over the distant ranges. A sudden breeze sprang up, bringing with it the distinct scent of rain.

'Looks like a storm, miss,' Alice said. The wind gust lifted the fair hair from her sweating brow.

'I must lock the chickens up for the night.' Kitty leant the broom against the wall. She went around to the lean-to and using the scoop, tipped grain into a bucket. Thunder rolled again as she walked to the hen coop. Clucking a silly noise, which the hens knew at once meant food, they followed her back into their pen. She threw handfuls of grain onto the ground until all the chickens were inside, then locked the gate.

Going back to the lean-to, she found that Alice had placed the vegetable scraps out for her to feed the pigs. Kitty jumped when another loud thunderclap banged overhead. Staring up at the sky, she stood in fascination as the fierce clouds raced across the purple sky. Lightning flashed to the east, spurring her on to feed the pigs quickly. She checked the milking cow making sure it was tied securely. Connie dashed to the clothesline to take down the dry clothes and Kitty ran to help as the wind grew wild.

The roaring gale made it a difficult job of fetching the washing off the line. Large bed sheets flapped about, snapping in the wind. One slapped Connie's face, making her gasp. Kitty looked over and grinned. Working her way down the line, she reached Connie as she struggled with another sheet. It whipped out and slapped Connie again as she wrestled with it, and Kitty chuckled at Connie's outraged face.

'Lord! I'll be black an' blue at this rate,' Connie called.

Kitty winked. 'Who's going to think a sheet did it?'

They struggled with the washing, giggling some more. Finally, they had it all in the basket and turned for the hut. The sight of thick smoke coming out of the front door stopped them mid stride. Kitty dropped the basket and, picking up her skirts, ran to the hut with Connie close behind her.

'Alice!' Kitty called at the doorway, coughing from the billowing smoke.

Inside the hut, through the smoke, Alice whacked a cloth against the flames of the fire, which spread from the cooking area out over the floor. The children's cries came from the bedroom.

'Get the children out, Connie!' Kitty yelled. 'Hurry!'

Connie darted into the bedroom. Alice was choking from the smoke, her eyes watering. She walked backwards from the fire trying to take a breath, but as she did so a flame attached itself to the bottom of her skirts. Within seconds, it was creeping up the material.

'Alice! Your skirt!' Kitty searched for something to stop the flames.

Alice screamed, flapping at her burning skirts with the towel she held. In her haste, she fell backwards, knocking over the table and the lantern placed upon it. The crashing sound was magnified by Alice's screams and the whoosh of flames that fed on the spilt oil from the broken lantern.

Kitty raced around the flames and, taking a bucket of milk standing by the back door, she threw it on Alice's skirts and put the flames out. Coughing and spluttering, she helped Alice to her feet. They stumbled out the back door, through the lean-to and outside.

Running around to the front, Kitty heard Connie calling from the bedroom. The fire had cut off their means of escape and she stood by the small bedroom window begging for help. Kitty bolted to the open window. She pulled Little Rory through and placed him on the ground, before reaching for Adelaide, and after putting her down, she grabbed Charles.

'Connie, stand on the bed and lift one leg through the window.' Kitty panted, her lungs seemed fit to burst.

'I won't fit,' Connie cried, her eyes wide.

'Nonsense. Hurry up, now.' Kitty looked over her shoulder, relieved that Alice hobbled away with the children.

'I'll get stuck. The window is too small.' Connie coughed and smoke billowed out between them.

Over Connie's shoulders, the flames flickered through the open bedroom door. Thick smoke surrounded them, seeping out through the gaps in the roof and walls. The old wood and dry bark structure could not stand against fire. Lightning flashed close by and thunder shook the ground. Alice screamed and all three babies cried in utter fear.

'For heaven's sake, Connie! Climb through the window,' Kitty yelled, frightened and frustrated. 'Get onto the bed and lift your leg through. I will pull you.'

'I can't, lass.' Fear made Connie rigid.

Something in the main room exploded, likely the other lantern they had.

'Do it,' Kitty screamed, reaching in. She would not lose any more of her family.

With jerky movements, Connie stood on the bed and, pulling up her skirts, lifted one leg through the window. Grabbing her calf, Kitty yanked her until Connie had to scrunch down to get her upper body through. With a cry, Connie and Kitty landed heavily on the ground.

Scrambling upright again, Kitty helped Connie to stand. Connie took two steps before falling to her knees again.

'Me foot. I've hurt me foot.' Connie groaned, holding her ankle.

'Lean on me,' Kitty shouted against the howling wind and the roar of the fire. Red, glowing fingers now spread across the bedroom's ceiling. The fierce heat pushed them away.

Struggling, they shuffled across the clearing to where Alice and the babies sat at the edge of the bush. Kitty lowered Connie to sit and the twins clambered across to her crying. Little Rory huddled close to Alice as Kitty ran back towards the hut.

'Where you goin', lass?' Connie wailed.

'I must fill the buckets. I have to try and save what I can,' Kitty shouted back, turning to run again.

'You can't! It's too late!' Connie struggled to get up, but her ankle gave way and she feel back to the ground with a grunt.

Kitty ran around to the back of the hut and moaned as flames tore apart the lean-to. Coughing, she hastened to the edge of the lean-to and heaved and dragged out sacks of grain and supplies. She made trip after trip back into the dense, choking smoke until finally the flames and the heat forced her to stop.

The wind howled around her, whipping her hair into her stinging eyes. She clutched at an intense pain that throbbed in her side and stumbled away as the flames rose high in the air. Overhead the thunder roared, dark angry clouds scudded across the sky, but not one drop of rain descended down onto the hell below.

Jessup and Holby, having been out with the cattle, rode in hard. Their horses skittered to a halt in a dust cloud and the two men jumped off their animal's backs and ran to her.

'You all right, miss?' Jessup frantically looked towards the small group at the edge of the bush. 'Everyone is safe?'

Kitty nodded slightly but said nothing as the roof structure cracked and crumbled into the middle of the main room. In turn, it caused the lean-to to topple inwards. Heat and smoke ballooned out, covering them in ash and hot embers.

It was all gone. All that represented her home was gone, and Kitty couldn't even summon a tear for it. She was dried out, emotionally and physically. No more, she could do no more. She'd had enough.

'Come away, Miss. There's nothing to be done.' Jessup gently turned her away. Black ashes carried by the wind coated her and he furiously brushed them off.

By sundown, the fire was just a smouldering heap of charcoal timber and a few glowing embers. Every now and then a thin sliver of smoke escaped, but there was naught left standing, except for the outline of a few tin items. The storm clouds still threatened, however, the thunder and lightning had stopped, and the wind had died down to a stiff breeze.

Jessup had bandaged Alice's leg burns and strapped Connie's ankle.

Kitty stood apart, her mind vacant, staring at the smoking wood. When Holby lightly tapped her arm to get her attention, she slowly gazed up at him.

'Miss, I'll harness the horses to the cart now,' he said in his quiet way.

'Why?'

'To go to Grafton. If we leave now, we'll get there just before midnight. I can wake one of the hotel owners to get you a room.'

She looked away. 'I am not going to Grafton.'

'Are you all going to sleep in the other hut then?'

'Yes.'

'But, miss, there is not enough blankets, food and things.'

'We will make do.' She edged away from him, not wanting to think. Somewhere in her body a stubborn ache pounded, but she refused to identify or dwell on it.

Connie called her over. 'Are you all right, lass?'

'Yes.'

Tears slid down Alice's cheeks. 'I'm so sorry, Miss. I spilt-'

'It does not matter.' She walked back towards the glowing embers. A fat raindrop landed on her head like a stone and then another and another.

Drizzle turned to heavy rain within minutes. Holby and Jessup helped Alice, Connie and the babies over to the other hut. Connie called, but Kitty ignored her. She let the rain soak her as the embers sizzled and spat. The smoking ruins fizzled out and Kitty felt her heart grow as heavy as the wet clothes on her back. The pain in her stomach grew with every moment.

She bent and picked up a chewed stick Charles and the puppies played with. Kitty prodded the ashes of her home as the rain splashed her in sooty muck. The remains of the tin trunk that once held all her important belongings emerged when a beam rolled away at her prodding. Grabbing the edge of her skirt to protect her hand, she walked over the embers caring nothing as they burned the soles of her boots.

The trunk's buckled tin lid wouldn't budge, but with perse-verance, Kitty lifted the lid a little and propped it open with her stick. She slid her hand into the hot interior and rummaged around until she felt another box of steel, her mind focused on one thing only. Dazedly, she felt the soles of her feet becoming uncomfortably warm. With a last desperate tug, she wrenched the heavy steel box out of the trunk. The motion nearly toppled her over into the wet, smoking remains, but she managed to stay upright and stumble out of the black charred coals.

Kitty staggered across the grass on hot, sore feet. The pain from them and her stomach made her fall to her knees. Jessup hurried to her, but she stopped him. 'Leave me,' she demanded coldly.

Seating herself more comfortably on the grass where she fell, Kitty took from around her neck a gold chain that held a small key. Fitting the key into the lock on the box, she opened it. She sighed with relief on seeing her documents still intact. Underneath them was a leather drawstring pouch with the initials BK stitched in gold thread. She tipped out her engagement ring from Benjamin and gazed at it. After kissing it, she replaced it in the pouch, returned it to the box and locked the lid. It was over.

Miles Grayson found her sitting in the rain a few moments later, when he and his men rode into the clearing. He dismounted before his horse came to a complete stop and was beside Kitty in a heartbeat.

'Kit. Are you all right?'

She stared up at him, not really seeing him. Grayson wiped his hands over her cheeks to clear them of dirt. 'Stay away from me, Grayson. I am a curse to all who know me.'

He gazed into her eyes. 'I am willing to take the chance.'

'I cannot let you. I...I...cannot go on and let others...get...hurt.'

'You don't know what you are saying, Kit. Listen to me now, I...' He got no further as blackness beckoned her and she gladly gave in to it.

Chapter Twelve

Kitty woke to the sun streaming across the bedroom. A rose-coloured quilt covered her and she lay between crisp white sheets. It took her a minute or two to gather her bearings and realize she was not in her own bed she shared with Connie, but in a beautiful room decorated with soft rose wallpaper and polished, dark mahogany furniture. Blue sky peeked through the fine lace curtains blowing at the window. A delicate breeze lifted the dust motes floating on the sun's rays.

Not caring where she was at the moment, she yawned, stretched and became aware of her bandaged feet. She frowned. She had no memory of hurting her feet. Then, the events of the fire flooded into her mind. She bit her lip and whimpered. Where are Connie, the babies and Alice?

Before she could throw back the bed covers, the door opened, and a young maid came in carrying a tea tray.

'Oh, Miss. You're awake. I was hoping you might be. How you are feeling?' The cheery maid smiled.

'Well, thank you,' she lied. Her bones ached, her muscles were sore, and an uncomfortable heaviness weighted her stomach.

'Everyone will be pleased to hear that. Mrs Spencer and the master have driven poor Dr Saunders nearly mad with their questions.' The maid placed the tea tray on the bedside table.

'The master?'

'Mr Grayson, Miss.'

Kitty shivered. 'I'm at Blue Water?'

'Yes, miss, you came here last evening after the fire at your home.'

Kitty nodded miserably. 'Is Mrs Spencer close by?'

'Just down the hall, Miss. The children are with her too.' The maid poured a cup of tea and passed it over. 'Are you hungry, miss?'

'No, not really.'

'I'll ask Cook to fix you something light anyway. Feeding people up is what she does best.'

'What is your name?'

'Leah, Miss. Mr Grayson said I was to see to your every need.' Leah nodded seriously for a moment and then grinned. 'Some say I talk too much, Miss. So, if I do, just tell me to hush. Being the youngest of fourteen children I had to talk to be seen.' Leah laughed at her own joke and Kitty smiled a little.

'Where is my dress? I would like to leave this bed.'

'Why, miss, it is ruined. Mr Grayson is waiting on a delivery of clothes this very day. He had someone ride to Grafton late yesterday and buy material for you all. Mrs Gates, the head dairy-man's wife, is a fine seamstress and she is going to be making up some dresses and things for you and Mrs Spencer, and some other women are making clothes for the children.'

'That is awfully good of them.'

'I best go tell Mr Grayson you are awake.'

Leah had only been gone a short time when there was a tap on the door, and it opened. Miles stood in the doorway, looking worried, but he gave her the slightest of smiles. His gaze scanned her face and her heart somersaulted. 'How are you?'

She had the awful urge to cry. 'I am well, thank you.'

He stepped further into the room. 'Dr Saunders says you need plenty of rest. He took care of your feet. There is no real damage, but they might be tender to walk on.'

'Thank you for bringing me and my family to Blue Water. It was a noble thing to do.'

A flush stained his cheeks. 'Do you really think so little of me that I would leave you all there to struggle alone?'

'Mr Grayson, I do not wish to argue with you. I have neither the inclination nor the energy.'

'I am sorry, Kit. I should learn to not speak so rashly.'

She tilted her head. 'Why do you call me Kit?'

He shrugged. 'Kit is a stronger name than Kitty, and you are a strong woman.'

'Or just a very stupid one.' A wry smile tugged at her lips.

Miles walked to the window and gazed out. 'I took the liberty of installing Mrs Spencer down the hall. She seems to be happy there with the children. I gave her a nursery maid to help her. One of my workers has a daughter, May, who is about fifteen, I think. She seems to be a good assistant.'

'You are kind. Is Connie's ankle very bad?'

'It is strapped. Saunders said she must stay off it, hence the need for a nursery maid.'

'And Alice?'

'Mrs Jessup? She is back at your property with her husband and your other man. Saunders said her burns are not too severe. With regular dressing changes, her injuries should heal within a month or so.'

'Dr Saunders must have been busy.'

'We are lucky to have him on the station. I found it wiser to have a doctor here all the time. Dr Saunders is retired and likes the easy life here, though sometimes he is busier than other doctors. We have nearly the population of a small village.' He turned towards the door as it opened, and Leah entered once more carrying another tray. Miles straightened and marched for the doorway. 'I will leave you to your meal. You should enjoy it; Cook is very good at her job.' Miles inclined his head and left.

Kitty watched him go, puzzled by the way he blew hot and cold with her. One minute he was so angry with her it seemed he'd take to her with a whip, and then the next he was quiet and concerned. He drove her mad. She didn't know how to handle him when he was nice to her. She much preferred them to be at each other's throats, that way she knew the rules and where she stood.

No sooner had she finished picking at her meal, then Dr Saunders arrived. She had not seen him since Rosie's death. The sight of him brought back memories too dreadful to deal with right now.

'How are you, Miss McKenzie?' He placed his black medical bag on the bed.

'Fine.'

'I shall look at your feet in a moment. First, I wanted to talk to you about your pregnancy.'

Kitty's eyes widened in surprise, but she remained silent, her stomach fluttering.

'Mrs Spencer told me in confidence.' Dr Saunders smiled and took her hand to feel her pulse. 'It's a wonder you haven't lost it. Do you have any pains?'

'No, not now, at least not pains, an ache.'

'But you did?' Dr Saunders raised his bushy eyebrows.

'Yes.'

'You feel nothing now?'

'Just a heaviness deep down.' Kitty shrugged. She forced herself to think very little of the child she carried. She couldn't let her guard down living so close to Grayson and thinking of the child as his weakened her reserves of strength.

Dr Saunders examined her and frowned. 'I insist you do not leave this bed for a few days. It's January fourteenth, when was your last menstruation?'

'September. The...the act was in early October.'

He felt her stomach. 'Around three to four months then. After what you've suffered in recent times, you could still lose this child. You need total rest, is that clear?'

Kitty gripped his hand. 'You will not tell anyone, will you?'

'Of course not.'

When the doctor left, Kitty swung the sheets back and put her feet to the floor. She swayed a little, but taking a deep breath, stepped across the room. At the door, she paused, grasping it to steady herself. The hall was deserted and silent. She shuffled along, peeking into rooms, until she found Connie sitting by the window knitting with her leg raised on a soft footstool.

'Nay, lass! What you doin'?'

'I had to see how you are.' She staggered to a chair. Sweat broke out on her forehead.

'Get back ter bed, you daft lump. We're fine.'

Kitty gritted her teeth. A throbbing pain vibrated through her stomach and back.

'I'm goin' ter try an' get on me feet later.' Connie gave her ankle a little wiggle. 'It's much better now.'

'Good.' Kitty tried to pay attention.

'May, the nursery maid 'as been a wonder. I don't know how we coped before without her. Yesterday evening she just came an' took over, it were wonderful.'

'I'm pleased,' Kitty mumbled. Gripping the back of the chair, she shakily stood.

'An' that Miles Grayson 'as been nowt but a gentleman to all of us.' Connie's knitting needles click-clacked as she worked them. 'Nay, credit where credit's due, he's been a true neighbour this time.'

'I'm going back to bed for a while, Connie,' said Kitty, heading for the door.

'Aye, lass, 'ave some rest.'

With a strength of will she didn't know she possessed, Kitty made it to her room and crept across to sit on the window seat. The pain receded for a moment and she gratefully breathed easier. She could not stay here. It was too difficult to live in Miles's house while secretly carrying his child. Connie was right, he'd been kind and generous, but that only made her feel worse. How could she stay living near him and bear his child? He'd know sooner or later and then what? The thought sent shivers up her spine.

There was a sharp tap on the door before Miles entered. 'You look deep in thought.'

'Do I?' Kitty winced. He was smiling, something he rarely did, and it softened his stern features. Indeed, he looked very handsome. Kitty felt an overwhelming longing for his powerful arms to hold her. So strong was the need that it momentarily blocked out the returning pain. The admission surprised and appalled her. She was disappointed in herself for wanting something she could never have. That same sharp disappointment, and her pain, made her tone edgier than she wished. 'I must leave here, Miles. I thank you for your hospitality, but I really must—'

'I hope you are not worrying about your home? Your cattle are feeding well on my pastures and both your men are adding another room to the smaller hut as we speak.'

Pain ripped her. 'I have to go.'

'What is the problem? I tried to make sure you had everything you needed, and your family was taken care of. I wanted to ease your suffering as much as I could. Did I overstep the boundaries? Did I anger you in some way? There is no need to rush back now. There is no room in the other hut for you all and—'

'I am going back to Sydney,' she whispered, as though she were committing treason. She bit her lip to stop a moan escaping. She needed the doctor badly, but not while Miles was present.

Miles stepped away and ran his fingers through his dark silver-grey hair. 'What about Rosie's grave?'

'I-I am giving the property to Alice and Jessup. They will look after it for me.'

He frowned. 'You cannot do this. You simply cannot give away a property. It is not a book or a sheet of music.'

'Thank you for all you have done. I...I shall never forget it.'

'Please stay a few more days,' he begged. 'You need to rest. In fact, you look pale.'

'I-I am tired. Can you leave me, please?'

'Certainly. Is there anything you need?'

She shook her head, not looking at him. Once the door clicked close, she stumbled and fell onto the bed as a deep red stain began to spread through her skirts. Another pain gripped her stomach like a vice. Closing her eyes, she stuffed her knuckles into her mouth to stop from crying out.

A knock sounded on the door and Connie hobbled into the room. 'Look, lass, I'm not doing too bad, am I? Dr Saunders said—' She paused mid-sentence. 'Oh, my God!' Connie hopped back to the door and called for help.

Miles rushed into the room. 'What's happened? Good God. Kit?' Gently, he and Connie lifted her into a better, more comfortable position on the bed, then he went to the door and yelled for Saunders.

'It's all right, lass. You'll be just fine,' Connie soothed as Kitty moaned, clutching her stomach.

'What's the matter with her?' Miles crouched beside the bed and repeatedly stroked Kitty's arm.

'Can you go hurry up the doctor, Mr Grayson?' Connie asked.

Suddenly, writhing around on the bed, Kitty screamed. She looked wildly from Miles to Connie.

'What is it, Kit?'

Kitty panted. 'Ohhh...Connie, help me!'

'I'll help you, Kit,' Miles told her, pulling her against him as though transferring his strength to her.

Her cries filled the room.

'Where is bloody Saunders?' Miles roared, looking through the open bedroom door.

'Connie? It hurts so bad,' Kitty ground out through clenched teeth.

'I'm 'ere, lass, I'm 'ere.'

'Connie?' Miles stared at her in confusion.

Connie closed her eyes and sighed. 'She's carryin' your child, but I think she'll lose it this day.'

Chapter Thirteen

The sun shone in a shimmering haze, but the breeze off the water made it pleasant to sit and enjoy the day. Sydney's harbour was, as always, very busy. Only, being Sunday, it hosted more pleasure crafts than the hustle and bustle of commercial vessels. High cliffs from behind to the east and west sheltered the little bay where the family had set up their picnic.

Dan lay on his side on a thick, navy-blue blanket reading the newspaper. 'The attempted assassination of His Royal Highness, The Duke of Edinburgh a month ago is still all the news. For such an event to occur in Sydney is so shocking, it has rocked society to its very core.'

Beside Dan, Ingrid sat watching the children playing in the sand. 'Indeed, it should. Disgusting behaviour to show visiting dignitaries.' She grinned and pointed to Joe and Martin sitting out on a rock with the waves lapping beneath. 'Are those two actually fishing or just relaxing in the sun?'

Clara kept an eye on the lace-covered food for descending flies and little black ants. She giggled. 'Joe's never caught a fish in his life.'

'This weather I like.' Connie sighed, watching Adelaide build a sandcastle. 'Not too hot an' not too cold.'

'Yes, May is wonderful for mild weather in Sydney,' Ingrid agreed, her face shadowed by the large hat she wore.

'Would you like a drink, lass?' Connie asked, looking at Kitty who stared out over the harbour.

'No, thank you.' Kitty rose from the blanket. 'I think I will walk a little.'

'Would you like me to come with you?' Clara asked.

'Next time.'

They watched silently as Kitty walked down the beach, her shoulders stooped; head hung low. She was a thin, pale creature and everyone despaired of her ever being well. Only Connie knew the real reason. The excuses Kitty gave for returning to Sydney were the failure of the property and losing Rosie, which was partly true.

'It's been nearly four months since you all came home, Connie. Surely she should be feeling better now?' Clara asked.

'I told you, love. Everythin' 'appened at once up there with our Rosie, the fire, the failure of the cattle an' all the other hardships. Her spirits are down, but soon she'll pick herself back up again, you'll see.'

Connie watched her dearest friend stroll away. In truth, Kitty was a woman eaten by so much sadness and hurt it was a wonder she was still sane. All the harsh, tragic events of her life had changed her little by little, slowly eroding her spirit. However, the greatest change occurred the day she lost her child, the day Miles Grayson swore he would never forgive her for killing the one thing he wanted more than anything else in the world, a child.

'Nothing is the same,' complained Clara.

'Things will come right again, Clara dear.' Ingrid smiled. 'We must give her time to readjust. Though, I do think it's time Kitty was taken out of herself. She has spent too long mooning over what is lost. What do you say, Connie?'

'Nay, I'm not sure.' Connie was hesitant. Kitty was fragile at the minute, but no one understood this, no one knew the truth of what she went through.

'Dan and I are invited to a ball tomorrow night hosted by the Ashford-Smith's. I think Kitty should go too.'

'She won't,' Connie was quick to reply.

'I will work on her.' Ingrid nodded. 'She cannot be left to mope forever. It is simply not healthy.'

Connie swatted at a pestering fly. It would be nice to see Kitty smile genuinely again. 'I suppose you right. But I doubt if you'll succeed.'

Kitty poured a cup of tea for her friend. 'I am not going, Ingrid. I told you so yesterday at the beach.'

'Well, I thought I would give you time to sleep on it.' Ingrid accepted the cup and saucer. 'Besides, you cannot refuse me now, I have already had your dress made.' She played her trump card.

'What?' Kitty whipped her head up so quickly her neck creaked.

'Yes, it is beautiful. Even Dan said you would look stunning in it.'

'No!' Kitty jerked up from the sofa. Socializing filled her with horror.

'It was made to order. You know I have good taste.'

'Ingrid, I am not going to any ball. Besides, I'm in mourning as you well know.'

'Yes, but sometimes one needs to trounce the standards and I think this is the perfect opportunity. You need to face the world again. No one would deny you that after all you've been through. Wear black if you must, but you will go.'

'I don't want more gossip spread about me and attending a ball will certainly do that.'

'Oh, do not be such a bore, Kitty,' scoffed Ingrid, becoming annoyed. 'Your self martyrdom is paling now.'

'My what?' Her temper, dormant for some time, now flashed through her ready to choke her.

Ingrid put down her teacup. 'What happened in the north is over and forgotten about. You've been back now for months and hardly left the house. Get on with your life.'

'How dare you?' A red mist blurred Kitty's vision.

'Oh, I dare all right. For it seems I am the only one who will. Everyone else is too frightened of your delicate constitution. Which is so laughable, for I've never known anyone as strong as you.'

'You go too far, Ingrid,' she whispered.

'Good. It's about time someone did.'

'You know nothing—'

'Dan and I will collect you at eight.' Ingrid gathered her gloves. 'I gave the dress to Hetta on the way in. It should be hanging in your room now.'

'You are wasting your time.'

Ingrid shrugged. 'Then I will no longer be your friend.'

Surprised, Kitty stared at her. 'You will stop being my friend?'

'Absolutely.' Ingrid stood. 'Connie has shielded you from anything to do with living a full life again, and I've had enough of it. You need to face the world and your past and conquer both. I want my old friend back, the one I first met with shining emerald eyes and a tinkling laugh.'

'It has been hard—'

'Of course, it has, no one doubts that, but are you going to live a half-life because you are frightened or it's hard?'

'You don't understand.' Kitty glanced around, looking to escape the conversation. Ingrid was stirring up thoughts and memories, dreams and hopes. She welcomed none of them. Not now, not ever. She had nothing to offer anyone. 'I...need some air.' She stumbled to the door.

'I am determined to find you a husband.'

Kitty spun at the door. 'Never will I marry.'

'Nonsense.'

'I had my chance, there will not be another.'

Ingrid gave an unladylike snort.

'Stop it!'

'Did he break your heart?'

The blood drained from her face. 'What are you talking about?'

'You tell me,' Ingrid said airily.

Kitty's heart twisted. She hoped it would stop altogether and liberate her from this life.

Ingrid stepped towards her but faltered. 'Kitty...'

Tears ran slowly down her face, but Kitty didn't brush them aside. It felt good to finally let them fall. She had not shed a tear over the loss of her baby, or the awful words Miles had thrown at her. She did not cry when she said good-bye to Rosie's grave or to Alice and Jessup or the land Benjamin gave her. She kept it all locked inside and now, it called for release.

'Darling, I am sorry.' Ingrid rushed to lead her back to the sofa. 'Let it out, my dear. It is long overdue.'

'I...I did not love him. I could not,' Kitty whispered through her tears and sobs. 'Ben was there between us and then...then the b-baby was.'

If Ingrid was shocked, she did well not to show it.

'I didn't want the baby, hated it even, because it was his, and now he hates me because I killed it.'

'How did you kill it?' Ingrid asked angrily, giving her a handkerchief. 'Why did he say such things to you?'

She dabbed her eyes. 'I worked like someone demented, trying my best to miscarry it. I hardly ate, never slept, worked harder than any man just to rid it from my body and deny its existence. Dr Saunders said I didn't take care of myself properly, lost too much weight and so on.' She gulped on a sob. 'The...the day of the fire was the beginning of the end. I tried to clear the lean-to of supplies, all the stress and heaving of sacks of grain brought on the first pains, but I ignored them.'

'Oh, Kitty.'

'Miles is right, I did kill my...our baby.'

'No—'

'I defiled Ben's memory in taking another man. A man I did not even like at the time, and then I killed the result of the awful act. What kind of person am I?'

'You are too hard on yourself. You must understand that Benjamin is dead. He would want you to find love and be happy. He adored you and your happiness would have been the uppermost of importance to him.'

'There will never be a man like him again.'

'No, but there are other good men. This Grayson fellow Dan told me about, is he Miles?'

Kitty nodded.

'Did he love you?'

'No.'

'But didn't he take you in after the fire?'

'Yes, but then he found out about the child.' Kitty closed her eyes, not wanting to remember the anguish on Mile's face as she bled away their baby.

'He is kind then?' Ingrid persisted. 'Perhaps, he does think well of you?'

'We had an a-attraction, that is all. I was lonely and upset when we...when I virtually attacked him. I really don't know what came over me. I am appalled at myself. I behaved disgracefully. No better than a woman off the street.'

'You are being ridiculous, dearest.' Ingrid kissed her cheek.

'No, it's the truth.'

Ingrid sighed heavily. 'Well, all I have to say is that it is time you put it behind you and start again. And tonight's ball will be the beginning. You know the Ashford-Smith's. Pippa is a delightful friend and it's so rare they leave Berrima to come to Sydney.'

'I cannot go to a ball, Ingrid.' Kitty dried her eyes with the crumpled handkerchief.

'Yes, you can, and you will. You need some happiness, Kitty. Your run of bad luck ends here, today. You need lightness and joy, to be surrounded by lovely gowns, fine wine and beautiful music.' Ingrid threw her hands up. 'You need your dance card to be full.'

'Oh no. No men, please,' Kitty agonised.

'You will dance, and much, much more. There will be no more sadness, no more tears.'

'I feel as though I have cried for the last twenty-four years.'

'So now it's time to smile for the next twenty-four years.' Ingrid grinned.

Kitty gripped Ingrid's hand. 'Do you think less of me for what I have done?'

Ingrid leant back on the sofa and frowned. 'Why, no. Good heavens, there are many secrets in most families. Mine included. Do you know that my uncle married a native Hawaiian woman? The scandal rocked my family to its very foundations. And closer to home, my eldest sister married beneath her and four months after her wedding she gave birth to a baby girl. So, I am not scandalised, dear Kitty. Never fear, you cannot get rid of me that easily.' Ingrid chuckled.

'I would hate to lose you.'

Ingrid winked. 'No chance of it.'

—ella—

Kitty knew she did not do justice to the beautiful black satin gown she wore. She was too thin, too hollow featured, and the shadows beneath her eyes showed no matter how much powder she applied. Her spirit was not in this ball, but she smiled at Ingrid and Dan to show them she was having a good time.

Indeed, the glorious ballroom was decorated to tantalize every one of the five senses. Beautifully gowned ladies and huge floral displays lent a swirl of colour and a heady mix of perfume to the scene. Fine wine and delicious food tempted any palate and laughter and music rung in eardrums.

The dance card suspended from Kitty's wrist was in fact full, but she possessed no knowledge of the young men who descended on her the minute she entered the ballroom. This did not bother her too much, for when she was dancing, she need not talk to people. However, the delights of the evening were lost to her. It hurt to see lovely young women laughing and talking animatedly to desirable young men. She wanted to be light-hearted and gay, but something inside her refused to be drawn to the appreciative glances that came her way. She had no energy to spend long nights at silly balls.

Spying an empty chair by the dance floor, Kitty walked towards it.

'Er, Miss McKenzie? I believe this is my dance?' A young man nervously offered his arm.

Kitty smiled a tight smile, trying hard not to sigh in disappointment as he led her onto the dance floor. She neither looked at nor talked to him as he turned her expertly around the floor. The music held no meaning and her feet followed his wherever he led.

At last, the dance came to an end. She thanked her partner and turned to flee, but instead bumped straight into a man's chest and stumbled back, apologizing.

The man remained motionless. Kitty glanced up to apologize again, and her heart turned over. She stepped back in horror, her stomach quivering.

The cold, steel- grey eyes of Miles Grayson narrowed. 'We meet again, Kit.' His voice was bitter, distant.

'I-I... Excuse me...' Kitty spun away, but Grayson's hand shot out and caught her elbow. The music began again, and Grayson drew her close to dance.

Kitty closed her eyes, shuddering as he clamped her fingertips within his large hand. Stumbling in his grip, her heart seemed suspended midway between her throat and feet. She felt the smooth material of his jacket under her left hand and shivered. If she turned her head just the slightest, she would be able to brush her cheek against his chest. The very thought made her blush and she groaned inwardly. This closeness sent her mind into a whirl. She had no warning of him even being in Sydney, let alone at this very ball.

'Just dance, Kit,' Grayson instructed, his jaw clenched tight, as he moved her majestically around the dance floor.

She hadn't seen him since the night of her miscarriage, when he had come into her bedroom, his eyes full of hate, and told her he would never forgive her deception. She had been allowed to stay until she was well, but three days later, she and Connie, with the babies, left early one morning without seeing Grayson. The housekeeper informed her he had gone to Bathurst. She never expected to meet him again and that thought had hurt her more than she cared to admit.

The waltz ended and Kitty sagged in relief at the idea of being away from Miles. Only, he held her tightly by the elbow and drew her away from the ballroom, past the refreshment room and out onto a large terrace. Other couples either stood in small groups or sat on benches chatting. Seeing this, Grayson led Kitty down a set of steps and into the landscaped gardens. Without speaking a word, he steered her across lawns, like carpet beneath their feet, and into a white-painted summerhouse. The structure was open on all sides and built in the shape of a hexagon. Bench seats lined each side and onto one of these Grayson pushed her none too gently.

Kitty sat with her head bowed and shoulders slumped. She could not fight him. She had no fight left in her.

'Have you nothing to say?' Grayson's scorn stripped away any defence.

She glanced up. 'I...must get back inside, Dan and Ingrid will be looking for me.'

'Someone like you should not even be in decent society!' Grayson exploded, but he suddenly hung his head and Kitty knew he had suffered too. Before, his hair had been dark grey, now it was noticeably lighter.

'Why did you bring me out here?' she whispered, not looking at him. She didn't want to see the anger burning inside him. 'Why did you dance with me if you think so ill of me?'

'I...because...' Grayson swore violently. 'I cannot even speak of my...disappointment and frustration.'

Slowly, she raised her gaze, hiding none of her pain and torment. 'There is nothing you can say or do that will make me feel any worse than I do already.'

He went to speak, but Kitty raised her hand, stopping him. 'I let my brother walk away from us in our weakest hour, because

I was too proud to go begging to our parents' former friends for handouts. That one action has kept him from us for nearly four years. I made my fiancé leave for Australia without me, when he so desperately wanted me to be with him. I spent so much time making my business a success that my younger brother ended up in prison. Again, my selfish need to live on Benjamin's land meant Mary eloped with some evil blackguard and I have not seen her since. My obsession with Ben's land killed Rosie. My anger made me with child when I ravished you and my prominent selfishness made me lose it. I have put my family through so much, Miles. There is nothing you can do to make my life worse. You were right that night when you came into the room and called me all those names. I am nothing. I deserve nothing.'

Slowly, he hunkered down in front of her and took both her hands. 'I am sorry, Kit. I shouldn't have reacted the way I did. I know it was an accident and I should never have said what I did. I'm not proud of my actions. My temper is appalling, it nearly matches yours.' He gave a wry smile. 'As to your family's fortunes, they are up to fate. You are not to blame yourself for every bad thing that happens.'

'I am to blame.'

He shook his head. 'No.'

'It is my role to take care of them.'

'Yes, you love them and provide for them, but it is the fates that decide people's destinies. Just as it decided we should meet.'

Kitty looked deep into his eyes, and for once their greyness was soft and warm. 'I am sorry about the child, Miles. I did not want it, and I deserved to die with it.'

'Stop speaking that way. You are a good, decent person, Kit McKenzie, and I mean every word. What I said before was simply my anger talking. I was wrong to speak so. I've been torturing myself about it ever since and hoping I'd have the opportunity to ask for forgiveness.'

Tears welled at his tenderness and she desperately wanted to rest her head against his shoulder. Kitty sighed. Tiredness wearied her. 'Can you take me back inside?'

Miles stood and held out his arm to her. She took it and they walked through the gardens. Back on the terrace once more, they found it free of people. The music drifted through the open windows and Miles swung Kitty around to face him.

'Dance with me?' he whispered close to her ear.

'Miles...I...'

'Please, Kit?'

'Very well.' Kitty slid into his arms and they moved beautifully in time with the music.

'Grayson is comin' 'ere?' Connie stared, amazed by Kitty's announcement.

'Yes. We talked a little at the ball and he apologised for his conduct about...well, you know what about.' Kitty sipped her tea.

'But lass, he's not good for you. What you both do t'each other is not right. You're in no state to manage another bout with him.'

'We aren't going to argue. He is just coming to talk.'

Connie smirked. 'Oh aye, that'll last five minutes. The two of you can't see each other without a slanging match.'

The doorbell rang and they heard Susie answer it. Miles's deep, strong voice made Connie raise an eyebrow at Kitty, who stood and straightened her skirts.

Susie entered the dining room. 'Mr Grayson is waiting in the parlour.'

'Do you want me ter stay here?'

Kitty shook her head. 'No. Come with me.'

He stood by the mantelpiece looking at a miniature portrait of Benjamin. He turned to face them as the rustle of their skirts alerted him.

Connie paused by the door. He smiled at Kitty as she came further into the room.

'Good morning.' Kitty held out her hand. He took it and pressed his lips to it.

'You look lovely, Kit.' His eyes danced with some hidden delight and his handsome face broke into a grin.

Connie sniffed. 'Mr Grayson, nice ter see you again.'

He bowed. 'And you, Mrs Spencer. Are you and the children well?'

'Aye, very well, thank you.'

Kitty indicated to a chair for him to sit. 'Would you like some tea?'

'No, thank you. I was hoping you would like to go for a drive. I have my gig outside. It is a lovely day for it.'

'I would like that, yes.'

'Wonderful.'

'I shall not be more than a minute.' Kitty swept from the room.

Connie waited until Kitty was out of sight and then narrowed her eyes at Grayson. 'I'll not mince me words.' She shook her finger at him. 'How you behaved on that certain night was unforgivable. After the tongue lashing you gave her, she barely ate for months. You damned nearly killed her! So, I'm tellin' you now, you do any more harm t'that lass, an' you'll 'ave me t'deal with. Now don't think I'm just a silly woman mouthin' off, because I'm warnin' you. She's suffered enough. I'll not let you hurt her anymore. Do you hear me?'

He nodded. 'Yes, Mrs Spencer, I do.'

'Right then, just as long you know.'

'May I ask you something?'

Connie crossed her arms over her flat chest, not giving an inch. 'Aye, go on then.'

'Actually, can you keep a secret?'

She eyed him suspiciously. 'Aye.'

'I want to ask Kit to marry me, but I will wait a while yet. I want to show her I am not the devil she thinks I am.'

Connie had no time to comment, much to her disgust, as Kitty swept in. They left soon after and Connie sat on the sofa and rubbed a weary hand over her eyes. She knew without a doubt that Kitty would marry Miles. She knew Kitty loved the man, even though the poor lass was still unaware of it herself. Connie gazed around the parlour and sighed at the thought of living here without her dear lass. Blue Water Station was a long way from Forbes Street.

Chapter Fourteen

Kitty sat upon the bay horse and rolled her eyes at Miles. 'I will fall,' she muttered, adjusting her position on the sidesaddle. Her new, dark blue riding habit was comfortable and in the latest style, but it didn't give her the confidence she needed.

'No, you will not. Just relax,' Miles encouraged. He sat his horse well, even though it was a borrowed mount.

'Promise you will not go faster than a walk?' She held the reins in a fierce grip.

'I promise, even if it is a hunt.' Miles laughed; a sound not often heard from him. The others in their group, good friends of his, smiled at each other.

A runner heralded the signal that a kangaroo had been sighted and the chorus of bugle noise hurt her ears. The hunt began, but Kitty's mount, an old mare, was happy to plod along at the back as the rest of the high-spirited horses galloped away to a blare of hounds barking and bugles calling.

Kitty stayed well away from the pack and was happier doing so, only Miles and his horse were impatient to be away. However, keeping to his promise, Miles made an effort to control his horse and remain beside her.

'Oh, go.' Kitty laughed at him. 'I can see you are desperate to be in the thick of things.'

'Don't be silly. I said I would stay with you.' Miles cursed at his horse as it threw its head in temper.

'I am fine, Miles, really. You go and I will see you back at the lodge.'

He hesitated. 'Are you sure?'

A rider drew alongside. Kitty softly groaned as Serena Feldon reined in her horse and smiled sweetly at Miles. 'You are being cruel to that horse, Miles, by refusing to let it have its head. It longs to be away. I shall stay with Miss McKenzie.'

Miles needed no second bidding and Kitty gripped the reins tighter. Serena Feldon was not her favourite person. In the two months Miles had been calling, Miss Feldon had managed to be frequently amongst the parties and groups of people she and Miles associated with. She even stayed on in Sydney when the Graysons' went back to Bathurst after a two-week visit to the city.

Kitty always grew uncomfortable and suspicious when Serena was around. The woman was sly, and Kitty didn't trust her. Serena pouted and simpered behind her fan to men at parties and won Miles's and any other man's attention easily. Whenever she spoke to Kitty, it was usually something spiteful, but so well hidden with her sweet smiles no one noticed.

'You must find it tiresome to follow Miles everywhere?' Serena inquired now. Her dark, chocolate-brown riding habit fitted her tall gracefulness well.

'Not at all. I only go where I am invited,' Kitty replied, conscious that wispy tendrils of hair fell out from under her hat.

Her thick, unruly hair was a complete contrast to Serena's dark sleekness.

'Miles is indeed a kind and generous man, he gives his attention to those who would otherwise not be comfortable in certain societies. I believe it to be his only weakness.'

Kitty chuckled. 'Lucky Miles, to have only one weakness.'

Serena scowled. 'I do not know of a better man.'

Kitty stared out over the rolling fields. A fleeting thought of Ben crossed her mind. 'Only the good die young,' she whispered, then instantly regretted the comment.

'I believe Miles is going back to Blue Water soon.' Serena steadied her horse as it pulled.

Kitty's stomach plummeted at the thought, which didn't surprise her. Their friendship meant a great deal to her. 'I am astounded he has stayed in Sydney as long as he has. After all, Blue Water demands so much of him.'

'I have decided to go with him. I love Blue Water so. It is like home to me. Miles and I go riding every day when I am there,' Serena gushed, her eyes bright.

'It is indeed a beautiful place.'

'When Miles and I marry, I am determined to host the biggest wedding the North has ever seen.'

Serena's words cut into Kitty like sharp slivers of glass, just as she had meant them to do. Taking a deep breath, Kitty tried to think logically. She knew without a doubt that Miles had feelings for her, though he never mentioned it. Their friendship grew stronger each day, but she was unsure whether Miles wanted more. Maybe he thought she could be used again without being wedded first? Maybe he held no intentions of being anything more than a friend. He never touched her in any way except as a perfect gentleman would. Her own frequent wanton feelings shamed her.

She longed to feel his lips on hers, his hands on her body. Of course, these thoughts and longings made her feel guilty. No lady should have such feelings. No lady should want a man with the intensity she wanted Miles. Why could she not be a genteel lady of refinement? She admitted silently that she was cursed with her mother's passion. She clearly remembered her mother and father kissing and canoodling in dark corners of the house when they thought no one was around. However, it was a scourge to have such feelings for a man to whom you were not married. There was a rightful censorship of anyone who merely looked a little too long at another person, never mind such sinful thoughts.

'I think I shall turn back now, Serena. I have a headache. You go on and meet the others.' Kitty tugged on the reins and swung the horse about.

'Very well,' Serena answered happily. 'I shall find Miles.'

Back at the lodge, Kitty dismounted and handed the reins to the groom. She went upstairs to her room and washed. Drying her hands, she gazed out the window at the surrounding fields, gently rolling hills, clusters of trees and scattering of cows. Quietness reigned now the squabble of hounds, horses and riders had gone. The sun disappeared behind a cloud and shadows threw the lodge into cool winter shade. Kitty shivered. What does he want with me?

The last couple of months had shown her his better temperament. She thoroughly enjoyed his company and the more time they spent together, the more they learnt about each other. A year ago, Kitty would never have thought she would be able to converse with Miles in a sociable way, never mind enjoy his company.

She smiled, remembering the events of the last two months. The first outing after the ball had been a nervous occasion for both of them, but they soon found themselves talking naturally about many subjects and the delightful day passed by very quickly.

From that day on, Miles accompanied her and Connie to various places. They boated on the harbour, walked around the parklands of the city, and he even showed her how to pick the right horse to win a few shillings on at the races. They went out to the theatre and museums. Miles took her and Connie, much to everyone's amusement and Connie's dismay, to dinner at an expensive restaurant. In turn, he was invited to dinners and afternoon teas at Forbes Street and slowly, he was winning Connie over again.

Although Miles, with his stubbornness and proud superiority, was maddening at times, she also knew of his unique tenderness and compassion. He was a man of many facets, and whether they be good or bad, they made him the man he was, the man she knew she loved.

Admitting her feelings allowed her some relief. The mourning for Ben was easing and becoming less powerful. He would always be in her heart, for he had been her first love. He opened her heart and eyes to what emotions men and women could share. She was fortunate to have known a good, decent man's love. Not everyone could say that. However, she now needed to live her life and grab whatever happiness she could. She was tired of being alone, tired of having no one to hold her.

A tap on the door interrupted her musings. Calling the person to come in, Kitty turned to find Miles hovering in the doorway, as though afraid of what he might find.

'Is the hunt over already?' She smiled.

'No, not quite. I just wanted to make sure you are all right.' Miles looked at her in a way he hadn't done before. A pulse ticked along his jaw, and when he ran a hand through his hair, it shook.

'I am fine, thank you. I just had a slight headache.'

'I had a strange feeling you might have gone back to Sydney.'

She frowned. 'Why would I do that without telling you?'

'Serena mentioned it.'

Kitty raised an eyebrow. 'I never said any such thing to Serena. Although, I imagine she would rather I did.'

'Why would she?'

Kitty shook her head at the idea of such an intelligent man not knowing what kind of woman Serena really was. 'She gave me reason to think that the both of you would soon be married.'

His eyes widened. 'She said that?'

She nodded.

'I don't want to marry Serena, Kit. She is like a sister, for I have known her all her life.'

'I think that is something you should discuss with her.'

'You are mistaken.'

'She said it to me, Miles. I didn't make it up.' Kitty tried not to be argumentative.

'I am sure you misread the conversation. It is easily done.'

She stiffened. 'Why are you so confident that I am at fault? Why can you not believe what I say to be the truth? Have you not seen how she looks at you?'

'What nonsense. As I said, we are like sister and brother, ask Campbell.'

'She may feel as though Campbell is her brother, but you do not fall into the same category.'

'I will not discuss this. Serena is my mother's godchild and has lived with us all her life. I didn't realize you were one to make up such malicious, distasteful gossip.'

'How dare you?' Kitty exploded, the short fuse to her temper ignited. 'My Lord. Again, I was so wrong about you.' She jerked her luggage onto the bed. 'Serena does her best to insult me at every opportunity.' She grabbed her toiletries off the desk. 'And you! You are nothing more than a wolf in sheep's clothing.

I loathe how you manage to have such false decency. You and Serena are well suited.'

Miles sighed dramatically. 'Oh, calm down, Kit. For pity's sake. You sure know how to turn on an act. Just admit you were wrong. It will not go beyond these four walls, I promise you.'

'I was not wrong, you blind fool. Why do men fall for her simpering ways? I will not demean myself a minute longer by partaking in this conversation.'

'Kit, this jealousy is unbecoming.'

'J-jealousy,' Kitty spluttered, amazed at his stance of self-righteousness.

'There is simply no need for you to be. I do not want to marry Serena because I want to marry you.'

Kitty stopped mid-stride and stared open-mouthed at him. 'What did you say?'

'I happen to think we should get married. It is a sensible conclusion to our friendship. I have found we get along well enough whenever we are not arguing. I need a wife and I believe you would be a wonderful asset to Blue Water.'

Kitty blinked rapidly, absorbing his carefully selected words. 'What about my needs?' she croaked.

Miles shrugged. 'I will give you whatever you want. You will be mistress of Blue Water and all that entails. I have a large fortune that would be at your disposal, as you need. I give you free reign of the house to control and decorate as you wish. All you need is to ask, and it will be yours.'

'And my family?'

'I have already thought of that. I know you will not leave Connie or the children, so I will make the attic rooms available as a comfortable nursery suite. The entire floor is Connie's to do as she wishes. Clara and Joe can come and live with us too, and Martin is welcome to call Blue Water home whenever he is in the country.'

He made it all sound so simple and easy. Her mind whirled at the enormity of what he offered. Never again would she have to carry alone the burden of worry. With Miles as her husband, she would be safeguarded against poverty and an uncertain future.

Kitty's thoughts drifted to her family and how well they would be cared for by her as Miles's wife. Joe and Clara would be introduced to the right people and their futures would be certainly more secure. She was quick to think about her family's benefit, but deep down she also wanted Miles for herself. He was a maddening, arrogant and unbending swine at times, but she had seen the softer side and that was the side she loved. She wanted him, it was as simple as that. He made no mention of love and she balked at that, but she had to be practical, and being Mistress of Blue Water and helping her family would have to be enough.

She raised her chin as though mentally preparing for the battle ahead. 'Very well, I will marry you.'

Chapter Fifteen

The fireworks lit up the night sky. The gathered crowd oohed and ahhed with each exploding boom of bright stars. Miles allowed all the servants, farm workers and their families to assemble at the edge of the garden to watch the event with his family and friends. Some of the elder farm workers, grumbling about scaring the animals, stayed behind to soothe the frightened beasts, but everyone else was enjoying the festivities as Blue Water ushered in the New Year of eighteen hundred and sixty-nine.

'Cor, I'm tired,' Connie said, in a pause of the fireworks display. Adelaide and Charles each held her hands.

'The three little ones will be tired too. The twins have not stopped all day, they were so excited.' Kitty heaved Little Rory up higher in her arms. He was growing too big and heavy for her now. He smiled, showing his little white teeth and she kissed his cheek. Soon, they would celebrate his third birthday and he was the image of his father.

'Are you exhausted, lass?' Connie asked concerned.

Kitty smiled and patted her rounded stomach. 'Do not worry, Connie dear. Miles does enough of that for everyone.'

'You can't blame him, lass.'

'I have taken no risks, have I?' demanded Kitty, finally putting Little Rory down to stand beside her.

'Just as well.' Miles come up behind them.

Kitty turned to look at him and her foolish heart skipped a beat. Their marriage was quite normal by most people's standards and she could not complain, for she had everything a woman might want, except the one thing she desired most. In six months of marriage, Miles had never said he loved her. Even in their most intimate moments, he never said the three words she longed to hear. It was the only problem in her marriage, but it was a large problem and she shared it alone. She would never humiliate herself to ask him if he actually did love her. He treated her well, giving her control of the house and servants. She was allowed to spend whatever amount of money she wished. However, it all seemed a little hollow when she did not have the closeness of his love.

Kitty put on a brave face when, at times, she longed to tenderly hold his hand or place a simple kiss on his cheek. He never encouraged any tenderness between them, though in the marriage bed he was considerate and gentle. Only, she wanted passion and intensity. She blushed at how she longed for him in the same way they had come together by the creek. Then, it had been spontaneous and explosive. Now, it was just two bodies coming together with no heart. She didn't understand why Miles behaved in this fashion. Why did he not want passion too? To her, he appeared to be the kind of man who would want and need it. Obviously, she was wrong and the tension in their marriage continued to build. Soon, it would be beyond repair.

'You should say good night, Kit. You need your sleep,' Miles said, picking Little Rory up. He smiled into the boy's face as the child pointed to the fireworks breaking out above their heads.

'I will go when the fireworks are over, Miles, and of a time when I choose.' She whirled away from him.

'What is wrong with her now?' Miles asked Connie as they watched her storm off and go talk to the Freemans.

'She's bound t'be tired an' out of sorts, Miles. She's near six months pregnant.'

Miles brooded. 'I cannot seem to say or do anything that brings a smile to her face.'

'The lass has a lot on her mind.'

'She has?' Miles scowled. For the life of him, he could not think what would cause her worry.

'No word of Rory and she's received no word from our Mary. It worries her, 'tis been too long now. One letter since you marriage is not enough. She was terribly disappointed that Mary didn't attend you wedding.'

'I shall write to Mary and invite her here to stay for a while. Do you think that will help?'

'It might. Though our Mary will be gettin' a lashin' of me tongue when I do see her. Selfish little wench.'

'I will look into the situation. The Ascots are known to some business associates of mine. I did not want to interfere before, but if it eases Kit's mind then I will find out what I can.'

'Aye, Miles, it would be good t'know what's what. Kitty was so happy to get Mary's first letter and wrote straight back saying she was forgiven, but Mary won't leave Goulburn.'

'I'll see to it, Connie.' Miles nodded. 'Well, I think it is time all small people were in bed,' he said, tickling Little Rory's stomach. 'The fireworks are finished, my man.'

'Give him 'ere, Miles. I'll tekk him an' the twins upstairs t'bed. It's been a right treat for them.'

Miles bent so Little Rory could kiss his cheek and as always experienced a sense of warm emotion. He had never been used to children, but the house now rang with the noise of the twins and Little Rory where before there had been only silence. In the past, he'd refused to believe his life was missing something, but with the house full, he knew the truth. People made a house a home.

Miles scanned the dwindling crowd, satisfied they all enjoyed a good time. His whole family surrounded him, and it gladdened his heart.

With a deep sigh, he searched for Kit. She was talking to Ingrid further along the veranda. His stomach clenched as he gazed at her beautiful face and swollen body. His heart thudded at the thought of her carrying his child beneath her heart. He ached with wanting, he could never have enough of her. She delighted him beyond reason, and he wondered how he lived his bleak life before she entered it.

However, he wished he could show her his love, but he refused to take that risk. She gave him no encouragement in forging a great love between them. So, he made himself content with what he had. Maybe one day she would unbend enough to allow him into her heart where Benjamin reigned.

Kitty sat in her day room, which was decorated in pale lemon and white. At the window the soft breeze lifted the cream lace curtains. She loved this room. It was solely hers and in it she read, sewed and discussed the day with Mrs Morris, the housekeeper, but mainly she used it as a writing room. The solid oak desk was placed close to the window to achieve maximum light for her to read her correspondence. In this peaceful room, she pondered and dreamed.

Alma, the parlour maid, tapped on the open door. 'The mail has arrived, Mrs Grayson.' She set a silver tray on the desk and left.

Kitty studied each envelope in turn. She carefully opened the one letter she dreaded seeing. Since her marriage, she had received a note once a month from Timothy Ascot. In every missive, he requested money for Mary and every month, she sent him twenty pounds. Kitty wrote a letter every week to Mary, with no reply. The situation was intolerable.

She had been correct to be angry and disappointed at Mary for her disgrace, but the damage needed to be repaired. Kitty was tired of her family being separated. She wanted for nothing now and longed to share that good fortune with her family. Am I asking too much to have them here with me? Rory was still missing, Mary refused to speak to her, Martin was sailing the high seas and Clara and Joe wished to go back to Sydney at the weekend with the Freemans to finish school.

'Why, Kitty, I do hope I am not interrupting you?' Serena glided into the room, wearing a satin gown of pale yellow.

'Is there something I can help you with, Serena?' Kitty tucked Timothy's letter in the drawer of her desk.

'No, not really.' Serena fiddled with the framed miniatures on the mantle. 'Aunt Blanche was wondering where you were hiding yourself. A good hostess always stays with her guests, you know.'

Kitty gave her a withering look. 'Blanche and the others are quite happily going about their business. This is their home too and they are quite used to it and its pleasures. I was simply taking a few minutes to attend to my correspondence.'

Serena gazed around the little room. 'You must be proud of yourself, achieving to dupe Miles into marrying you?'

'Dupe Miles?' Kitty chuckled. 'What drivel. Miles is the least of men one could dupe.'

'Miles and Blue Water were mine.' Serena's harsh words cut the air.

'Then why are you not sitting here instead of me? Come, Serena, if Miles wanted you for his wife then he would have asked you.'

'You took them both from me!'

She stood and Serena's eyes narrowed at her swollen stomach. 'Go home, Serena. It does you no good to torment yourself by coming here anymore, and why you do it is beyond me.'

'Do not dare to pity me.' Serena gripped a book on the desk. 'You think you are so clever but look at yourself and your family. Why, your brother is a wastrel and your sister are married to a man who has more mistresses than clean shirts!'

Kitty jerked. 'What are you saying?'

Serena sauntered around the desk. 'Timothy Ascot is a scoundrel and a drunkard.'

'What do you know of him?' Kitty whispered, dreading the words Serena would delight in speaking.

'Oh, now that would be telling, would it not?' Serena stared, laughter filling her eyes before she strolled out of the room.

Kitty followed her into the hall. 'Wait, Serena!'

'Is everything all right, Kitty dear?' Blanche stepped out of the sitting room opposite.

Serena went out through the front doors and Kitty sighed in frustration. 'Do you know where Miles is, Blanche?'

'I do believe the men have just come in from their ride. They are out on the veranda having a cool drink. Shall we join them?'

Kitty nodded and linked her hand through Blanche's arm. She desperately wanted to see Mary and she needed to discuss it with Miles.

However, it wasn't until they were preparing for bed later that night that she managed to speak of her problem. Kitty, clad in only her nightgown, brushed out her long hair. 'Miles, I must go to see Mary. I know Goulburn is a long way from here, but I feel that I must go before the baby is born.'

Turning to face her, Miles grinned as he climbed into their four-poster bed. 'The situation is in hand, Kit. I have written to Mary and her husband, inviting them to stay with us. I should receive a reply by next week.'

'You have?' Kitty stared in amazement. 'What made you do that?'

'I thought you both needed to forgive and forget. Besides, I wish to meet my sister-in-law.'

She lowered her hairbrush. 'Why did you not tell me?'

He shrugged and scratched one naked shoulder. 'I wanted to surprise you.'

Kitty moved to the bed and folded back the crisp, white sheets. 'I worry about her, Miles. Serena indicated, and reaffirmed my initial feelings, that Timothy Ascot was not—'

Miles pulled her to him and kissed her tenderly, effectively cutting off her flow of words. 'Enough talk, Mrs Grayson. Your husband wants you.'

'But, Miles...' She groaned as he nibbled her neck. Warmth coiled like a spring in the pit of her stomach. All thought of Mary and Timothy Ascot fled her mind as she surrendered to her body's demands.

'Kiss me, wife...' His nose nudged hers and she sought his mouth as tingles of desire fired her blood. She felt his need of her hard against her thigh and revelled in the power she had over him. Sometimes he seemed awed by the fact that she wanted him just as much as he wanted her. Despite her pregnancy, they made love frequently. Miles would hold her gently, almost reverently, never demanding anything, though sometimes she wished he would. She pushed away the thought that the only time they were close was in bed. She had to make that enough and not want his heart too.

———ele———

Kitty bent and pulled out a rogue weed growing in the rose bed.

'Lass, stop bendin' and fussin' in your condition, there's enough gardeners here ter see it.' Connie shook her head and steered Kitty along the path. 'Let's walk by the river.'

Kitty sighed. 'It is pleasant to have the house to ourselves again, although I will miss Clara and Joe.' She chuckled. 'I like our other visitors too, but it's nice when they go.'

'Aye, that Serena is a nasty piece of work. I'm glad ter see the back of her.'

'Indeed.'

'Shame Miles has gone away for a few days. What's it all about anyway?'

'He is riding the boundary fences with his men. There have been frequent spates of cattle stealing in the far reaches of the property, so Miles and the men are camping out in the bush to try and apprehend the thieves. They knew it not to be the local aboriginals for some of them work for Miles and they told him the thieves were white men.'

'Well, I hope he's careful.'

They paused at the riverbank and gazed at the flowing water. On the opposite bank, a platypus dived into the shallows.

Kitty raised her face to the warm sun. 'The head butcher's wife, Delia Trent, has asked us over for tea tomorrow.'

'Oh aye?' Connie threw a pebble into the water. "Tis grand how everyone has accepted us.'

'Yes, we are fortunate.' She linked her hand in Connie's. 'Apparently, Mrs Trent makes wonderful scones.'

'I hope she medd fresh cream an' all.'

Kitty laughed and looked over to where Mrs Morris rushed across the lawn towards them.

The housekeeper waved a piece of paper in her hand. 'Oh, Mrs Grayson!'

Mrs Morris's agitation surprised Kitty and at once filled her with dread. 'What is it?'

'It just arrived.' Mrs Morris puffed, handing a telegram to Kitty. The blood drained from her face as she read it.

Connie instantly moved closer to her. 'What's up, lass?'

Stunned, Kitty raised her gaze to Connie. 'Mary is very ill, close to death. That is all it says.'

'Nay, lass.' Connie's hand flew to her throat.

'Mrs Morris, organize for my things to be packed immediately. Also have the carriage brought around, I must get to Grafton straight away, I cannot lose any more time.'

The housekeeper's eyes widened. 'Mrs Grayson, I beg you to wait for Mr Grayson. I can have a man sent for him right away.'

'No, I cannot wait. It would be hours before a man could locate their camp. Miles can follow me later. Now please, do as I ask.'

'Steady now, lass,' Connie admonished, following her across the lawns and into the house. ''Tis a long journey you've got ahead of you.'

Upstairs, Kitty took underclothes out of her drawers. Leah, her maid, hurried in carrying a small trunk and began to pack. 'I am relying on you, Connie, to explain to Miles why I did not wait for him. You know how he will react.'

'He's goin' t'be as mad as a bull, you know that, don't you?' Connie collected Kitty's toiletries off the dressing table.

'I cannot think about that now.' Kitty donned traveling clothes. Her only thought was to get to Mary and help her before it was too late. She'd failed Mary before but not this time. Her sister needed her, and nothing would keep her from being there.

'Tekk Leah with you, lass. 'Tis too far ter go on you own.'

Kitty nodded and looked at her maid. 'Leave this, I will see to it. Go and pack.'

Within fifteen minutes, Kitty's carriage trundled down the dirt road away from Blue Water. Connie stood on the veranda with the children and waved her off, wishing she could go with her. When the carriage disappeared from view, Connie called for Mrs Morris.

'Yes, Mrs Spencer?'

''Ave you sent for Mr Grayson, Mrs Morris?'

'Aye, Mrs Spencer, before the carriage left.'

'Good. How long do you think it'll tekk for him ter get home?'

'Four to five hours at least, but he'll ride hard. I told the rider to tell Mr Grayson it was urgent. So, she'll not have too much head start, and if she doesn't get a boat until morning then he'll be able to catch up with her in Grafton.'

Connie frowned, worried.

'Come, Mrs Spencer, let us have a cup of tea while we wait.' The housekeeper's tone was gentle. 'I, too, am fond of our spirited young mistress.'

'I'd like it better if you were t'call me Connie, since we're cut from the same cloth. I don't try ter pretend what I'm not.' Connie sniffed.

'Well, that would be grand, Connie, and I'm Sybil. Shall we go to the kitchen and sample Cook's delicious fresh biscuits?'

Hetta hugged Kitty to her ample breast as she stumbled across the threshold. Even Susie looked happy to see her. Kitty led Leah to the sofa, for the girl looked ready to fall down.

'Eh, miss, I'm that surprised to see you,' Hetta gushed, her eyes shiny with tears.

'It is good to see you too, Hetta. I am in sore need of a bath and a meal, but first, we must help poor Leah. We have endured a sensational voyage from Grafton in a tiny cargo boat. She has been seasick the entire journey.'

'Aww, poor lass. Here, Susie, help this lass upstairs and make a bed up for her.'

Kitty sighed as the two maids left the room. She ached in every part of her body. 'Send Susie out to buy me a first-class train ticket to Goulburn and find out when the next train leaves. I must be on it.'

'Goulburn?'

Kitty yawned. The trip had been a nightmare as rough seas tossed the small boat around. Yet, she had been lucky to secure a passage on it immediately arriving at South Grafton wharf. 'Leah will have to stay with you. She is too weak to be of any use to me.'

'Are you visiting Miss Mary?'

'Mary is ill and needs me.'

'Why that skank never said,' Hetta muttered.

'Who?' Kitty spun around.

'Mr Ascot. He were here just yesterday.'

'Here? Why was he here?' Her tiredness left to be replaced by frustration and anger. Why had he left his ill wife?

'He allus comes here when he's in Sydney. He told me you allowed it.'

Thunderstruck, Kitty gaped at her. 'What does he do here?'

'He stays the night and has a meal and a bath. I thought it was him when I heard you at the front door.'

Kitty held onto the back of the sofa for support. 'I never gave him permission to use this house when he was in the city. Why didn't you write me a note to confirm it?' Her fury was such it made her shake.

'He's your brother-in-law, I just thought it to be true. He said you and he were writing to each other and all was forgiven. He keeps telling me that next time he'll bring Miss Mary with him, but each time he comes alone.' Hetta was red-faced with shame.

'That...that...' She wanted to hit something, hard. Damn him!

Hetta screwed up her apron in anxiety. 'I'm so sorry, Mrs Kitty, I just thought you knew.'

'I need a bath, Hetta,' Kitty whispered, trying desperately to remain calm. Her child kicked in her womb and Kitty closed her eyes. She must stay calm for the child's sake. She couldn't do anything to jeopardize the child.

Kitty's head fell against the window with a thump, instantly waking her. The rattling of the train was bone numbing, but with each mile, they traveled the closer she became to Mary.

Her emotions alternated between fear and anger at the fates that seemed determined to wrench her family apart. She thought being married to Miles would save her from dealing with these situations alone, but she had come to realize Miles only offered her protection from poverty. The emotional needs she craved from him were never going to be hers. He married her for an heir, and she him for security. Of course, she was fooling herself, pretending she could ignore her overwhelming love for him, and love him she did, foolishly, completely. She thought she could live as his wife without him loving her in return. Now, she knew she was wrong.

Finally, the body shaking stopped as the train rattled into the last station on the new railway line to Moss Vale. The railway to Goulburn was not yet completed and this little village was the railhead. Here, coaches lined up to take the train passengers onto the next step of their journeys. Kitty fumed at this new-found knowledge and silently cursed herself for taking things for granted in this young country. She assumed the train would take her straight to Goulburn, now the journey would be slower, and every minute spent away from Mary was a minute too long.

Kitty stepped down from the train and gazed around at the mass of people disembarking. The noise of the steaming train, the yelling baggage handlers and the whistle of conductor hurt her ears. She only carried a handheld bag, having left the rest of her things at Forbes Street, and so was able to move off to the waiting coaches without the holdup of searching for luggage.

Twenty minutes later, after a quick refreshing cup of tea bought at a stall on the platform, Kitty squashed into the coach with five other people. The driver wasted no time in whipping up the horses and over the rutted roads the passengers were tossed against each other. The man seated next to her apologized profusely for the next ten minutes, then after that gave up.

'I hope we aren't stopped by bushrangers,' an elderly woman sitting opposite spoke.

'I have travelled this route many times, madam, and not once have we been stopped,' another occupant replied. 'Besides, the driver and his man both have weapons,'

'A shootout is the last thing we need,' a man put in.

The elderly woman clutched a small bag to her chest. 'My sister warned me not to travel with my jewels, such is the barbarism in the country. London is much more civilized.'

A heated discussion on the outlaws of the world took place for a short while before the passengers fell into a subdued silence once more. Kitty closed her eyes and tried to relax her weary body. She had not claimed a decent rest since the night before she left Blue Water, three days ago. The steady fall of rain only increased her despondency.

The clouds hung low above the town of Goulburn, which grew year by year in prosperity. Large sheep stations dotted the outskirts of the area and the town itself was cradled in the midst of a shallow valley.

Another day ended as the coach rolled into the wide, muddy, well-defined streets. Buildings of architectural design gave Goulburn, the largest town in the surrounding district for many miles, a sense of permanence. Thank goodness that at least Mary did not have to endure the hardships of living miles and miles from any source of comfort.

The steady rain became a downpour and Kitty, along with many others, ran for cover. Inside the coach inn, the odour of wet clothes and stale beer sickened her. Faint, she raced outside once more. She preferred the teeming rain to that of the rank air in the stuffy coach house.

'Are ye needin' a lift, missus?' an old man with a weather-beaten face called out to her from across the muddy coaching yard. He was draped in a large sack and the brim of his hat dripped water in front of his squinting eyes.

She lifted her hand to signal yes and waited while the driver steered the horse about. Kitty gave him the address of what she hoped was Mary's home. It was the only address she had, the one she used when sending money to Timothy. At least it was a place to start.

The cold cab seat chilled her, but she was unconcerned. Mary filled her mind. How would she cope if Mary was taken from her also? Was it not enough to have buried her parents and little sister in York, then Max, Ben and Rosie, to now face the prospect of doing it again with Mary. No!

A few minutes later, the driver pulled his horse to stop outside of a two-storied, stone house. The green-painted front door led straight off the roadside path. With her heart lodged in her throat, Kitty paid the driver and then rapped the brass knocker three times.

A middle-aged woman wearing a black servant's frock and white cap and apron opened the door a crack. 'Can I help you?' she whispered, gripping the door.

'My name is Kitty Grayson. I am looking for my sister Mary Ascot.'

The servant's solemn face relaxed ever so slightly, and she quickly beckoned her in. 'Oh, Mrs Grayson. I never thought you'd come.' The woman ushered Kitty into the small hallway. 'I'm Jane Giles.'

'So, my sister is here?' Kitty swallowed back threatening tears.

'Yes, Mrs Grayson, but she awful bad. I'm expecting the doctor again any minute. Come upstairs.'

The maid stopped at the top of the landing. 'The doctor calls every day, sometimes twice a day. She floats in and out of wakefulness.'

'What is exactly wrong with her?'

The maid's expression altered, and her gaze darted away. 'She...er, well, Mr Ascot and she were arguing like, and um...he...'

An icy shiver ran down Kitty's back. 'Are you saying my brother-in-law hit my sister?'

Tears came to the woman's kind blue eyes. 'Yes, Mrs Grayson, but he not only just hit her the once, you understand?'

Kitty placed her hand against the wall to steady herself. How dare he? She would kill him with her bare hands!

The maid entered the bedroom and Kitty hesitated, wondering what she would find. Straightening, she took a deep breath and walked in. The fire shifting in the grate was the only sound in the stark, white room. The double bed had a plain iron bedframe and its smooth white quilt barely showed the outline of the thin ghostlike figure sleeping beneath. Kitty stepped to the bed and stifled a moan with her hand as she looked down on her once beautiful sister.

Bruising covered Mary's face like a hideous mask, swollen eyes and split, bloodied lips completed the destruction. Along her jaw and cheekbones, the bruises mingled and joined, creating a mottled colour of blue, black and purple. Mary's thin body hardly moved; such was the shallowness of her breathing. Her long black hair lay lank on the snowy pillowcase, but on closer inspection Kitty saw bloodied white patches on Mary's scalp where the hair had been pulled out. Dried blood also knotted her long tresses.

'I can't wash her hair until she wakes up proper like,' the maid explained as if reading her thoughts.

Carefully, Kitty raised the quilt and looked down the length of Mary's body. Tears trickled down her cheeks at the wasted flesh. Mary wore no nightgown, for her ribs were bandaged and she had bruising over her arms, stomach and legs. Her hipbones struck up clearly against her pale skin.

'Why did this happen to her?' Her fury-laced whisper broke the silence of the room.

'I don't know what to say...' The other woman shook her head. 'She wouldn't go to you and she wouldn't let me write to tell you how he treated her. But once this happened, I had to let you know. So, I went through her things and found your address. The doctor didn't know if she would survive.'

'Timothy Ascot did all this?' Even though the evidence was before her, it was too hard to understand that a man could do this to his wife, the one he supposes to love.

'Yes, Mrs Grayson, only, this time he's gone too far. The doctor sent for the constable and they want to arrest him for attempted murder.'

Murder.

Kitty shivered, horrified. 'H-he fled?'

'Aye, straight after he did this.'

Kitty's lips curled in white-hot anger. 'Well, he better keep on running for, if my sister dies, I will not rest until he is swinging off the end of a rope.'

An hour later, the doctor arrived, and after examining Mary, he sat with Kitty downstairs. They discussed Mary's condition and Timothy Ascot for some time.

Dr Blewitt stirred his tea. 'I'm glad Mary has family. She's too fragile to be left alone with that blackguard. I often saw her in the street, but she never stopped to talk. She always had the look of a frightened doe about her.'

'I had no idea, or I would have come to see her sooner and taken her home.' Kitty sighed, pain encircling her heart. 'I waited for her to come to me, which was arrogant, and I am ashamed of myself.'

'You weren't to know what kind of man he is.'

'Yes, I did. From the very beginning, I didn't like him. I refused him permission to marry her, but they eloped. I should have tried to find them and bring her home. Instead, I went on my way. I wanted to punish her, teach her a lesson. I will never forgive myself.'

Dr Blewitt's kind brown eyes softened. 'You are too hard on yourself, Mrs Grayson. We all make our own paths in this world.'

'She will get better, won't she?' Her vision blurred with tears.

'In time, I hope. Though if she does, it'll be her damaged mental state which will last the longest and be the hardest to overcome.' He stood and reached for his hat. 'From what the maid has told me, the husband has tortured her since the beginning.'

'I want to take her home with me, away from him,' Kitty said, rising also and walking with him to the door.

'That won't be for a long while yet, at least a month or so, if not more.'

Kitty nodded. She watched him run into the rain-sodden night and climb into his buggy. With a deep sigh, she closed the door and went upstairs to Mary. 'Has she woken?' she asked Jane.

'No, Mrs Grayson. Shall I make you a meal now?'

'Thank you, that would be greatly welcomed.' She rubbed the back of her neck. 'Thank you, Jane, for taking care of my sister.'

'I wish I could've done more, but he always went for her when I ran errands. It got to the stage where I was frightened to leave her.'

Guilt ravished Kitty. 'Well, he will never touch her again, that is for certain. Are you the only help there is?'

'Yes. He couldn't afford to keep the others on, I only stayed because I had nowhere else to go and I knew someone had to take care of Mrs Ascot. But I haven't been paid for many months.'

Kitty stared, amazed. 'I sent him money.'

'We never saw any of it. I thought something was up though, because once a month, he would disappear to Sydney and not come back for a week or two and then the bills would start arriving and he'd go mad again.'

Kitty sat on the chair by the bed and held Mary's hand. 'I shall sit with her for a while. Then, I'll attend to the bills. Can you find them, please?'

'Very good, Mrs Grayson.'

It was close to midnight by the time she and Jane sorted through the unpaid bills. Ascot owed money to nearly every merchant in the town and many in Sydney too.

By late evening on the second day, Kitty grew restless. She read some but found it hard to concentrate on the words. She drew the curtains and lit the bedside lamp and then paced the floor for lack of anything better to do. She turned at the end of the bed and her heart nearly stopped beating as Mary stared at her through puffy slits.

'Mary!' Kitty dashed to her sister's side.

A single tear squeezed out of one damaged eye. 'Kitty?'

'Yes, dearest, I am here.' Emotion thickened her voice as she kissed her sister's cheek. 'You have nothing to fear, I shall take care of you now.'

'Timothy?' Mary croaked.

'He is gone, dearest. He will never hurt you again.'

'Promise?'

'Yes, I promise.'

Mary relaxed and then frowned. 'You are having a baby?'

Kitty grinned and patted her round stomach. 'Yes.'

'I am...sorry...'

'There is nothing to be sorry for now. Don't worry about it. Would you like a drink or something to eat?'

'A drink.'

Kitty poured a glass of water from the jug on the bedside table and then placed her arm under Mary's shoulders to help her up to drink.

Mary managed to take a few sips. 'My whole body feels sore...'

'It will take some time to heal, pet, but between Jane and myself you will soon be well.' Kitty kissed her forehead. 'Now, I'll go downstairs and tell Jane to make something light for you. I shan't be a minute.'

Jane cried at the news Mary was awake. She set to work making a tea tray. 'Lots of eggs and milk and chicken broth will have her up and about in no time at all.'

'We must not mention Ascot or the police until she is able to cope with such news.'

A knock on the front door prevented any more discussion. Kitty went up the hall and answered it. Her shock could not have been greater if the devil himself stood there. 'Miles!'

He grabbed her elbow roughly and marched her further in with him. 'I want to shake the very breath out of you, you selfish, ungrateful, wilful bitch!'

She gasped and stepped back, his vice-like grip hurting her. 'Miles—'

'Don't speak, don't open your mouth!' He turned as Jane came rushing up the hallway. 'Get out!' he spat at her.

His fury fed Kitty's and she yanked her arm out of his steel grip. 'Enough! Upstairs my sister is recovering from a near-death experience. So, you can damn well show some respect.'

'Respect?' He laughed without humour. 'What about you showing me some respect?' She frowned and he laughed again. 'That confuses you, doesn't it? You have no idea how to respect me, do you?'

'That's a lie!' She indicated for Jane to return to the kitchen and then stared at her husband, whose body virtually shook with suppressed rage. 'I know you must be...annoyed with me Miles.'

'Annoyed?' His cold eyes darkened to near black and his face looked pinched, unreadable. 'Yes, I guess you could say that.'

'I had to leave straight away, please understand.'

'All I understand is that you risk the safety of my child.'

His cruel words hit her between the ribs, crushing all hope that he loved her. His child. That's all that mattered to him.

Unable to answer, too hurt to think clearly, she led Miles into the little sitting room. He took off his traveling coat and threw it on a chair. He looked magnificently male and virile. Kitty ached with love and need. She longed to run into his arms, but that would never happen, not now. She'd been put in her place and was sensible enough to not expect more, but the knowledge hurt more than she could abide.

His narrowed gaze surveyed the bare, uninviting room before roaming over her body. 'Your sister?'

'I believe she is out of danger now.' Kitty wrung her hands, hating this coldness between them. 'She awoke properly just a little while ago.'

He raised a haughty eyebrow. 'What is her illness?'

She crossed her arms in disgust. 'A terrible beating by her husband.'

Miles frowned. 'She was beaten?'

'Yes.'

'Where is Ascot now?'

'I don't know.' She tossed her head. 'He is wanted by the police. He nearly killed her.'

'He will be caught, Kit.'

She nodded.

He picked up his coat and pulled out a small package. 'I brought your mail.' Miles placed it on the small table by the sofa. 'I collected it while waiting in Grafton for a suitable boat heading for Sydney.'

She made no move towards him. His aloofness settled around her heart. 'Thank you.'

A light tap on the door made her turn.

Jane dithered holding the meal tray. 'The tray is ready, Mrs Grayson. Do you want me to take it up?'

'No, Jane, I will do it.' Kitty took the tray from her and over her shoulder looked at Miles. 'Do you wish to come up with me?'

'Very well.'

Miles's face paled at the sight of his sister-in-law. Mary became distressed by his presence in the room, but he smiled and eased his large frame into the chair by the bed. 'Mary, I am Miles,

Kitty's husband. You have nothing to fear from me. In fact, when you are well, I wish for you to come to our home and live with us.'

Mary trembled and peered through her slits at Kitty.

'It is all right, my dearest.' Kitty put down the tray and took Mary's hand and kissed it. 'We are going to take care of you. Eat up now, Jane will be disappointed if you do not.'

Miles nodded. 'Yes, you must eat and get well. Many await your arrival at Blue Water.'

'Blue Water?' Her gaze shifted to Kitty. 'I know nothing of your life now.'

Kitty smoothed the back of Mary's hand. 'Have you received any of my letters?'

Mary shook her head.

'We have plenty of time to fill you in.' Miles rose and left the two sisters.

Kitty joined him downstairs shortly after and he poured them both a glass of red wine from a bottle of at the back of a drink's cabinet. Jane had left them an arrangement of cold meats, bread, pickles and salad in the dining room. Miles carried in their drinks while Kitty went to the sideboard and filled two plates with food.

'Was that the first time Ascot had done such a thing?' he asked, as Kitty placed his plate before him.

'Apparently not, from what Jane tells me.'

'The man should be shot.'

'I agree totally.' She stabbed at the slice of ham on her plate.

'I wish you had waited for me, Kit.' Miles muttered. 'Where is Leah?'

'Sick. She is at Forbes Street.'

He pushed his plate away untouched. 'I nearly died of heart failure at the news you had gone.'

She studied her glass of wine. 'I had no time. Did Connie not show you the telegram?'

'Yes, she did. Still, a woman with child traveling the country by herself is totally abominable. Anything could have happened.'

'My sister needed me.'

'You should have put the child first!'

'I was never in danger, Miles. For heaven's sake, some women work right up to the time of birth. Women are stronger than you realize.'

He slammed his fist onto the table. 'Not you! You have already lost one!'

Kitty raised her chin, biting back the stinging words she longed to throw at him, but knew he spoke the truth. 'I promise you, the child was never in danger.'

'It was in danger the minute you were away from Blue Water!'

She glared at him, hating him for only wanting the child and not her. Oh, he wanted her body, she knew that, but it was not enough. She loathed it when they argued, but she was determined not to let him rule her. His bearing and superior manner could easily crush her spirit. If she must fight him for the rest of their lives she would, but never would she change. It simply wasn't in her nature to do so.

Miles took a sip of wine. 'I cannot stay too long. There is a lot I need to attend to at Blue Water. I will stop over in Sydney on my way back to see to other business matters too.'

'I understand.' Kitty nodded, though it was like someone had put a knife through her heart. Their relationship was sinking fast.

'You will stay here with Mary for some time?' Miles's tone was distant.

She shifted her food around with her fork. 'Yes, until she is well enough to travel. Naturally, I am not sure when that will be. A month or so.'

'Nothing I could say will change your mind to come home, will it?'

'No. I'm sorry, but she needs me.'

He nodded.

Tears burnt her throat and she pushed back her chair and stood. 'I must get back to Mary.'

Miles rose. 'If I hurry, I can take the last coach back to Moss Vale. I'll leave money on the table for your expenses.'

'Thank you.' She left the table and hurried from the room.

Later, in the early hours of the morning, Kitty couldn't sleep, her mind and heart full of Miles. Wrapping a blanket around her, she sat in bed and read the letters he brought her. The first one was from York. It informed her that four months ago, Dorothea Cannon died in her sleep. The other letters fell slowly to the floor.

Chapter Sixteen

Three yellow-tailed black cockatoos flew high overhead outlined against the clear blue cloudless sky. Their eerie screeching rent the air, shattering the quietness of the glorious day. Kitty and Mary sat in wicker chairs in the back garden of the house under the shade of a large, weeping willow tree. Jane poured them a cup of tea each, while encouraging them to try her ginger biscuits fresh from the oven. It was Mary's first venture outside since her beating three weeks ago. Her bruising had diminished in ferocity, leaving yellowy-green shadows around her face and other parts of her body. Her ribs, though still sore, began mending and the puffiness left her eyes except for a little tenderness and blackness underneath.

A small brown and orange butterfly fluttered over the newspaper Kitty read and she made a comment to Mary about it. Mary smiled, however, her eyes held a faraway look. Kitty frowned. Mary had reverted back to the shy and quiet sister she was before meeting Gina and Timothy Ascot. She took no interest in anything and spent every day in near silence.

Kitty did her best to keep their conversations light and entertaining, but it wasn't easy. Jane spent nearly all her time cooking and baking delightful tasty treats to tempt Mary's appetite. Nevertheless, Mary remained reed thin.

'There is a show on tonight, a traveling theatre production. They are performing Shakespeare's A Midsummer Night's Dream.' Kitty grinned over the rim of the newspaper. 'Shall we go and see it?'

'As if I'm able, Kitty, with my face.' Mary lowered her head.

'We could put powder on it and with a low hat and veil no one will see anything at all. Besides, it will be dark. Oh, say yes, Mary. We both need a little entertainment.'

'No, I don't think so.'

Kitty sighed and tried to concentrate on the newspaper. The baby kicked and she rubbed the spot.

Mary leant forward. 'Is something wrong?'

Kitty smiled. 'No, just the baby kicking. He is especially active at the moment.'

Something died in Mary's eyes as she stared at Kitty's stomach. 'My baby would have been a few weeks old by now.'

Kitty's eyes widened. 'Your baby?'

'I lost it.'

'Dearest...' She reached out a hand to her.

Mary looked away, her voice a mere whisper. 'I suppose babies cannot be hit even in their mother's body.'

'He hit you when you were—'

'Yes, why should that stop him?' Mary shrugged.

She tossed the newspaper aside. 'You should have written to me. You should have left him!'

'Why? So that you could say I told you so?'

Kitty jerked, shocked. 'As if I would say that. You know me better, Mary. Indeed, you have hurt me saying such an awful thing. Am I such an ogre?'

'I'm sorry.' Mary grasped Kitty's hand. 'I know you would have received me. Only, I was ashamed.'

'Well, the important thing is we are together now and always will be.'

A tear slipped over Mary's lashes and trickled down her cheek. 'Can we leave here? I am tired of this house and the memories it holds.'

'That is a splendid idea. Do you feel well enough to leave to-morrow?'

'Yes, tomorrow.'

'Very well, let us begin to pack. We will break our journey in Sydney and stay at Forbes Street. Who knows? Maybe Martin is in dock.' Kitty grinned, pleased to see a small sparkle back in Mary's eyes.

By nightfall, the three women were tired, but happy. White dustsheets covered the furniture and all the window coverings were drawn. Jane had booked the tickets for the morning coach and then spent the rest of the day cooking the last remaining food to either be eaten themselves or taken and given to the poorer families in the nearby streets. A youth who lived next door was hired for the afternoon to carry the heavy trunks downstairs and do other odd jobs Kitty found necessary. There were few valu-ables in the house to be packed away and so their task of leaving was simple.

Jane was to accompany them to Sydney, where she would have a better chance to find employment. She was to live at Forbes Street until she found her own rooms. With two very good ref-erences, from Kitty and Mary, she would be in a good position to begin a new life.

'Do you feel tired, dearest?' Kitty asked entering her sister's bedroom, wearing her nightgown and a fine white-laced shawl.

Mary sat in bed brushing her long black hair. 'Yes, I am, though very relieved to be leaving in the morning.'

'Sleep the best you can, for tomorrow will be a long day.' Kitty kissed her cheek.

Mary hugged her. 'Thank you for everything.'

'Fiddlesticks. You have no need to thank me. I am your sister, and this is what sisters do for each other.'

A loud bang from downstairs echoed around the house.

'What is that?' Mary whispered, her eyes wide in her pale bruised face.

'I'm not sure...' Kitty left the bedroom and went onto the landing. The banging started again on the front door and someone shouted. Jane, dressed in her nightwear, crept up the hallway.

'Jane, don't open the door, just ask what the person wants.' Kitty stepped down the staircase.

Jane stopped and called, 'Who is there?'

The thumping stopped. 'Listen to me, you silly wench. Open this door at once!'

Wide-eyed, Jane turned to Kitty who stood on the last step. 'Oh, my Lord. It's him, he's back!'

A tingle of fear trickled down Kitty's spine. She pulled Jane away from the door. 'I will let you out of the back door. You must run for the police and then Doctor Blewitt, understand?'

Jane nodded.

The thumping on the door began again. 'Let me in!'

'Go away, Ascot,' Kitty shouted. 'You are not wanted here.'

There was a pause and then Ascot laughed. 'Is that the lovely Mrs Grayson? My, my.'

'Leave us.'

'It is my house!'

'No, I believe it is the bank's now.'

'You soulless witch!'

Kitty ignored him as he yelled abuse and banged again. She and Jane stole down the hallway to the kitchen and through into the scullery.

'Go carefully, Jane.' Kitty pulled back the bolt and opened the heavy door enough for Jane to slip through. The pitch-black night greeted them. Her heart thudded as Jane disappeared into the darkness.

With shaking hands, Kitty closed the door. Abruptly it was wrenched out of her grasp and flung against the wall. She stumbled back and stared in horror at Timothy Ascot.

'Not very smart.' He advanced into the scullery.

Kitty turned and fled. She reached the kitchen table before he grabbed her hair and wrenched her head back. She yelled and twisted in his grasp.

He wrapped her long hair around his fist so tightly she screamed. 'Now, my beauty, let us understand each other,' he sneered into her face. 'You and your pathetic bitch of a sister are going to do exactly what I say, do I make myself clear?'

'Let me go,' Kitty cried in frustration. The pain was excruciating, but her temper rose.

Ascot flung her away from him with a force that sent her toppling to her knees.

Kitty pulled herself up by holding on to the table and turned to face him. A red mist of anger made her tremble. 'You are stupider than I thought. Imagine returning to the place of crime.'

'I shan't be here long. I need to get a few things I unfortunately left behind.'

'I understand running away from the police, after nearly killing your wife, would make you forget certain belongings.' Disgust filled her. She was ready to pounce on him and tear his eyes out.

'So, she lived?' Ascot snickered.

'Longer than you will.'

'Really? I doubt it.' He looked around the kitchen unconcerned. 'Now, where's that wench, Jane? I want something to eat while I retrieve my belongings.'

Kitty gripped the table edge. 'Jane is not here.'

Ascot advanced, his fist raised. 'Where is she? I heard her before.'

'She is bringing the constable,' Kitty gloated.

Confusion checked him. 'I thought you were the one going?'

'No, you were too late. I was merely letting Jane out, not going myself.'

'You bitch!' Ascot's fist flashed out and hit her jaw with such power she catapulted across the room and landed on the floor by the cooking range. Dazed, she cowered into a ball as he stepped closer and lifted his foot, ready to kick her.

Movement at the door caused Ascot to spin around. He faced his wife.

'You are not going to hurt anyone anymore.' Mary stood by the doorway, showing no emotion.

'Shut up!'

Mary moved further into the room, closer to the large Welsh dresser lining one wall.

'Why didn't you just die when you had the chance?' he scorned. 'You are so pathetic. Is there nothing you can do well?'

'I can certainly pick no-good husbands.'

'Well, you would never have had me if I had known the truth about you. I only married you because I thought there was money. Wasn't I fooled?'

'I never gave you cause to think I was wealthy.' Mary seemed totally uninterested.

'You never told me otherwise either.'

A sudden thumping came at the front door and the constable called out.

Ascot looked at the scullery.

Mary pointed to the easy escape. 'You run now, and you will be doing it all your life.'

'Shut up.' He scratched his head in panic. 'There are documents in the bureau in the sitting room.'

Mary stared at him with cold eyes. 'Deeds? All your inheritance? They are gone. All gone to pay what you owe.'

'Liar.' He crept towards Mary.

In a clamour of noise and confusion, two policemen burst into the kitchen from the scullery. They skidded to a halt at the sight of Ascot advancing towards Mary.

'Stop right there!' One constable pointed his pistol directly at Ascot's chest.

'I haven't done anything!' He ran for the hallway.

A single shot rang out and Ascot stumbled and fell against Mary as he slid to the floor. A gaping wound wept blood from between his shoulder blades. Within seconds, the house filled with police officers, as well as Doctor Blewitt, Jane and nearby neighbours.

Kitty heaved herself up from the floor and staggered to Mary leaning against the dresser. As Kitty went to hold her, a strip of steel winked within the folds of her skirts. Without taking her gaze off her dead husband, Mary carefully replaced the long-bladed knife into the drawer.

Chapter Seventeen

Kitty knew that for as long as she lived, she would never be used to traveling long journeys through the wild and in-hospitable Australian bush. Even though the carriage seat was leather padded, she ached in every part of her body. She looked across at Mary and Leah. They slept lightly, their heads swaying in rhythm with the rumbling carriage.

Kitty gazed out the window at the passing bush. The unique, sharp scent of the eucalyptus trees filled her nostrils and she breathed in deeply. Out here in the middle of nowhere, the scent was headier than in the cities. Native birds sent out their calls, the laughing kookaburras, the black and white magpies and the mocking lyre birds all sang as though to greet her.

They journeyed through rain forest that edged Miles's property and she sighed in wonder, as she always did, at the sheer height of the magnificent hardwood trees and the green tropical palms and ferns. They crossed the last creek bed by way of a small wooden bridge built by Miles's men and were at last on the well-constructed road winding through the cultivated fields of wheat, barley and hay. Workmen and women toiled to bring in harvest.

She couldn't believe the excitement building inside her, even the baby turned in her womb as though picking up on her anticipation. How she had missed Blue Water in the two months she had been away.

She and Mary had spent a month in Sydney relaxing with Martin, Joe, Clara and the Freemans until Connie's note arrived telling her to return home. Miles had not written to her since his hasty departure from Goulburn and he knew nothing of Ascot's assault.

At first, Kitty didn't want to leave Sydney. She didn't want to live with a man who possessed no deep feelings for her. However, and unfortunately, her heart missed him. Her body missed sleeping beside him and her soul craved his smile. She needed to try harder to win his love and never being one to turn away from a challenge, she left Sydney determined to make her marriage work.

Closer to the house, the drive wound its way through the worker's cottages. Kitty smiled and waved to the workers they passed. Their good wishes warmed her, and she grinned at Mary and Leah who awoke at the noise. Her heart raced as the carriage rocked to a stop in front of the veranda steps. An adoring sigh escaped as she looked at the large beautiful house. She was home.

Mrs Morris rushed out onto the steps, clapping her hands in pleasure. 'Oh my, Mrs Grayson, it is so good to have you back.'

'I hope you are well, Mrs Morris.' Kitty looked beyond the housekeeper for Miles, but he wasn't there. She stepped down and turned to assist Mary. 'Please let me introduce you to my sister, Mrs Ascot.' Kitty linked her hand in Mary's arm. 'Mary, this is Blue Water's wonderful housekeeper, Mrs Morris.'

A squeal erupted to the side of them as the children hurtled through the gardens and into Kitty's arms. 'My darlings, I have missed you.' She kissed the three of them a dozen times.

'We missed you,' Charles told her, with Adelaide and Little Rory chiming in.

'Well, 'tis about time an' all.' Connie stood at the edge of the drive with her hands on her hips. 'I never thought you were comin' home.'

Kitty grinned. 'Dearest Connie.' She hurried to hug her friend.

Connie squeezed her tight. 'Don't you ever leave me again, understand?' she whispered into Kitty's ear.

She nodded. 'Now come and see Mary. She needs you.'

Tears brimmed in Kitty's eyes as Connie walked over to Mary, paused and then pulled her into her arms.

Kitty took Little Rory's hand and addressed Mrs Morris. 'Is Mr Grayson close by?'

'Er...no, madam. He's...out riding at the minute. Er...Miss Feldon is visiting.' Mrs Morris avoided looking at her by studying her boots.

Serena is here. Kitty's happiness at being home plummeted. 'Thank you, Mrs Morris. Could you arrange for our luggage to be taken up?'

'Certainly, madam, and would you like a refreshing cup of tea?'

'Yes, out on the back veranda would be lovely.' Kitty left the others and hurried upstairs, her stomach churning at the thought of meeting Miles again.

In the bedroom, she took off her gloves and little black felt hat. On arriving at Grafton, she had used a room at an inn to change into a beautiful maternity frock that flowed out from under the bust in the shade of grape with the neckline embroidered in black ribbon. She had wanted to look fresh and attractive for Miles, but it was all for nothing. Serena ruined it all.

Downstairs once more, Kitty sat on the veranda and sipped tea waiting for Connie and Mary to join her. Sounds from further along the garden caught her attention. Laughter reached her, feminine laughter, high and sweet. Kitty shrivelled and died inside. They strolled closer, Serena in a silk pastel pink gown and Miles smiling indulgently at her. Neither of them wore riding clothes.

Connie and Mary arrived and sat at the table. 'By, lass, that tea looks grand, don't it our Mary?'

Kitty didn't comment, causing Connie to turn and stare too. Connie swore violently as Miles and Serena laughed walking through the rose beds.

Eventually Miles glanced up at the house and stopped. He stared at Kitty for a long time before he strode towards her. Beside him, Serena lifted her skirts and ran to keep up.

'Kit.' It was all he said, but it was enough to make Kitty die for him. She was unable to reply as Serena asked questions at a rapid rate.

'What a surprise! Are we not surprised, Miles?' Serena pouted. 'When did you arrive? How well you look, Kitty. Being with child suits you, and that colour. Why plum is so obliging when one is your size.'

Connie glared at her before patting Miles's hand. 'Now then, Miles, isn't it grand ter 'ave our lass and Mary home?'

He smiled, finally taking his eyes off Kitty. 'I am very pleased. How are you, Mary?'

'Well, thank you,' answered Mary quietly.

Kitty seethed. It was bad enough Serena was present but for him to only say he was very pleased irritated her. Had he missed her, or did Miss Wonderful Serena comfort him? Her heart ached. She rose and noticed that Miles's eyes widened at the size of her stomach, which had been partly hidden under the table. 'I wish to lie down for a while.'

'I think I will also.' Mary joined her and they went inside.

Miles looked desperately at Connie. 'Is she all right?'

'Nay, lad,' Connie said, using the tender term for they had been alone and getting to know one another for weeks. 'I don't know what ter say ter you.' She glanced at Serena. 'I want ter speak in private please.'

Serena's look was full of loathing. 'Very well. Excuse me.'

Connie waited until she had left and turned on him. 'Why in blue blazes did you have ter let her stay 'ere?'

'Who? Serena?'

'My God. All men must be daft. Kitty'll never accept her cos she knows Serena wants you.'

'Not this again?' Miles erupted. 'I have told Kitty this kind of thinking is nonsense.'

'Don't get all tetchy with me, my lad. Do you want ter be with our lass or not? Cos she'll be back in Sydney before you know it. Her an' the babby. I only just got her to come back as it is.'

'All right, all right.' Miles sighed and ran his fingers through his steel- grey hair.

'She loves you, Miles. Show her that you love her too.'

'Are you sure she does though? I'm just security to her.'

Connie shook her head in frustration at such foolishness. 'Show her that you love her,' she said slowly, looking earnestly into his doubtful silver eyes.

'I will try.' Miles rubbed his hand wearily over his face.

'An' get rid of Miss Slimy Feldon.'

'Connie! She is still my family.'

'Aye, an' Kitty's you wife.'

ele

As the days and weeks went by, Kitty made a determined effort to become closer to Miles. She wanted her marriage to be a success. She'd been partners with failure for too long. Being home at Blue Water settled her spirit and renewed her hope that her life and that of her siblings would be better from now on.

She took long walks with the children and Mary around the property. They went to see the baby farm animals and helped to feed the pigs and chickens. They visited the wives of the workmen and spent hours down by the river looking for wildflowers and wombat burrows.

Kitty was due to deliver her baby any day, but that didn't stop her visiting Alice and Jessup and their new baby. She drove a small gig by herself over the rough track towards their property. The pleasant drive in the fresh autumn air lifted her spirits. The sun shone brightly but was not too hot. After an hour, Kitty arrived.

Jessup had proven himself, and with the help of Holby and Miles's men, he now had two new barns, a larger cottage, plus more pigpens, a bigger vegetable garden and even a well. The milking cow had been joined by another, and the entire beef herd had doubled.

Kitty called to the two men, who stood in the middle of the pigpen. They quickly jumped the low fence and hurried to her. They virtually carried her off the gig such was their concern.

'Lord, Mrs Kitty. I'd thought we'd seen the last of you for a while.' Jessup laughed.

'Oh, the children have a slight cold and Connie told me I was not to take them wandering around the property today.' Kitty grinned. 'I was a little restless, so I thought I would come and pester you all.'

'Miss Kitty!' Alice called from in front of her cottage. She wiped her hands on her white apron. Her hair was put up in a haphazard way and on closer inspection she had flour smudged on her nose. Kitty embraced her and they went into the cottage.

Baby Paul lay awake in his wooden cradle, waving his small fists in the air. Kitty immediately picked him up. 'Have you been good for your dear mother, my precious?'

'Sit down, please. I honestly didn't think you'd be back for a long time.' Alice set out her best tea service. 'I thought I would see you next when I came to Blue Water to visit the new addition.'

'Oh, I think this baby is never coming. It is quite happy where he is. Though, I believe I will never walk straight again. My back aches something terrible.'

Alice chuckled. 'I know exactly what you mean.'

They talked and laughed for the next hour, and then went to put the fresh flowers Kitty had picked from the extensive gardens at Blue Water on Rosie's grave.

For a while, she stood by the little girl's grave. She missed her darling Rosie and hoped she was at peace with their mother and father, little Davina, Max and Ben.

Kitty sighed. She had not thought of Ben for some time and was thankful she could do so now without pain.

'Would you like to come in for another cup of tea, Mrs Kitty?' Alice murmured.

'No, thank you, Alice. I'd best head back. If I don't make a start now, you may have a lodger for the night.' She grinned as she rubbed her aching back.

She bade them all good day and drove the gig back out onto the bush track. Her bones seemed to ache, and the gig's seat became awfully uncomfortable. Towards halfway home, the twinges in her back grew steadily worse. At one point along the track, Kitty drew rein and shakily climbed down. She walked a few paces bent double when a sharp pain stabbed her in the back. She moaned.

The horse whinnied and sidestepped in fear. Another pain rendered Kitty to her knees. Her cry echoed around the treetops and ricocheted back to her. She knelt on the ground and breathed deeply.

With a shuddering breath, Kitty pulled herself up into the gig. Slapping the reins, she urged the little mare to go faster. Only, the jarring hurt so much she cried.

After a short way, she pulled the mare back to a walk and gritted her teeth as another pain ripped at her. In a daze, she allowed the mare to take her home. Sweat poured from her body and soaked her clothes. Her moans grew louder. She glanced up when the mare stopped.

'Mrs Grayson? Mrs Grayson, are you hurt?'

Kitty tried desperately to focus on the man speaking to her, but another pain struck, and she groaned deep within her chest.

'I'm Wilf Daniels, a stockman.' His old weather-beaten face hovered before her. She blinked as his image wavered. 'Mrs Grayson, is the baby coming?'

'M...Miles...the baby...'

Wilf Daniels climbed onto the gig, squashing Kitty in his haste. He took up the reins and sent the mare into a wild gallop.

'Stop! Stop,' she cried. The shaking nearly made her swoon.

'I've got to get you back, Mrs Grayson.' He urged the poor mare on.

Kitty gripped the sides as she swayed to and fro with the rolling gig. She clenched her teeth and closed her eyes, trying not to cry. The mad dash slowed somewhat when they reached the house drive. Wilf's frantic calling brought many from what they were doing to clamber about the small gig. Everyone uttered an opinion on what was best to do, but nobody actually did anything. A bellow made them all turn and run at Miles.

He pushed his way through the crowd to Kitty's side just as another pain wrenched at her body. She cried out as Miles reached for her. His roar for help and the doctor lifted the fine hair on the back of her neck.

'Kit, my darling, I've got you now. It will be all right,' he murmured, holding her dead weight close to his chest.

Wetness on her thighs caused her to look down, a dark red stain seeped through her skirts. 'Miles!' She gripped his shirtfront. 'It cannot happen again. I won't lose another one!'

'You won't, sweetheart, I promise.'

Doctor Saunders pushed his way through the crowd to them. 'Miles, get her into the house.'

Miles mounted the staircase, yelling for Mrs Morris and Connie, both of whom came running and followed him into the bedroom.

Connie and Mrs Morris undressed her before Dr Saunders examined her. Resting back against the pillows, Kitty gazed at Miles as he wiped the sweat off her forehead with his handkerchief and murmured endearments.

The doctor and Mrs Morris with Connie, Mary's and Lena's help worked hard for the next ten hours. Their efforts, however, did not help Kitty's progress. She fought to be brave and held Miles's hand tightly. As the sun went down, Connie lit lamps and candles.

Miles flatly refused to leave the room when ordered to by Saunders and any attempt to dislodge him from her side led to violent arguments, but eventually he was pushed out the door by Connie. She told Kitty he was pacing the pattern off the carpet outside the bedroom.

By early morning, Kitty was so exhausted she wept softly. The pain was too much and too long. She read the anxiety on the doctor's face and knew the labour was not going well. She turned her head slightly to stare at Connie. 'Fetch Miles, Connie.'

'Nay, lass.'

'I mean it. I want to speak to him.'

With a glance at the doctor who nodded, Connie hurried to the door and beckoned for Miles, who entered hesitantly, his face pale with fatigue.

Kitty smiled and lifted her hand, and in a leap, he was beside the bed kneeling, kissing her hand.

'Do you suffer greatly?'

She raised her eyebrows but shook her head. 'Not too much.'

'Liar.' He rose to kiss her forehead.

Her love for this hard man at her side filled her heart. 'Miles?'

'Yes, darling?'

'Tell Saunders to save the baby, not me.'

'Never,' Miles croaked.

'Listen to me.' Kitty grasped his hand. 'The baby comes first. He is your son. You can always have another wife, but maybe not a child.'

'I shall not listen to another word, Kit.'

She closed her eyes and held her breath while another pain descended.

Dr Saunders patted her leg to get her attention. 'Mrs Grayson, I want you to breathe through this and when you get the urge to push, tell me.'

'I do not need...to...push!' Kitty panted. Swiftly everything changed. She arched her back and cried out. Miles reeled backwards in shock.

'Do you need to push, Mrs Grayson?' Saunders asked.

'Yeeesss!' Kitty strained and her grip on Miles's hand drew blood. She pushed hard, wanting to cry at the agonizing pain that ripped her insides.

The moment passed and she rested. She yearned to close her eyes and sleep. Miles stroked her hand and it annoyed her as too quickly another pain grew. Kitty groaned as she pushed again.

'You need to leave, Miles,' Saunders murmured, not really caring as he gave full attention the business end of the bed.

Miles kissed her hot cheek. 'I am sorry, Kit. I will never let you go through this again. I promise you.'

As he took a step away, she gripped his hand for dear life just as the baby's head emerged and its cry shattered the room.

'Steady, now,' Saunders cautioned.

Kitty's body took control and sent the child slithering into the world.

'You have done it. Kit, the baby is here!' Miles wiped the tears from his eyes and kissed the top of Kitty's head.

'Is he all right?' Kitty, trembling and exhausted, leant back against the pillows.

'Yes, he is perfect,' Dr Saunders raised his voice above the cries of the baby, 'and he has a pair of lungs on him too.'

Connie washed him and then wrapped him in a soft woollen blanket. She placed him gently into Kitty's arms. 'Baby Grayson is a good size.' She grinned.

'Look at him.' Kitty gazed in weary amazement at the little body she brought into the world. He was the very image of his father and she loved him immediately.

'He is a miracle, just like his mother,' Miles whispered, touching a fingertip to his son's soft cheek.

Kitty glanced over to the doctor who still messed about down the end of the bed.

He looked up and winked. 'Not all the work is over, my dear.'

She groaned. 'Miles, take the baby. My arms are shaky.' Miles took him from her quickly and held him close.

'So, what's his name then?' Connie asked, taking a clean night-gown from the drawer.

Kitty looked at Miles, her heart full of love. 'That is Miles's choice. I have done my bit.' Tiredness swept over her.

'Adam Gabriel Grayson,' Miles said without hesitation, smiling at his newborn son.

Connie came over to him and kissed the baby on his soft downy head. 'Welcome then, Adam Gabriel Grayson.'

Chapter Eighteen

Kitty pushed the perambulator down the gravel path between the garden beds and smiled at her sleeping baby son. He was all of two weeks old, and a major source of excitement to everyone at Blue Water. She waved to the head gardener as he passed with his wheelbarrow. She knew many were surprised by her early appearance but staying in bed for more than three days had frustrated her.

She steered down the drive and smiled at the workmen's greetings, pleased to have brought happiness to the station. An heir to Blue Water and another generation to ensure its continuity delighted everyone. The celebrations lasted for two days. Miles had corked a barrel of ale for his men and the women cooked up a feast fit for a king. Kitty heard that blessings to the new Grayson were toasted with every lift of a glass or jug.

It was a perfect day of sweet fresh air and sunshine. She raised her face to feel the sun's morning warmth. She felt, maybe for the first time in her life, an inner peace. Her relationship with

Miles had altered somewhat for the better. He was gentle and attentive towards her and even though she needed his love, she was sure she could live without it, if they continued to have this new closeness as it was better than nothing.

He worshipped their son, but he still held himself back from her and this puzzled and hurt her. She had to summon the courage to hope that one day he would feel more than just concern and friendship.

'Good morning, Mrs Grayson'

Kitty looked up as she neared the steps of the veranda. 'Good morning, Mr Downs.' She smiled at her husband's station manager as he doffed his hat.

'Would you know where Mr Grayson is likely to be at present?'

'Well, no. My husband is gone by sunlight and I rarely see him before noon. Is it urgent?'

Mr Downs carried the perambulator up the stone steps for her. 'No, not really. Only the new man we hired is proving to be difficult. I think we should give him the heave-ho.' Downs bent to peek at the baby.

Adam made grizzly noises and Kitty rocked the baby carriage. 'What trouble is this fellow causing?'

'Oh, he's acting the big shot and is making a name for himself. He talks like a gent but is as scruffy as a beggar.'

This description caused Kitty to look up at Downs for it was close to what Bess White had said a couple of years ago. For some reason, she shivered despite the day's warmth. 'What is this man's name?'

'John Smith. Well, I better be off about me duties.' He replaced his hat. 'Good day to you, Mrs Grayson.'

Kitty took the baby inside. She sat with him in the drawing room, and within a few minutes, was joined by Connie.

'Mary's got the bairns playin' happily, so I thought I'd escape for a minute ter see how little'un is doin'.'

'He is fine.' She frowned and looked out the window.

'What's up, lass?'

'There is a new worker who is causing trouble amongst the men, apparently. Mr Downs said he is well-spoken but scruffy looking.'

'Aye, so?'

Kitty blushed. 'Well, I instantly thought of Rory.'

'Nay, don't be daft. Besides, wouldn't Miles tell you if a fellow came 'ere with the name Rory McKenzie?' Connie scoffed.

'This man goes by the name of John Smith.'

'Listen, lass. This colony is full of misplaced people. Thousands of bodies are 'ere lookin' ter escape their pasts, not just Rory.'

Kitty nibbled her bottom lip. 'I have placed so many advertisements in nearly all the papers around the country. I just wished I knew where he was.'

'Lass, he could've gone elsewhere be now. He might have gone ter the Americas for all we know.'

She nodded and gazed down at her son with a great weight about her heart. Yet, something niggled away at her.

Later, Kitty left Adam with Leah and strolled to the farm buildings situated a mile down the drive. The area was large, for it was here all the work was done to keep Blue Water running smoothly and profitably. Before the farm buildings, the cottages for the married couples lined the road, but Kitty merely smiled and waved to the workers' wives and walked on. She had no wish to linger at the moment. Instinct urged her on.

The main farm buildings contained their own yards, and here too, were the sleeping quarters for single men. Interlocking storage barns, equipment sheds and holding yards surrounded the mill, dairy, shearing shed, piggery and stables. It was a place of activity, noise and smells. Men shouted, whistled, cursed and laughed while going about their hot and dirty hard work. The aromas of leather, hay and grains, horses, cows, sheep and pigs, dust, manure and sweat all mixed together in the hot sun.

She didn't know why she came down here to search the men's faces, but some nagging unease kept taunting her.

Kitty skirted the dairy yard, empty of beasts until the evening when they were brought in from the lush green fields especially cultivated for the herd. She hesitated only for a fraction and then headed for the single men's sleeping quarters. Thankfully, Miles was away from the house due to some water crisis in another part of the property. She knew he would be displeased with her being amongst the men.

Kitty rounded the corner of a long timber building. Ahead a cloud of dust rose, and a crash of wood splintering halted her. A group of men crowded into a circle, yelling and shouting. Rushing to them, she pulled at their arms and wedged herself through them to get a better view.

In the centre, dust flew so thickly it obscured her sight. Two men fighting hurled her way and thumped into her with such force Kitty fell and landed with a thump on her bottom.

'My God, Mrs Grayson?' The men closest to her suddenly realized their mistress was in the middle of the mayhem and their faces paled. There'd be serious trouble now.

'What the hell?' One of the fighters stared incredulously at Kitty, while the other bent to retrieve his fallen hat out of the dust.

'What is the meaning of this?' Kitty flung away the helping hands and dusted off her skirts. 'My husband will not tolerate this kind of behaviour at Blue Water.'

'Sorry, Mrs Grayson.' A bystander slid away and disappeared into a building. Others soon followed him.

She raised her chin. 'What started this?'

An older workman shifted his weight from one foot to another. 'Er, well, you see...this is nowt but a bit of fun.'

'Nonsense. These two men were trying to kill each other.' Kitty stared at the group. 'Get about your business the lot of you while I deal with this matter.'

She waited until the crowd dispersed and then glared at the two fighters, though only one looked at her, the other had his back turned which incensed her. 'You there? At least have the decency to look at me when I address you!'

Slowly, the tall man turned to look at her. His blond hair fell over his eyes, but not before Kitty saw the blueness of them. Her knees went weak and she swayed in shock. 'Rory?' Were her eyes playing tricks?

His eyes widened before he lowered his head.

She blinked, not believing it could be true. 'I-I cannot...believe it. Is it really you?'

He wiped his sleeve across his filthy face. 'I am afraid so, dear sister.'

'I have looked for you everywhere.'

'Now you have found me.' Rory grimaced, his face hard and unyielding, his eyes cold.

She waved away the other fighter and once alone, she humbled herself. 'Are you not pleased to see me?'

Rory slapped his hat against his leg and swung away.

'Rory?'

He paused but did not turn around. 'I have to go, Kitty. It is better this way.'

'No!' Kitty ran after him and swung him around to face her. 'You cannot leave now. I have only just found you. We can be together again for always now.'

Rory finally looked deep into her eyes. 'Are you married to Grayson?'

'Yes, I am.'

'Then our lives are vastly different. I no longer have a family, I haven't since that day in the cellar.' The words were said casually, but Kitty heard the unspoken pain behind them.

'Yes, you do.' Her throat clogged with tears. 'You have more than you realise.'

'Don't remind me, Kitty. A man can only take so much shame.' Rory walked away.

His retreating back and slumped shoulders reminded her of his cowardice. Fury and love waged a war inside her. She took one step. 'Don't you dare walk away from me again! You have a son. Are you walking away from him too, just like you walked out on us?'

Rory paused mid-step. Slowly, he turned around. 'What do you mean, a son?'

'Mrs White, do you remember her? She found out who I was and left a baby on our doorstep. She said you had got her daughter with child. Her daughter died. So, I took him in. I have no doubt she is speaking the truth, for he is the image of you. He is a McKenzie.'

'She died?'

'The mother? Yes.'

'I tried not to think about her. I had hoped she would have married and raised the child with someone else. I...I simply couldn't stay...'

'I will not let you run away anymore, Rory. You call yourself a man, well, it is time you began acting like one.'

'Running away is what I am good at. I've been doing it long enough.'

'Do you think it has been easy for me? You don't have the monopoly on living a harsh life. We all suffer at times.'

'Look at you in your fine clothes.' He sneered. 'You know nothing.'

She laughed without humour. 'I know what it is like to be poor, to be hungry and to be so down in spirit I thought I would die.' She tossed her head and swallowed her tears. 'I wanted to run away too, but I did not.'

He flung his arms wide in a savage gesture. 'Do not lecture me, Kitty. You have no idea what the last few years have been like for me. I have been reduced to living like a dog, begging for scraps, for somewhere to sleep—'

'I don't know what you went through. However, you will tell me about it later. Right now, you need to bathe and change your clothes. Then, you shall meet your son.'

Rory's gaze darted around as though looking for an escape. 'No, Kitty. I-I cannot do it.'

'I told you, Rory, the time for running has come to an end. Be a man and face your responsibilities. It's not hard to do, I've learnt to.' Kitty stared defiantly at him, then allowed her face to change and show her love. 'I have missed you, brother.'

Rory's face crumbled and tears trickled slowly down his face leaving streaky dirt marks. Kitty opened her arms. At long last, she hugged her beloved Rory.

The joyous noise of children's laughter floated on the cool breeze. Every now and then, an adult called, reminding the children not to go too close to the edge of the riverbank.

Miles smiled. The sound of his wife's voice always brought a smile to his face and worship to his heart. He had tried to show his love and she welcomed his presence, but not once did she open her heart to him. Rory's appearance had begun to lay her ghosts to rest, but he wondered whether she would ever rid her heart of Benjamin Kingsley.

He wandered along the path between the garden beds towards the river and the group of people he had come to love nearly as much as his wife. Through the tall silver gum trees lining the water, young Charles dashed away from his sister who was doing her best to catch him.

On a blanket surrounded by food sat Rory, Mary and Connie all watching the antics of the three active children. Rory and Kitty had talked about the years apart. They had laughed and cried as a family, and got to know one another again, especially Rory and his son. They visited Rosie's grave and any day now, they expected Joe and Clara's arrival. Mary too, was slowly coming out of the shyness that consumed her. The effects of her dreadful marriage with Timothy Ascot were receding a little.

Miles crossed the lawn and spotted Kitty in the shade. She stood and put their son in his perambulator. Tenderly, she covered the carriage with a fine lace shawl to keep the flies from him while he slept. It pleased Miles to observe his beautiful Kit glowing with contentment.

Since Adam's birth they had slept in the same bed without touching and he ached to hold her.

She was now surrounded by her family. Did that complete her? Does she have room in her heart for me?

'There you are, Miles! Come an' have a bite ter eat,' Connie ordered, causing everyone to turn to look at him.

'I will, Connie, in a minute.' Miles went and gazed at his son.

Kitty fiddled with the lace cover. 'Have you finished your business for today?'

'Yes.'

'Adam has been awake for quite a while. You missed him, for he will sleep now a good few hours.' She sat on the blanket with the others.

While Miles ate the plate of food Mary handed to him, he listened to them talk.

Abruptly, Rory jumped up from the blanket and faced them. 'I have been doing a lot of thinking, Kitty.'

'Oh?' She smiled at him, her emerald eyes shining with love.

Miles, knowing what was coming, groaned inside. Kit wouldn't be pleased to hear Rory's words.

Rory cleared his throat. 'I have decided to return to Sydney and go into business. I have the opportunity to finish with my wandering ways. It is time I accepted responsibility for my own life.'

'P-pardon?' Kitty frowned, bewildered.

Rory flushed. 'I need to make something of my life, and Miles has offered to help. We are going to be partners.'

Kitty's face paled. She stared at her brother in a way Miles knew was not good. 'Doing what exactly?'

'I wish to open a small shop, along the lines of a general store. Miles said he would help me.'

'You both discussed this without informing me, without including me?' She jerked to her feet, her eyes flashing, and Miles groaned. 'Did you not think I might like to be included?' An angry stain crept up her cheeks.

Miles stepped forward to calm her. 'Kit, I think you should commend Rory for—'

'Do not begin to tell me anything, Miles Grayson!' She spun on him like a spitting cat. 'He is my brother and he should have come to me for help! It is I who has been searching for him for four years. I took in his child when he could have been living in the slums!'

Rory reached out his hand. 'Kitty, please. Of course, you are included in my plans. I just thought Miles would understand my needs better and have the contacts in Sydney to help me.'

Mary quietly rose to take Kitty's arm. 'I have offered to return to Sydney and live with Rory and help him in his business, Kitty. He will be well looked after, I assure you. Indeed, I believe we shall look after each other.'

Kitty stared at them wide-eyed. Her mouth opened and shut wordlessly.

Miles closed his eyes momentarily, knowing she would blame him for this.

'How can you decide this without me?' She backed away from them a little. 'I have striven to keep us altogether and just when I achieve it you leave me?'

'Kitty, let me explain.' Rory appealed to her. 'I...I thought we might take Little Rory with us. I want to raise him, and Mary will be there to help.'

Her wild gaze raked them in one violent look. She stumbled backwards with her hands over her ears blocking out their pleading.

'Kit.' Miles took a step towards her.

She turned on him. 'Leave me! This is all your doing. You didn't want them here. Now I am to be left alone. Well, I will not. I cannot stay here by myself and suffer your coldness.' She turned and ran along the riverbank.

'What's she on about?' Connie said, rising. 'We're not all leavin' her.'

Stunned by her reaction, Rory looked at them. 'I never meant to hurt her, but it is the best decision for me, and with Mary's help, Little Rory will not want for anything, I promise you. Besides, we're not going right now, we thought in about a month or so, when my son has grown to know me more.'

Connie patted his arm. 'I know, lad. You both need ter start again an' Little Rory should be with you, he's your son after all. We'll miss him sorely, but he'll be fine with you an' Mary.'

Miles placed his plate on the blanket. 'I will find Kit.'

He walked for a few minutes before he found her sobbing on a large outcrop of rock that partially hung over the water. It was a pleasant spot to sit and fish, as the rock was wide and flat and easy to walk onto. Large trees threw shade over the water, turning that part of the river to a deep olive green. A lone call of a magpie high in the treetops echoed over their heads, and the slight breeze rippled the water, stirring a dragonfly to hover just inches from the surface.

'Kit.'

She jumped when he spoke her name.

'Go away, Miles.' She turned her back to him.

'No.'

'I don't wish to talk to you.'

Miles looked out over the river. 'Why does the thought of them leaving hurt you so much?'

She raised her head, but still didn't look at him. 'I stood by my parents' graves and vowed to keep the family together. I have been trying to do that ever since. Now, we are finally all together, and I thought I was finished worrying over them. I thought here we could live in our own paradise. But you have ripped my plans apart!'

'They are welcome to live with us if they wish, but Rory is proud, Kit, that's what you don't see. He wants to be independent, his own man. Can you allow him that? You cannot control people.'

She twisted to face him. 'I do not want to control them!'

'Then let them go.'

'We have only just reunited.'

'We will make plenty of trips to Sydney and they to here.'

She studied a slow-moving fish visible in the shallows. 'I cannot stay here without them.'

'Why?' His voice cracked and he sighed at his pain.

'Because as much as I love Blue Water, the thought of being alone here with you and your rigid emotions is horrifying. I have given you an heir, I have kept my part of the bargain.'

'Bargain?' Incredulity drove his voice high. 'Our marriage is a bargain?'

'Well, it was no love match, was it? Let us at least be honest.'

'Very well, it is time the truth was told.' Miles braced himself to say the words he should have said a long time ago but lacked the courage to do so for fear of her total rejection.

'I don't want to hear anymore, enough has been said already.'

'This is not about them, but about me.'

'You?' She sneered. 'You have done enough by helping them to leave me.'

He flinched but persisted. 'Why do you think I asked you to marry me?'

'Because you needed a son.'

'Yes, I did. However, the love I felt for you played an enormous part.'

'Love?' she mocked him. 'I believe you are mistaking that for the ugly word called lust.'

'Wrong. I know the difference. I have lusted after you, I will admit to that. But it turned into love very soon after.' He took a deep breath. 'I want to ask you a question and I need an honest answer, if you please.'

She nodded while wiping away her tears.

Miles clenched his fists, wondering if the outcome would favour him. 'Do you have any...feelings towards me?'

'Feelings?'

'Yes.'

She gazed out over the water. 'You have asked for an honest answer and so I will give it, even though it makes me feel defenseless and weak.' She looked into his eyes. 'Yes, I have feelings for you.'

'Enough feelings to call love?'

She nodded. 'I believe it could be called love.'

A pulse twitched along his jaw and he relaxed his shoulders. 'You understand that I would do nothing to make you unhappy?'

'You do make me unhappy.' Kitty's deep sadness etched her fine features, dampened the spark in her emerald eyes. 'I am unhappy because you do not tell me of this so-called love you have for me. You showed me a glimpse of a wonderful man in Sydney and that is who I hungered for, but then you changed as soon as we married. You drew away... Yet, in the bedroom, you make me weep with your tenderness, but you never say the words I long to hear.'

'Is it any wonder?' He ran his hand through his hair. 'I can't continue fighting a ghost, Kit. It's too hard.'

She whipped her head up to frown at him. 'A ghost?'

'Ben, your fiancé. I can't compete with him.' He shrugged in hopelessness, feeling like his heart had been ripped into pieces by a rusty blade and left to bleed, drop by drop. 'I've tried to compete, but right from the beginning you put him between us. He was your first love, he was taken from you tragically and then you met me, and our meeting wasn't great...'

'Ben is the past.'

'Is he?' Miles wondered if he begged on his knees would she think kindly of him. 'I'd like to believe he was in the past.'

'He is. Trust and believe in me. I want you to be my future.' She stood and lightly placed her hand in his. 'I want you to be the one who holds my hand as we walk by the river. It is you who I need to hold me when I close my eyes at night.'

He pulled her closer, his heart pounding. For her, he would die. 'Speaking of my emotions does not come easily to me, but please believe me when I say...' he sucked in a breath, '...with all my heart I love you, Kit.'

A smile quivered on her lips. Her eyes mirrored his love. 'And I love you.'

- Read more about Kitty's family in the third book in the series, Southern Sons, which focuses on Kitty's grand-children.

About the author

Author of over thirty novels, AnneMarie Brear has crafts sweeping historical fiction with atmosphere, emotion, and drama aplenty that will surely satisfy any fan of the genre. AnneMarie was born in a small town in N.S.W. Australia, to English parents from Yorkshire, and is the youngest of five children. From an early age she loved reading, working her way through the Enid Blyton stories, before moving onto Catherine Cookson's novels as a teenager.

Living in England during the 1980s and more recently, AnneMarie developed a love of history from visiting grand old English houses and this grew into a fascination with what may have happened behind their walls over their long existence. Her enjoyment of visiting old country estates and castles when travelling and, her interest in genealogy and researching her family tree, has been put to good use, providing backgrounds and names for her historical novels which are mainly set in Yorkshire or Australia between Victorian times and WWII.

A long and winding road to publication led to her first novel being published in 2006. She has now published over thirty historical family saga novels, becoming an Amazon best seller and with her novel, The Slum Angel, winning a gold medal at the USA Reader's Favourite International Awards. Two of her books have been nominated for the Romance Writer's Australia Ruby Award and the USA In'dtale Magazine Rone award and recently she has been nominated as a finalist for the UK RNA RONA Awards.

AnneMarie now lives in the Southern Highlands of N.S.W. Australia

http://www.annemariebrear.com

Also by

Kitty McKenzie
Kitty McKenzie's Land
Southern Sons
The Slum Angel Series
The Slum Angel
The Slum Angel Christmas (novella)
The Marsh Saga Series
Millie
Christmas at the Chateau (novella)
Prue
Cece
Alice
The Beaumont Series
The Market Stall Girl
The Woman from Beaumont Farm
The Distant Series
A Distant Horizon
Beyond the Distant Hills
The Distant Legacy
Contemporary
Long Distant Love
Hooked on You
The War Nurse's Diary
Short Stories
A New Dawn
New Beginnings: an anthology